'I want to take you away from here, Louisa,' he said eventually. 'I want to take you somewhere safe whilst I figure out exactly what's happened.'

Her eyes narrowed suspiciously. Robert surmised that she hadn't had much reason to trust people in the last few years. She wrapped her arms around her body protectively and started to hunch into herself.

'I promise I won't hurt you,' Robert said, kneeling down in front of her and gently taking her hand. 'I won't let anyone hurt you ever again.'

She flinched as his skin touched hers, not pulling her hand away but cowering a little, as if she expected him to hit her.

'Trust me,' he said quietly.

Louisa regarded him for almost a minute in silence, staring into his eyes, and Robert felt as though she'd studied his soul. Eventually she gave a small, almost imperceptible nod.

AUTHOR NOTE

Ever since I can remember I have been fascinated by the workings of the mind: what makes one person thrive whilst another will be made to withdraw. One thing that has particularly intrigued me is how society's perception of mental illness has changed over time. This is demonstrated perfectly by our treatment of those suffering from mental illness. Hundreds of years ago such people were shunned by society and cast out of their communities. In the Regency period common practice was to lock away anyone with unexplainable behaviour and pretend they didn't exist. This led to an increase in the number of unregulated and unlicenced institutions where the unfortunate inmates received no rehabilitation or medical care, worsening their conditions. Stories abound about unfortunate individuals discarded in asylums by their relatives who, despite having no reason to lock them up, wished to gain from their disappearance.

Another psychological theme runs through this book. For centuries men have fought in wars which have left mental as well as physical scars. The symptoms of shell-shock, or post-traumatic stress disorder, have only recently been recognised as a consequence of the strains that battle places upon the psyche. However, the soldiers of the Napoleonic wars would have been subject to many of the same stresses as soldiers of today. SECRETS BEHIND LOCKED DOORS explores how such mental scars can be a barrier between the sufferer and the wider world. In writing a character with some features of PTSD I hoped to portray how the disorder can impact on every aspect of life—including love.

SECRETS BEHIND LOCKED DOORS

Laura Martin

Published in Great Britain 2015
by Mills & Boon, an imprint of Harlequin (UK) Limited,
Eton House, 18-24 Paradise Road, Richmond, Surrey, TW9 1SR

© 2015 Laura Martin

ISBN: 978-0-263-24761-9

Harlequin (UK) Limited's policy is to use papers that are natural,
renewable and recyclable products and made from wood grown in
sustainable forests. The logging and manufacturing processes conform
to the legal environmental regulations of the country of origin.

Printed and bound in Spain
by CPI, Barcelona

Laura Martin writes historical romances with an adventurous undercurrent. When not writing she spends her time working as a doctor in Cambridgeshire, where she lives with her husband. In her spare moments Laura loves to lose herself in a book, and has been known to read cover to cover in a single day when the story is particularly gripping. She also loves to travel—especially visiting historical sites and far-flung shores.

Books by Laura Martin
in Mills & Boon® Historical Romance:

THE PIRATE HUNTER
SECRETS BEHIND LOCKED DOORS

Visit Laura Martin's profile page at
www.millsandboon.co.uk

For Dad, for all the inspiration and encouragement.
And for Luke. I couldn't do it without you.

Chapter One

Robert fought the urge to turn around and flee. He wasn't a man who had ever run from anything. Six years he'd fought in the army and he'd never backed down from a fight, but right now his courage was deserting him.

'Ready, sir?' asked Yates, his agent, apparently oblivious to his discomfort.

Robert nodded, raised his hand and knocked on the imposing front door.

The stench hit him as soon as he walked inside. It was a mixture of sweat and cabbage and something else he didn't even want to guess at. He wondered how the staff coped with it, the smell permeating their clothes and lingering as they returned home to their families. At least they could return home though, he supposed. Some of the inmates wouldn't ever leave the confines of the Lewisham Asylum; they'd spend long years cooped up in the dreary rooms with only their screams for company.

'Lord Fleetwood—' a grubby little man hurried out to greet them '—it is such an honour to meet you. I'm Symes, the humble proprietor of this establishment.'

Robert nodded silently in greeting. He wanted to get his business here sorted as quickly as possible and escape. Already he was feeling despair, the same sensation the patients must have felt as they were dragged out of the sunlight one last time.

'I said to your man there must be a mistake,' Symes said as he led Robert into his office. 'None of our patients are gently born, we haven't got any ladies here.'

Robert very much hoped so, but in the ten years Yates had worked for him he hadn't known the man to be wrong.

'You have a patient listed as Louisa Turnhill?' Robert asked.

Symes flicked through the ledger in front of him, his short, pudgy fingers crinkling the paper.

'Louisa Turnhill, aged nineteen. Came to us just over a year ago.'

Over a year in this place. Robert couldn't even begin to imagine it.

'What's wrong with her?' Robert asked bluntly.

Symes squirmed a little in his seat, but dutifully read out the entry next to her name. 'Melancholy and mania. Violent outbursts. Hallucinations.'

'And what is her treatment?'

Symes looked at the two men in front of him blankly.

'Treatment?' he asked.

'Yes, what are you doing to make her better?' Robert had a sneaking suspicion he knew the answer to this question, but he persisted anyway. 'How do you propose to cure her?'

'Oh, there is no cure, Lord Fleetwood,' he said, baring his yellow teeth in an uncomfortable smile. 'We don't deal in cures here, just room and board and a place for the wretched to stay out of the way of the rest of the world.'

Robert knew he'd never been in a more depressing place. Nearly one hundred poor souls locked in grim little cells with no hope of a cure and for many of them no hope of release.

'Tell me,' he said reluctantly, 'how is Miss Turnhill presently?'

Symes shrugged. 'I oversee the asylum, I don't visit the inmates. You can see for yourself.'

He stood and stuck his head out into the corridor, motioning for a middle-aged woman to come into the room.

'Show this gentleman to Room Sixty-Eight,' he ordered.

Robert followed the dowdy woman up three flights of stairs. All around him screams and moans were muffled by thick wooden doors. He wondered how anyone got any rest. He wasn't surprised they didn't hope to cure anyone at Lewisham Asylum; he rather suspected it would turn a sane person mad within a month.

'She's in here, sir.'

The female warden slotted a key into the lock in front of her and opened the door.

Robert steeled himself, then stepped inside. He turned to see the door closing behind him as the warden locked him in.

He waited a minute for his eyes to adjust to the darkness. There was a tiny window, high up in the wall, covered almost entirely with bars. It let in a sliver of sunlight, but nowhere near enough to illuminate the room. In one corner was a metal bed and in another a small pot. The walls were whitewashed and the floor beneath his feet bare floorboards.

At first glance Robert thought they'd brought him to the wrong room, an empty room. For a few seconds he didn't see the slender young woman crouching by the side of the bed, her wrist encircled by a manacle and a chain securing her to the wall. She was sitting completely still, regarding him with wide brown eyes.

'Miss Turnhill?' he asked.

She shied away from him as he took a step towards her.

'Louisa?' he tried again.

In his least threatening manner Robert ambled across the room and took a seat on the bed. It was hard, little more than a metal frame with an inch-thick straw mattress.

'My name is Robert, I'm here to help you.'

The young woman cocked her head to the side and scrutinised him. For an instant Robert wondered if she was dumb, or if she'd forgotten how to speak in her year of captivity.

'No one's here to help me,' she said eventually, her voice a little croaky as if underused.

'I would really like to learn a little more about you,' he said softly.

She chuckled and Robert wondered if she was about to become hysterical.

'No, you wouldn't.'

'How are you feeling today?' He tried a different tack.

She paused, regarding him seriously. 'Not too mad today, thank you very much.'

Robert felt as though he'd been transported to another world. He had no idea how to talk to this young woman. She didn't seem mad, at least not at first glance, but he wasn't exactly an expert.

'Are you going to hurt me?' she asked as if enquiring about the weather.

Robert looked at her carefully. Underneath her uninterested demeanour he realised she was scared. Petrified, even.

'I promise I'm not going to hurt you,' he said sincerely.

She relaxed a little. 'Have you brought any food?' she asked.

Robert wondered how she'd gone from violence to food so quickly. His confusion must have shown on his face.

'When people come in it's either to hurt me or bring me food,' she said calmly.

Robert Fleetwood, hardened soldier and celebrated war hero, felt his heart go out to this **scared young woman. In that instant he vowed silently to help her. Even if she wasn't the Louisa Turnhill he was looking for, he would make sure she was properly looked after, somewhere a long way from Lewisham Asylum.**

'Will you tell me how you came to be here, Louisa?' Robert asked.

She stood, the chain attached to her wrist jangling as she moved. He saw she was thin—a year of asylum food didn't seem to provide much nourishment. Her hair was long and straggly, falling most of the way down her back. There were bruises on the pale skin of her arms and dark circles under her eyes. She was in a poor state, but despite all of this Robert saw the spirit burning in her eyes as she watched him look over her. In her time at the asylum they hadn't broken her.

She came and sat on the bed next to him, making sure there was as much distance as possible between them.

'There's no point,' she said, turning her face towards him, 'you wouldn't believe me anyway.'

It was said with such certainty that Robert knew he had to hear her story. He wondered if she was deluded, whether she would tell him a different tale if he came back tomorrow.

'I might,' he said simply.

'If you stay here overnight, there's lots of screaming,' Louisa said. 'And moaning and shouting. Do you know the most common thing people shout?'

He shook his head.

'They shout "I'm not mad"—' she paused '—or "I shouldn't be here", which is much the same thing.'

Robert couldn't imagine spending a single night in this hellish place, let alone over four hundred as she must have done.

'Everyone says it,' she said with a small smile on her face. 'But I actually mean it.'

'You shouldn't be here?'

'I'm not mad,' she said, 'or at least I wasn't when they put me in here.'

He didn't know how to respond. He'd expected howling and writhing, he'd been prepared for that—this cool, detached statement of sanity he didn't know how to react to.

'I probably am a little bit mad now. Anyone would be after a few months in this place.'

She looked at him and Robert got the sensation she was assessing him, weighing up whether he was worth revealing more to.

'I said you wouldn't believe me.'

'What happened?' Robert asked simply, not trusting himself to say more. He got the feeling this strange young woman was very astute— she'd know if he lied to her.

'You actually want to know?'

'I want to know.'

'I had an evil guardian,' she said, then giggled. 'Your face is a picture.'

Robert hadn't realised he'd moved a muscle.

'My evil guardian locked me up here after I refused to marry him. Lecherous old sod.'

Sometimes she sounded so normal, so sane, but Robert knew there were some lunatics like that. So caught up in their fantasy world they could make others believe it was true.

'He wanted the money my parents had left to me. When I wouldn't give it to him through marriage, he bribed a doctor to certify I was insane and dumped me here. I should imagine he's worked his way through most of the money by now. Not that it's any use to me in here.'

Robert knew he shouldn't believe her. He knew he was probably being manipulated, conned into believing her fantasy, but the disbelief in his mind was giving away to horrified realisation.

He'd received a letter eight weeks ago, a confession of sorts. It had been sent the day before his great-uncle had died. In the letter his great-uncle confessed to committing a grave sin and asked Robert to put it right. The only other information the old man had supplied was Louisa's name.

Surely this wasn't the sin his great-uncle had talked of. Robbing a young woman of her fortune was one thing, but to rob her of her freedom and label her as insane was worse than murder.

He cursed the man again for not providing more details of his crime.

'And who was your guardian?' he asked, trying to make his tone casual even though he was holding his breath in anticipation of her answer.

'Thomas Craven,' she said. 'The name I curse last thing every night and first thing every morning.'

Robert felt the foundations of his world rock. This young woman *must* have been the ward of his great-uncle, Thomas Craven, otherwise there was no way she could have given him the right name.

When Yates had tracked Louisa down to the asylum, Robert hadn't known what to expect. He'd wondered if his great-uncle had somehow played a part in this young woman's descent into madness, maybe by robbing her of her innocence, an event she hadn't been able to recover from, and for which his great-uncle had rightly blamed himself. No part of him had been prepared for the possibility she'd been wrongly imprisoned for over a year.

'It's all right,' she said, patting him on the hand in a sisterly gesture, 'you don't have to believe me.'

Robert stood and paced to the other side of the tiny room, trying to buy himself time to figure out what he believed.

'I want to take you away from here, Louisa,' he said eventually. 'I want to take you somewhere safe whilst I figure out exactly what's happened.'

Her eyes narrowed suspiciously. Robert surmised she hadn't had much reason to trust people in the last few years. She wrapped her arms around her body protectively and started to hunch into herself.

'I promise I won't hurt you,' Robert said, kneeling down in front of her and gently taking her hand. 'I won't let anyone hurt you ever again.'

She flinched as his skin touched hers, not pulling her hand away, but cowering a little as if she expected him to hit her.

'Do they beat you here?' he asked, suddenly catching sight of the bruises on her arms for a second time.

She laughed in disbelief. 'Of course.'

Robert felt the rage building inside him, rage he thought he'd managed to control for so long. He didn't know if this young woman was mad or the victim of a very heinous deception, but either way she didn't deserve to be beaten. She shouldn't be chained to the wall, frightened of every person who entered her dismal cell. She deserved more than that, every human did.

'Trust me,' he said quietly.

Louisa regarded him for almost a minute in silence, staring into his eyes, and Robert felt as though she'd studied his soul. Eventually she gave a small, almost imperceptible nod.

Robert rose to his feet, strode the couple of

paces to the door and thumped hard on the wood with his fist.

He waited until he could hear footsteps approaching, then thumped again.

The female warden unlocked the door and stood aside for him to come out.

'Get me Symes,' he commanded. 'And give me the keys to unlock this poor girl's manacles.'

The warden just stared at him.

'I said give me your keys,' he growled in a voice that brooked no argument.

Wordlessly the warden handed over a key, unthreading it from the bunch.

'Go get Symes,' he repeated. 'I'm taking Miss Turnhill away from here.'

'Very Arthurian,' Louisa murmured as he unlocked the manacle from around her wrist.

He looked at her, puzzled.

'My knight in shining armour.' He saw the smile on her face and humour in her eyes and wondered how anyone could keep from utter despair after spending such a long time in the asylum.

'What's going on?' Symes asked as he blustered in. 'Lock her back up immediately.'

'I'm taking Miss Turnhill with me,' Robert said, 'and we're never coming back.' It was a bit of a dramatic statement, but the whole scene seemed a little farcical to him.

'You can't do that,' Symes said.

'I'm her legal guardian now, I can choose to do whatever I like. And I choose to take Miss Turnhill away from this dreadful place and into my care.'

With that Robert took Louisa's hand and tucked it into the crook of his arm. She took a couple of steps forward and stumbled. Robert realised she wasn't used to walking far and, adding to that the excitement of escape, he wasn't surprised she was a little overcome. Wanting to make their exit as quickly as possible, he bent his head to Louisa's ear and dropped his voice so only she could hear.

'I'm going to carry you,' he said.

'You most certainly are not.'

Robert blinked twice in quick succession. Most young ladies wouldn't give up the chance of being swept into a man's arms whatever the circumstances.

'I was dragged into this hellhole, but I will walk out on my own two feet.'

Chapter Two

Louisa stumbled, but only once. She righted herself, held her head high and walked out of Lewisham Asylum for the last time. They could threaten to poke out her eyes and hang her by the neck, but nothing would make her enter that vile place ever again.

'Where to now?' she asked, eyeing her saviour with a grin on her face.

He looked down at her with concern. Louisa supposed she probably did look a little mad, dressed in the grey sack of the madhouse, squinting into the sun and grinning like a lunatic. She didn't care. She was free.

'My home, perhaps?' Robert suggested.

She pulled a face. 'But there's so much to do. Over a year of things to catch up on. I was thinking a stroll in the park.'

She watched as he tried to hide the horror

on his face. She grinned again and waited as it dawned on him that she was teasing.

'Your home would be lovely,' she said quietly.

She'd always found it hard to be serious, her natural temperament was carefree and joyous. Even when her parents had died she'd tried to see the positive side to life. In the years she'd dodged her guardian's unwanted advances she'd almost forgotten how to smile. Then he'd dumped her in the asylum and she'd vowed she would be true to herself, no matter what hardships followed.

Gently Robert helped her up into his carriage. He followed her inside and banged on the roof, signalling for the driver to depart. Louisa watched as the facade of the asylum faded into the distance, then felt her body start to shake. She couldn't believe she was actually out of that place. She was free. She didn't know what life held for her now, but surely nothing could be worse than the eight long years with her guardian or the one in the madhouse.

She couldn't stop the shaking, she felt overwhelmed. She felt the tears start to pour from her eyes and run down her cheeks.

'It's all right,' Robert said soothingly. 'You're safe now.'

He moved from his position on the opposite side of the carriage to sit next to her. Gently he took her in his arms and held her. Louisa felt herself stiffen. She wasn't used to human contact, at least not of the friendly kind. No one had hugged her since her parents had died. Slowly she allowed herself to relax into his arms, soothed by the soft sound of his voice.

'You're safe now,' he repeated over and over again, and for a few moments Louisa allowed herself to believe it.

She wondered what was driving this man. She'd had to trust him in the asylum, she'd have trusted anyone who'd given her the chance to escape, but now she was free she could always try to make her own way. She watched as the carriage slowed slightly and wondered if she would hurt herself too much if she jumped. Being alone in London was a scary thought, but at least she wouldn't be locked in anywhere. For all she knew this man might be taking her somewhere worse than the asylum.

It was possible, but the rational part of Louisa knew to dismiss the thought. She might not know his motivations, but Louisa's instincts were that he was a good man. Maybe she would stick with him for a little while, just until she could make plans to be on her own.

Self-consciously Louisa wiped the last few tears from her cheeks and sat upright. As she wriggled free from Robert's arms she felt strangely bereft. She'd been on her own so long that just that little bit of human contact had been world changing.

'So what's the plan?' Louisa asked. 'Sell me into slavery? Banish me to work in a travelling fair?'

He was too easy to poke fun at, that was the problem. Robert Fleetwood was a serious man, too serious for a man of his age. She wondered if he'd been in the war. He had a scar running down his left temple that looked as though it had been inflicted by a sword. She supposed it could have been from a duel, but he looked like a soldier. He had that upright bearing, serious mien and a haunted, faraway look in his eyes that suggested he'd left a bit of his soul on the battlefield.

'You joke a lot,' he said seriously.

'I find when you're incarcerated as a lunatic it helps if you can enjoy the funnier things in life. It does get rather dull otherwise.'

Robert shook his head. 'It's not that,' he said. 'You use it as your protection.'

Louisa felt stripped, naked. It was as though he'd looked inside her very being and found each and every one of her weaknesses. And he'd only known her for an hour.

'I meant what I said back there, Louisa,' he said seriously. 'I'm not going to hurt you and I won't let anyone else hurt you either.'

She allowed herself to hope, to dream. It was

everything she'd ever wished for during her darkest hours at the asylum. A protector, a rescuer, someone who actually cared about her, but Louisa knew it was too good to be true. Life wasn't the stuff of fairy tales, she'd found that out long ago. She might have dreamed about a protector, someone to rescue her, but she'd known she wouldn't ever rely on anyone but herself again. Other people could hurt her, let her down. Even a knight in shining armour was too good to be true. No, Louisa had promised herself she would only ever depend on herself again, no matter how tempting the dream of someone to look after her had been.

'Why are you helping me?' she asked. It hadn't mattered before, but now she was free she needed to know.

Robert sighed, a small crease appearing between his eyebrows as he frowned. Louisa wondered what he looked like when he laughed. Handsome, she supposed, not that he wasn't handsome when he was serious, but a smile would change his face to make him irresistible to the ladies. Real ladies, not lunatic paupers like her.

'Eight weeks ago Thomas Craven died,' he said slowly.

Louisa didn't know how to react. The man who'd made her existence a misery, ruined her entire life, was dead. She felt a strange bubble of rage building inside her. It was as though she'd been robbed. She'd wanted to confront him, stand in front of him and tell him what an awful, wicked excuse for a guardian he was. Now she would never be able to.

'As his closest living relative I inherited his estate.'

Slowly realization dawned on Louisa. Robert hadn't been lying when he'd said he was her guardian. She'd assumed it was a ruse to trick Symes into letting her go.

'So you actually are my guardian?'

He nodded. 'The day before my great-uncle died he wrote a letter and sent it to me. In it he confessed to some awful wrongdoing on his part.'

Louisa sat paralysed, unable to move. She felt stunned.

'He gave me your name and asked me to put right the wrong he did you.'

'Did he tell you what he did?' she asked urgently. 'Did he say he'd had me locked up when I was completely sane?'

Robert shook his head. 'I'm sorry.'

Louisa felt the breath being sucked out of her. There was no proof, only her word, that she wasn't insane. That was why Robert had studied her so intently back at the asylum. He was weighing her up, deciding whether to believe her at all.

'So how did you find me?'

'I visited my great-uncle's estate and asked around. The servants were all very tight-lipped, but eventually someone talked. Said there was a big scandal and you were taken away to be locked up. My agent, Yates, has been scouring the country for you ever since.'

'What happens now?' Louisa asked, suddenly feeling very vulnerable.

'I don't know,' Robert said with a rueful grin. 'I've never been a guardian before.'

'I can give you a few pointers on how not to do it,' Louisa suggested, feeling some of her spirit returning to her. 'I've had plenty of experience.'

Robert looked at her tenderly and Louisa felt her heart start to pound in her chest. She clenched her fists so she wouldn't reach up and stroke his cheek. It would be entirely inappropriate. He was her guardian, her saviour, and no doubt he was still wondering if she was quite right in the head. What she was feeling was natural, Louisa reasoned, it was gratitude for his chivalrous rescue of her from the asylum. She forced herself to look away from his serious blue eyes or she knew she'd do something she would regret later.

Self-consciously Louisa stared down at her grubby hands and skinny arms. Her dress was shapeless and filthy, her hair hadn't been cut or styled for over a year and she probably stank like a sewer rat. There was no way a man like Robert would find her attractive. And even after a bath and a change of clothes she wasn't anything like the ladies he'd be used to. She'd spent her adult years festering in a cell or secluded in the country whilst her peers learnt to waltz around ballrooms and flirt with gentlemen. She was not fit to even fantasise about a man like Robert.

'Penny for your thoughts?' Robert asked.

Louisa desperately tried not to blush.

'I was wondering whether I smelt better or worse than a rotting pig,' Louisa said with a sunny smile, her defences back up. She took a sniff. 'Worse, I fear.'

Robert leant forward so his face was only inches from hers. Louisa had to remind herself to breathe. He inhaled deeply.

'Now I'm no connoisseur of rotting pigs,' he said, 'but I don't think you smell as bad as you think you do.'

It was the strangest compliment she'd ever received.

'We'll get you a bath when we get home,' he said.

Louisa immediately pictured Robert lathering her back as she luxuriated in a tub full of bubbles. The idea made her feel hot all over and she squirmed slightly. This was the last thing she needed: an infatuation with her guardian.

She settled back into the seat of the carriage and tried to look anywhere except at Robert. It was hard when her eyes were being so rebellious. Every few seconds she found herself staring at his face, watching the tiny changes in his expression.

'Where do you live?' Louisa asked, trying to use banal conversation to distract herself.

'Here.'

The carriage rolled to a stop and Louisa glanced out. She nearly had a heart attack. It was one of the grandest London town houses she'd ever seen.

'You can't live here,' she squeaked.

He regarded her strangely. 'I can assure you I've lived here for the last two years,' Robert said, 'but I'm always up for suggestions for more comfortable accommodation.'

'I can highly recommend the Lewisham Asylum.'

He turned serious again and took her by the shoulder. 'I want you to forget that place, Louisa. I will do everything I can to make you forget it.'

Louisa saw the care and sincerity in his eyes and already the asylum seemed a long way away.

Chapter Three

Robert glanced at the clock and tapped his fingers absent-mindedly on the arm of the chair. His years of service in the army had made him exceedingly punctual; he even turned up to dinner in his own house five minutes early.

Not that there was any rush, he thought, as he sipped from the glass of whisky in his hand. He'd planned for dinner this evening to be a very informal affair with just him and Louisa present. He didn't want to scare her, and after eating slop from wooden bowls with her fingers for over a year he doubted Louisa would welcome company at her first civilised meal.

He glanced at the clock again, wondering if he should check on Louisa. He'd handed her over to his housekeeper, Mrs Kent, a couple of hours ago. The older woman had clucked over Louisa's poor state and had whisked her upstairs to fuss over her.

A little bit of fussing would do Louisa some good, Robert thought. She'd been neglected for too long. He wondered if her experiences over the last few years had inflicted any permanent damage. Only someone with a very robust character would escape unscathed from a situation such as hers.

The door slowly swung open as Louisa stepped into the room.

Robert stood immediately, surprised by the difference a bath could make.

'Good evening, Lord Fleetwood,' Louisa said.

For a second Robert couldn't find the right words. She looked completely different to the scrawny little ragamuffin he'd swept from the asylum and into his carriage earlier in the day. Granted she was still all skin and bones, but Mrs Kent had scrubbed Louisa's skin until it was glowing, then must have turned her attention to Louisa's hair. In place of the lank locks that had hung down Louisa's back earlier in the day was a head of shining chestnut hair, secured into an elegant hairstyle.

The only thing that stopped Louisa looking like a young lady of the *ton* was the shapeless dress she'd had to borrow from Robert's middle-aged and voluptuous housekeeper. It hung off her like a sack, but at least it was clean and not that awful grey garment she'd spent over a year wearing.

'You look lovely,' Robert said.

Louisa scrunched up her nose as if she didn't believe him.

'You do.'

And she did. Robert wasn't in the habit of giving out compliments just for the sake of it.

'It feels wonderful to be clean,' Louisa said, fiddling with her hair self-consciously. 'For the first time in longer than I can remember I smell of roses rather than cabbage.'

'Shall we go in to dinner?' Robert asked.

He held out his arm and waited for her to slip her hand into the crook of his elbow. She hesitated before stepping forwards and Robert realised he had a long way to go before Louisa trusted him. She was scared of even the briefest human contact. He'd seen her flinch on a couple of occasions since he'd brought her home, as if she was expecting him to raise a hand to her. *Slowly,* he cautioned himself, *if you're gentle she'll start to trust you eventually.*

He made sure no part of his body brushed against hers as he escorted her into dinner. He watched her face as he pulled out her chair and waited for her to be seated before sitting down himself. She was wary of every movement, but seemed to relax once he'd sat down.

'We've got a lot to discover about each other,' Robert said as the footman brought the first course to the table.

Louisa smiled at him, but it didn't quite reach her eyes. He supposed she was nervous of giving too much of herself away.

'What you like to eat, for example.'

As she realised Robert wasn't going to push her for more personal facts quite yet, Louisa relaxed.

'I used to be rather fussy,' she said, eyeing the bowl of soup in front of her. 'My mama would despair at mealtimes.'

'And now?'

'Now I don't think there's much I wouldn't eat.' After a mouthful of soup she added, 'Except gruel. Serve that and I'm walking out.'

'I'll tell cook madam is not a fan of the gruel.'

'Or porridge,' Louisa added. 'I do like this soup, though.'

Robert could tell she was holding back. She wanted to spoon the deliciously warm liquid into her mouth and not bother with any conversation, but even after a year locked away, her upbringing as a well-mannered young woman shone through.

'What else do we have on the menu?' Louisa asked, her eyes sparkling in anticipation.

Robert was glad—she needed to put some

more flesh on her frame. A few weeks of good cooking and she'd be much healthier and able to face the world again.

He shrugged. 'I've got no idea.'

Louisa frowned. 'But it's your house, isn't it?'

He nodded.

'Then how can you have no idea what's for dinner.'

The truth was he had little interest in food. For years in the army he'd got used to eating whatever was available. More often than not it would be a sinewy rabbit or a watered-down stew. After a while he'd stopped noticing how the food tasted and had eaten it for sustenance only.

And since he'd returned from the war...well, nothing was the same, not even the fancy dinners he used to enjoy.

'I let cook decide.'

Louisa looked at him as though he were mad.

'Every night you could have anything, *anything*, you desire, and you let your cook decide.'

'She does make very good choices,' Robert said, motioning to the two empty bowls of soup the footman was whisking away.

'Even so, I'd love to choose exactly what I was going to eat each and every day.'

Robert decided not to reveal he wouldn't notice if it was a pheasant or a field mouse set down in front of him.

'At the asylum we had gruel every day,' Louisa said, surprising Robert with this little snippet of information, 'and porridge for breakfast.'

Hence her dislike for gruel and porridge, he assumed.

'And when I lived with my guardian he used to restrict my food if I did even the slightest thing wrong, but the servants often saved me a few scraps and leftovers.'

No wonder she'd devoured the soup as if it were her last meal on earth. Nine years of deprivation would do that to anyone.

'Would you like to help Mrs Rust plan the meals for the next couple of weeks?' Robert asked, surprising himself with the question.

For a second Louisa's eyes lit up with excitement, then she became suspicious.

'I'd love that,' she said slowly, 'if you truly are planning on keeping me around. But I'll understand if you decide to sell me to that travelling fair. I am quite expensive to feed after all.'

The humour was back, her protective armour against the world.

Robert stopped himself from reaching out and taking her hand. He knew she wasn't ready for that kind of contact yet. Instead, he leant forwards slightly and looked her in the eye.

'You're not going anywhere, Louisa,' he said. 'I'm your guardian and I promise you have a home here with me for as long as you want or need it.'

'The last thing you want is a half-crazy penniless orphan getting in your way.'

This time Robert couldn't stop himself reaching out to touch her, it was an automatic gesture.

'You're not crazy, Louisa,' he said seriously.

And he believed what he was telling her. All his doubts from the asylum had been quashed a while ago. Louisa wasn't insane, she was the victim of an awful old man's plot to steal her inheritance.

'Sometimes I feel it.'

It was said so quietly Robert barely heard her.

No, she wasn't insane, Robert thought, but she'd been badly hurt by her experiences and he'd have to remember not to push her too hard.

'You're not crazy,' he repeated, 'and you need to stop telling yourself that you are.'

The footman chose that moment to bring in the main course. Robert lifted his hand from Louisa's and sat back, watching as she tried to conceal her emotions.

They ate in silence for a few minutes. Robert could tell Louisa was still thinking about his declaration and wondering if she could trust him. He knew the best thing to do was to give her time.

'How will it work?' she asked eventually.

'What do you mean?'

'You being my guardian, me living here. The whole thing.'

Robert could tell that how he answered her would be very important.

'I've never been a guardian before,' Robert said, buying himself some time to think. 'I'm not sure what to do for the best.'

The military man in him perked up and Robert started to formulate a plan.

'But I guess it all depends on you.'

Louisa leant forwards. He'd at the very least got her to engage.

'For instance, would you prefer to live in town or the country?'

'You have a house in the country?' Louisa asked.

Robert thought of his extensive estate far away from the hustle and bustle of the city.

'I have a house in the country,' he confirmed.

She took another bite of beef and chewed whilst she thought.

'I've never lived in London before,' she said slowly. 'At least not as a free woman.'

The Lewisham Asylum didn't count.

'Would you like to?'

'I'd like to give it a go.'

'Then why don't we plan on spending a few

weeks in London. I will have to employ a chaperone for you, a companion.'

Society would be scandalised at the thought of a gently bred young woman spending even a night alone in a house with a bachelor such as he, but Robert knew his servants would be discreet and he had no intention of telling anyone.

Louisa nodded, spearing a piece of carrot with her fork. She lifted it up to her mouth and chewed on it thoughtfully.

'Tomorrow we'll visit the modiste and get you some clothes of your own,' Robert said, looking at Mrs Kent's sizeable dress.

The last thing he wanted to do was spend his days visiting dress shops and interviewing companions, but he felt as though he owed it to Louisa. If he palmed her off on some female friend, she would probably feel as though he was abandoning her. Not that he had any obliging female friends in any case, or many friends at all for that matter. The last few years he hadn't exactly been a social butterfly.

No, he'd have to spend a bit of time helping Louisa settle into her new life. Once she was used to living as his ward and had a suitable companion he would be able to back off a little and return to his normal life.

The footman entered one final time, bringing dessert. Robert watched as Louisa's eyes lit up at the sight of the fruit crumble that was placed in front of her.

'Do you like fruit crumble?' he asked.

Louisa nodded and Robert was surprised to see tears in her eyes.

'It was my mother's favourite,' she said.

He didn't know what to say. Louisa stared for a few long moments at the dish in front of her, then stood abruptly.

'Please excuse me,' she said, then fled the room.

Robert was left staring at the door, wondering whether he should go after her.

'Best leave her for the night,' Mrs Kent said as she watched Robert pace the hallway. 'Poor duck has had a hectic day, I'm sure she'll be happier in the morning.'

Robert glanced up the stairs one final time before retreating to his study. He'd never professed to understand women.

Chapter Four

Louisa dried the tears from her cheeks and tested the door handle for the tenth time. It was strange not to be locked in and every few minutes she wondered if she'd imagined her freedom and just had to test the handle again.

The corridor outside her room was quiet. She'd listened as slowly the household had retired for the night and now she was sure she was the only one still awake. She looked left and right, allowing her eyes time to adjust to the darkness. There was no one there.

With one final glance into the bedroom Louisa stepped out into the corridor. As she crept along in the darkness she allowed her fingers to trail across the plush wallpaper, luxuriating in the expensive textures. Everything in this house was the polar opposite of the asylum, from the wallpaper and plush carpet to the kindness of the inhabitants. For a second Louisa hesitated. Maybe she was being foolish.

She probably *was* being foolish, but in her mind it was her only option. For a little while, during the delicious dinner Robert Fleetwood had given her, she'd allowed herself to dream. She'd wondered if he had meant everything he'd said: the promise of safety and security, the life of comfort as his ward. On first impressions he seemed a good man, an honest man, but despite all that Louisa knew she couldn't stay with him.

She'd vowed to herself that if she ever escaped from the asylum she'd never be dependent on another human being again, and most especially not a man. Although in her darkest moments she'd dreamt of a man such as Robert coming to rescue her, Louisa knew fairy tales didn't exist and she was better off relying only on herself. She had resigned herself to a lonely life, but loneliness was better than betrayal.

Silently she crept down the stairs, pausing every few steps to check no one else was stirring.

Louisa knew the streets of London were cruel and unforgiving to young women with no money or connections, but at least she would be dependent on no one but herself. She couldn't bear growing close to Lord Fleetwood, starting to enjoy her new privileged lifestyle, only to have it ripped away again. It would be better never to experience it, to not know what that life could be like. Because it *would* be ripped away. It might be in a week or in a year, but Louisa knew that all good things in life didn't last. One day, when she was least expecting it, her life would again be turned upside down.

Louisa reached the front door and quietly started to unlock it. Only a couple of minutes and she would disappear into the anonymity of the London streets. As she pulled the door open she wondered if she should leave a note for Lord Fleetwood, an explanation of why she had left, but decided against it. Although he might protest otherwise, Louisa doubted she was little more than an inconvenience to his ordered lifestyle. He'd saved her from the asylum and she didn't doubt he was a good man, but he'd done it out of a sense of duty, to right the wrongs of his great-uncle. Within a few days she doubted she would even enter his thoughts.

Louisa wouldn't forget him quite so quickly, though. Her knight in shining armour, the man who had actually believed she wasn't insane and rescued her from a lifetime of misery locked in Lewisham Asylum. Louisa knew Robert Fleetwood's face would grace her dreams for many nights to come.

She slipped out into the darkness and gently pulled the door closed behind her. As she heard the latch click she knew there was no going back now. Taking a deep breath, Louisa pulled the shawl Mrs Kent had lent her across her shoulders and walked down the steps. It was a chilly night, the sky was clear and cloudless and the air crisp, but Louisa was no stranger to cold. In the asylum the winter nights had been almost unbearable. More than once Louisa had thought she would perish from the icy temperatures alone.

With one final look at the house she'd felt most at ease in for the last nine years, Louisa hurried off down the street. It wouldn't do to linger. Every second she remained, a little bit of her resolve weakened. She turned the corner at the end of the street and disappeared into the night.

Robert woke up, gasping for air. The screams and shouts that had been haunting him in his dreams faded into the darkness, but he was left with a pounding heart and his muscles tensed, ready for action. He knew if he closed his eyes he would see the faces of his fallen comrades as clear as the day they had died. He might have come home from the war over two years ago, but the awful sights he had seen still haunted him at night.

Slowly he sat up in bed and reached for the glass of water he kept on his nightstand. It was tepid, but as the liquid hit his throat, Robert didn't care—it was more about distracting himself from his nightmare than needing a glass of water.

He sank back down on to his pillows and lay staring up at the ceiling, knowing he would not get a wink more of sleep. Not that he wanted to. If he succumbed to the tiredness that flowed through him, making his eyes droop, he knew he would be right back on the battlefield, looking at the agonised faces of his friends as they took their last breaths.

As he lay in the darkness he listened to the sounds of the house. It was quiet outside. His closest neighbours on either side were elderly couples who didn't attend any social events and his house was off the main thoroughfare so they didn't get many passing carriages. Inside the house there was the occasional creak of wood, but it sounded as though all the servants had retired for the night.

Robert was contemplating getting up and heading down to his study to look over some papers when the distinctive click of the front door being closed came to his ears. He listened for any further sound, but the house was entirely silent.

Rising quickly from his bed, he strode over to the window and pulled back the curtains. He looked out into the moonlit street. Louisa was just turning away from the house, pulling a woollen shawl tighter around her shoulders and walking off down the street.

For a moment Robert froze as his mind tried to process what he was seeing. He couldn't understand why Louisa was out in the street, leaving his house.

After a couple of seconds he sprang into action. In this instant it didn't matter why she was leaving, it just mattered that she was. Or more specifically that she was out on the streets of London all on her own in the middle of the night. Even in a neighbourhood like this Robert doubted she'd survive more than an hour before she ran into trouble.

He pulled on a pair of trousers and threw a shirt over his head. The foolish woman would be a few streets away by now. He had to find her before she disappeared into the anonymous heart of London. Slipping his feet into a pair of boots, Robert threw open his door, dashed along the corridor and bounded down the steps. Within seconds he was out the front door and onto the street. He set off in the direction he'd seen Louisa take from his window.

When he reached the corner there was no sign of her and Robert felt a stab of panic. He couldn't lose her already, this young woman he'd promised to protect. He couldn't fail her.

He set off at a jog, all the time glancing left

and right, hoping to catch a glimpse of Louisa in her shapeless grey dress.

A coach sat at the end of the road, the driver leaning back against his seat. For a moment Robert thought the man must be asleep and cursed under his breath.

'Good evening, sir,' the man said without moving as Robert slowed his pace. 'Fine evening for a walk.'

'Have you seen a young woman walk past?' Robert asked, sparing no time for pleasantries.

'Oh, yes, sir, not two minutes ago. Pretty little thing in an awful oversized dress. Shouldn't be out on the streets alone at this time of night.'

'Which way did she go?'

The driver scratched his chin and Robert had to fight the urge to reach up and pull him from the seat. Didn't the man understand the urgency?

'Turned left on to Poplar Street,' he said eventually.

Without stopping to thank the man, Robert dashed off. He ran down the entire length of Poplar Street. As he was approaching the end he wondered if the coach driver had sent him the wrong way. Surely he should have caught a glimpse of Louisa by now. She'd had a few minutes' head start, but there was no reason why she'd be hurrying. He'd practically been sprinting for the last few minutes.

A cold ball of dread started to form in the pit of his stomach. What if she'd been snatched from the street, dragged into an alleyway, her screams muffled? He couldn't stop the image of Louisa being attacked from settling in his brain and he felt the anguish rip through him. Another person he hadn't been able to protect, another life destroyed because of his inadequacies.

Suddenly he was once again back on the battlefield, the unmoving faces of his fallen men surrounding him. He felt the darkness start to take over and his body start to shake.

A high-pitched scream drew him back to reality. Louisa. It had to be. No other woman would be foolish enough to be wandering the streets at this time of night.

He started running in the direction of the scream, all the time hoping he wasn't going to be too late.

Chapter Five

Louisa struggled against the hand that was pressed against her mouth, sinking her teeth into the fleshy palm. Her attacker pulled away from her for an instant and she took the opportunity to let out another scream.

'Shut up,' the man growled, slapping her across the face with such force her neck snapped back and her head hit the wall.

For an instant Louisa's world went black. She fought the urge to let the darkness take over her, knowing she wouldn't have a chance of escape if she lost consciousness.

As the world came back into focus Louisa opened her mouth to scream again, but quickly clamped her lips together as she saw the glint of light reflected off her attacker's knife blade.

'Good girl,' the man murmured. 'Just keep quiet and I won't hurt you too much.'

Louisa very much doubted that. She didn't

know if this man planned to rob her or do something much, much worse, but she hoped she wouldn't be around to find out.

She was just assessing whether she could outrun her attacker when a figure pounced from the shadows.

'Oof,' her attacker groaned as he received a fist to his abdomen.

Louisa backed away, glancing behind her and wondering if she should run. There was no guarantee her saviour was any nobler than the man he was now punching in the face.

She had just decided to make a run for it when a familiar voice growled, 'Don't even think of moving a muscle, Miss Turnhill.'

Her eyes widened with surprise. Her mysterious saviour, the man beating her attacker, was none other than Robert Fleetwood.

She didn't disobey him.

The man who'd been attacking her managed to wriggle free from Robert's grasp and without a backward glance scuttled off into the night.

Louisa was left alone in the alleyway with Robert.

Even in the darkness she could tell he was fuming.

'I am going to escort you home,' he said.

Louisa allowed him to tuck her hand into the crook of his elbow and pull her along beside him. He walked fast, his long legs eating up the distance in no time. Louisa nearly had to run to keep up with him, taking two steps for his every one.

She glanced up at him as they walked. His jaw was clenched and his eyes focused straight ahead. He didn't once look down at her.

Louisa opened her mouth to say something but immediately decided against it. She'd been scared in the alleyway, more scared than she'd ever been in her life. If she thought about it too much, she knew her legs would start to shake and give way beneath her. So instead she concentrated on keeping up with Lord Fleetwood.

It took only ten minutes to reach his house and within another thirty seconds they were behind a locked front door. Louisa was marched into Robert's study and deposited unceremoniously on a comfortable leather sofa.

Still Robert did not speak. He crossed over to a decanter and poured himself a generous glass of whisky, which he downed in one gulp.

Then he turned to face her.

Louisa felt herself shrinking back in her chair. He was angry, furious even. She knew she was in trouble, but strangely she didn't feel scared. At least not scared of him. Although she'd known Robert only a short time she somehow knew he

wasn't going to hurt her. He might shout and be-
rate her for putting herself in such danger, but he
wouldn't actually physically hurt her.

'Miss Turnhill,' he started, 'why don't you
talk me through your thought process when you
decided it was a good idea to wander the streets
of London in the middle of the night?'

Louisa swallowed. When he put it like that it
did sound rather foolish. She'd been so preoccupied with leaving, with standing on her own
two feet, she hadn't thought through the consequences of her actions.

She cleared her throat and moistened her lips
with the tip of her tongue.

'I thought the exercise would do me good before bed,' she tried to joke weakly.

The stony silence that met her comment was
enough to tell her he wasn't amused.

'No more jokes, please. Tell me what pos-
sessed you to leave in the middle of the night?'

Louisa swallowed. 'I don't want to have to
rely on anyone else,' she said eventually.

He looked at her as though she'd grown an
extra head.

'So you thought you would take off in the
middle of the night with no money and no means
of supporting yourself.'

She had to agree it did sound a little foolish.

'London is a dangerous city,' Robert said in a

low voice. 'What do you think would have happened if I hadn't followed you?'

Louisa felt her hands start to shake. She knew what would have happened. She doubted she would be alive now, or if she was she would probably be wishing she was dead. It was only luck that Robert had seen her leave and had followed her, and reached her in time to save her from her attacker.

She felt the tears building in her eyes and tried to hold then back.

'I know what would have happened,' Louisa said, her voice cracking as the tears started to roll down her cheeks.

Robert looked at her for a couple of seconds, but as the sobs started to rack her body Louisa felt him sit down beside her and suddenly she was in his arms.

Her body instinctively stiffened at the contact, but gradually she relaxed as he held her, glad of the comfort he provided. He made her feel safe, Louisa realised. In this world where it seemed everyone was out to hurt, her he protected her time and time again.

'It's okay,' he said soothingly. 'You're safe now.'

Louisa sniffed and tried to stem the flow of tears, but found now she had started she just couldn't stop.

'I've got you,' he whispered. 'I'm not going to let anything happen to you.'

In that instant Louisa was inclined to believe him. He'd saved her from the asylum and just now he'd saved her from her own foolishness.

With an effort she wiped the tears from her cheeks. She felt her fears slowly ebbing away as he held her, knowing somehow that with him she was safe, at least just for a while.

They sat in silence for a few minutes, Robert seeming to understand she needed a little while to collect herself. As she dried the last of her tears, she felt him pull away slightly so she was still in his arms but could look up at his face.

'We need to discuss what you're afraid of,' Robert said. 'And this time I need you to be honest with me.'

Louisa nodded. She supposed she owed him that much at least.

'I understand you haven't been able to rely on anyone for a very long time and I know me asking you to trust me is an impossible task when you've known me for less than a day, but I do need you to at least be willing to see if I can earn your trust.'

She looked up into his sincere eyes and wondered for a second what would happen if she did just trust her life to this man. He seemed so genuine and caring, yet Louisa knew it would be a mistake to trust him. It would be a mistake to trust anyone, but maybe she could just give him a chance.

'London is a very lonely city,' he said with a sadness that made Louisa wonder again why he was quite so serious all the time. 'And it is a dangerous city, especially for beautiful young women.'

She felt her pulse quicken at his description of her. Did he actually think she was beautiful or was he just being kind?

'I would feel much happier if you would agree to stay here with me, under my protection,' he said, 'but I'm not going to force you to.'

She couldn't quite believe what she was hearing.

'So I can leave at any time?'

He grimaced.

'Yes, you can leave at any time, although I'd prefer it if you didn't choose the middle of the night.'

'You wouldn't stop me?' Louisa needed the confirmation.

'I'm not going to lock you in, Louisa. I would much prefer it if you choose to stay, but if you want to go I will not protest.'

Louisa looked at him, still not quite able to believe what he was saying.

'I suppose you think with no money and no contacts I have no choice but to stay.'

'If you choose to go, I will give you money,' Robert said. 'Good God, Louisa, do you think I could let you go out on to the cruel streets of London without any means of supporting yourself? I'm not a monster.'

It was the first time since the asylum he'd called her by her first name. Louisa rather liked the sound of it coming from his lips.

'You'd give me money?' she echoed.

'Yes. And contacts. But I really hope you decide to stay, at least for a little while.'

She thought it over. Part of her wanted to grab the money and go, start a new life not having to rely on anyone but herself. The other part was still scared from her first experience of London on her own.

'If you do decide to stay, you can of course change your mind at any time,' Robert said.

'So I could stay for a week, but you'd still help me if I decided to leave after that?'

He nodded. Louisa felt torn. She looked up at Robert and searched his face. How could she tell if he would hurt her, if he would betray her trust at some point in the future? Everything she knew of him so far pointed towards him being honest and trustworthy, but how could she judge a man on such a short acquaintance?

'Maybe I could stay for a couple of days,' she

said, 'at least until I get to know London a little better.'

The relief that flooded over Robert's face was obvious and Louisa dared to wonder if she had found someone who actually cared for her. She suddenly had an overwhelming urge to lean forward and kiss him. His lips looked so inviting and the way he held her made her feel so safe and secure.

Stop it, she told herself, *do something like that and he'll march you out the door himself.*

Still, Louisa couldn't quite make herself look away.

She was suddenly very aware of every place his body was touching hers: the way their thighs were pressed up against one another, the bare skin of his arms looped around her back and how her body was cradled against his chest.

Louisa watched his face as he registered her desire for him and for an instant she thought he might lean in and kiss her. His eyelids seemed to grow heavy and Louisa thought she saw the flash of desire brighten in his eyes.

As quickly as the moment had come, it passed and Louisa was left wondering if she'd imagined it. Robert stood and paced to the window, a hand running through his hair.

Louisa felt suddenly bereft. She wasn't used

to such close contact, but it seemed she missed it when it was gone.

'You should get some rest,' Robert said, his voice thick and directed towards the window. 'Just promise me you won't leave again tonight.'

She owed him that much at least.

'I promise,' she said quietly. Standing from the sofa Louisa crossed to the window and waited until Robert turned to face her.

'Thank you,' she said, looking Robert directly in the eye. 'You've saved me twice in the space of twenty-four hours.'

She stood on tiptoe and planted a light kiss on his cheek, her lips brushing momentarily against the fine stubble, the sensation sending a shiver down her spine.

Louisa didn't wait to see his reaction, instead turned and walked from the room, knowing she would probably dream of this quiet, serious, chivalrous man when she eventually fell asleep.

Chapter Six

Robert sipped at the scalding cup of coffee and tried to focus on the newspaper he held in front of him. He'd been attempting to read the same article for the last fifteen minutes and he hadn't got past the first paragraph. Every few seconds he would find himself glancing at the door, wondering if and when Louisa was going to show up for breakfast.

He'd recovered from the scare she'd given him the night before and he thought she would probably decide to stay with him for the time being. Robert told himself it was just friendly concern that made him look up from his newspaper every time there was a creak in the hallway, but deep down he knew that wasn't true.

There had been a moment in his study last night, just as Louisa had agreed to stay for a while at least, when she'd swayed towards him. Her body had been pressed up against his after he'd cradled her in his arms for comfort. He'd become aware of her womanly curves under the sack-like dress and a flicker of desire had ignited within him. For a second he had nearly given in to his desires. Robert was certain Louisa had leant towards him ever so slightly and it would have been so easy to bend his head and cover her mouth with his own.

Easy but disastrous. Louisa was his ward, a young woman who had been through so much in the last few years. She didn't deserve to be pounced upon by her new guardian within hours of meeting him. And even if the attraction was mutual, it was still very bad idea. Robert had not been with a woman for a very long time. Not since…

With a gargantuan effort Robert dragged his thoughts away from that catastrophic night. The night he'd lost his best friend in the entire world and most of the men under his command. All because of a woman. No, he wasn't going to allow himself to get involved with anyone ever again. It was the least he could sacrifice for the men whose deaths weighed on his conscience.

Robert was distracted from his dark train of thought by the opening of the door. Louisa edged into the room and stood nervously in the doorway. He realised she wasn't quite sure how to behave in his house yet.

'Come and sit down,' he said, motioning to the seat beside him. 'How did you sleep?'

'Wonderfully,' she said with a sunny smile.

He studied her carefully, wondering if she was joking. After their midnight dash through the neighbourhood Robert hadn't slept a wink. He wasn't sure if it was because he'd lain awake listening for Louisa's footsteps, wondering if she would disappear into the night again, or if it was the knowledge that if he fell asleep the nightmares would return. This morning he felt haggard.

Louisa, by contrast, looked fresh and ready for the day.

'Are you ready for our shopping trip today?' Robert asked. If she was ever going to be seen out in public, she needed something suitable to wear and his housekeeper's dress really wasn't good enough.

Louisa looked down at her dress and ran the coarse material through her fingers.

'I've grown rather fond of baggy grey dresses,' she said with a grin. 'It would be a shame to change my style now.'

'And it is quite a style.'

He watched as she tucked into her breakfast and wondered whether this shopping trip was a good idea. He couldn't deny she needed some new clothes. The dress she'd worn home from the asylum had been consigned to the bin and she couldn't continue borrowing Mrs Kent's dresses. No, he knew she needed to go shopping, but he wasn't sure he was the one who should be going with her. If he'd found her attractive in the shapeless grey dress last night, he dreaded to think what response she might elicit from him as she paraded up and down in silks and satins.

Robert shook his head almost imperceptibly. This was ridiculous. He was a grown man, not a young boy unused to controlling his emotions. For years he'd been able to maintain a stony exterior, hide what he was really feeling from the world. Compared to that, concealing a modicum of attraction for Louisa should be child's play.

'Why don't we meet in half an hour?' Robert said, standing to leave. 'That will give you enough time to enjoy your breakfast.'

Louisa turned to him with a smile on her face. 'I'm very much looking forward to today,' she said.

Robert nodded, then beat a hasty retreat, not trusting himself to say a word.

Twenty-five minutes later Robert was standing in the hall, waiting for Louisa. He resisted the urge to check the clock again, knowing she would probably have interpreted his half-hour rendezvous time as flexible. Not everyone was as punctual to the minute as he was.

'So where are we going?' Louisa asked as she descended the staircase, a skip in her step. Robert thought she seemed more relaxed today and he knew his assurance she could leave at any time had helped her to trust him just a little more.

'There is a modiste not too far from here,' Robert said. 'I'm told she's one of the best in the city.'

'Wonderful, I wouldn't want anything less than the best. I am used to garments made of the finest fabrics and designed by the most talented dressmakers.'

Robert was slowly getting used to her sense of humour and even found himself smiling.

'I'm not sure we can quite match the quality of the clothes you're used to, but we can only try.'

He led her out to the carriage that waited for them at the bottom of the steps and took her hand in his to help her up. Her fingers were warm against his skin and Robert found himself holding on for just a little longer than was strictly necessary.

Once she was settled, he bounded up into the carriage and took the seat opposite her. They moved off almost immediately.

For a few minutes they travelled in silence. Robert watched Louisa as she stared out the window at all the grand houses. She was a little awestruck, but as they neared their destination he could tell she was becoming increasingly nervous. Although the expression on her face didn't change, she was absent-mindedly wringing her hands together. Robert's best friend, Greg Knapwell, had done the same thing before each and every battle they'd fought together.

He tried to work out why she was quite so nervous; it was only a dress shop after all. Then he realised she probably hadn't ever been to a dress shop before.

'There's nothing to be afraid of,' he said quietly.

Louisa spun to face him. 'Why do you think I'm afraid?'

'When I was in the army, a friend of mine used to wring his hands together before we went into battle, very much like you're doing now.' Robert surprised himself with his answer. He never talked about the war if he could help it. And if he was asked questions by some simpering debutante who thought he was 'ever so brave', he always answered in the vaguest terms possible. He didn't think he had voluntarily brought the subject of the war up in the two years since he'd returned to England.

Louisa looked at him silently with her big brown eyes and Robert felt as though she were looking deep into his soul.

'You lost your friend didn't you?' she asked eventually.

He nodded, not trusting himself to speak.

'I'm sorry. It must seem silly to you, my being afraid of visiting a shop, after all you and your friends went through.'

'No,' Robert said, 'it's not silly. Being nervous of the unknown is the most natural response in the world.'

'You must find everyday fears a little ridiculous, though,' Louisa said.

Wordlessly he shook his head, knowing he couldn't tell her sometimes he was afraid to go to sleep, knowing the nightmares could start as soon as he allowed his mind to drift into oblivion.

'There's nothing to be afraid of today,' he said, steering the conversation away from himself. 'I'll be with you all the time.'

'Surely not all the time,' Louisa teased.

'Well, not far away,' Robert said, his voice gruff.

'I worry what people will think of me.'

'Don't.'

He'd stopped caring what people thought

when he realised he'd lost most of the people who mattered to him.

'That's your advice?' Louisa asked. 'Just don't?'

'That's my advice.'

She grinned and turned back to the window. Robert was pleased to see she'd stopped wringing her hands together.

The carriage halted in front of a large shopfront and Robert watched as Louisa's eyes widened in amazement.

He quickly hopped down from the carriage and once again held out his hand to help Louisa down. This time he didn't let go, but tucked her hand into his elbow and escorted her inside.

They were met by a smiling woman who bobbed into a curtsy as soon as they walked inside. She looked from Robert to Louisa and back again, the confusion showing on her face. She had obviously seen the grand carriage stop outside the shop but was puzzled she did not know the mismatched couple who descended from it.

'Welcome, sir, madam,' she said.

'I'm Lord Fleetwood,' Robert said, watching as the woman's eyes widened in recognition of the name, 'and this is my ward, Miss Louisa Turnhill.'

'It's an honour to meet you both.'

'Miss Turnhill has come to stay with me, but

unfortunately all her clothes were destroyed in a fire.'

'All of them?' the modiste asked in disbelief.

'All of them,' Robert confirmed.

'My name is Mrs Willow, this here is Lucy,' the woman said as a young shopgirl stepped forward. 'And this is Prudence,' she added as another girl bobbed a curtsy. 'We would be delighted to be of assistance.'

Robert stepped back as the three women crowded around Louisa and bustled her farther into the shop. He found a comfortable chair, placed so that he had a good view of the proceedings but was tucked out of the way.

'How many items would you like to order for today?' Mrs Willow asked.

Louisa glanced back over her shoulder at Robert.

'Oh, just the one,' she said.

'She means one to wear away today,' Robert corrected her from his position in the corner, 'and six more to order.'

All four women looked at him in shock.

'Of course, sir,' Mrs Willow said. 'And would these all be daytime dresses?'

Again Louisa looked at him for guidance.

'For now, yes, let's focus on the daytime,' he said. 'But if you keep her measurements, then we can order evening gowns at some point in the future.'

'And what colours do you favour, Miss Turnhill?'

'Anything but grey,' Louisa said, smiling. 'The brighter the better.'

Robert watched as Louisa was led round the shop and roll after roll of material was presented to her. She seemed to come alive with every minute as she discussed the luxury of one material and compared it to the comfort of another. He could hardly believe this was the same scared young woman he'd found in a cell in Lewisham Asylum just yesterday.

Every so often Louisa would glance his way, uncertain about a decision, and Robert would give her an encouraging smile. He liked that a small gesture from him was enough to give her the confidence she needed to prosper in such an unfamiliar setting.

'So we have decided on materials and colours,' Mrs Willow said. 'Now we have to decide on style.'

Louisa was led behind a curtain by the two young shopgirls. Every few minutes Mrs Willow would carry another dress behind the curtain.

'What do you think?' Louisa asked shyly.

Robert looked up and felt his breath catch in his chest.

Louisa looked at him nervously, biting her bottom lip. Robert knew he had to say something, but suddenly his words had deserted him.

'You look beautiful,' he said eventually.

Beautiful didn't even begin to cover it. She looked stunning. He hadn't been able to even begin to imagine what had lain under the shapeless sacks he'd seen her in before. Now it was laid out for everyone to see. The dress nipped in at her slender waist and skimmed over her hips and the upper half accentuated her cleavage to maximum effect. Robert felt a sudden and unexpected stab of jealousy. He didn't want anyone else seeing her like this.

He told himself to stop being so ridiculous. She wasn't his to covet. She was his ward and he should be pleased she was so delighted with her new appearance.

'I feel like a different person,' Louisa said quietly.

As she smiled Robert knew it was a smile just for him and he felt the first stirrings of desire wake inside him. When she was happy, genuinely happy, she glowed.

The four women looked at him expectantly and Robert realised he'd cleared his throat in an effort to take control of himself. They were expecting him to say something.

'The colour suits you,' he ventured. He wasn't

an expert on fashion or materials, but no one could deny the emerald-green complemented Louisa's chestnut hair and deep brown eyes exquisitely.

'We'll take it,' Robert said to Mrs Willow. 'That's if you would like it.'

He turned back to Louisa and saw the hope burn in her eyes, but something was holding her back.

Discreetly Mrs Willow ushered the two shopgirls away so Robert and Louisa could converse in private.

'What's wrong?' Robert asked. 'Don't you like it?'

'I love the dress,' Louisa answered. 'And I love how it makes me feel. It's just…' She trailed off.

Robert smiled at her encouragingly.

'It's just I don't know if I can afford it.'

Robert frowned.

'I think Mr Craven spent most of my inheritance and I haven't exactly been able to earn a living this last year.'

'You're my ward, Miss Turnhill,' Robert said slowly. 'It is my legal obligation to provide you with clothes and food and shelter.'

He saw her face drop at being called his 'legal obligation'.

'What's more, it is my pleasure to buy this dress for you.'

'Thank you,' she said.

She said it with such sincerity he knew she appreciated him not treating her as solely his duty.

Louisa took a step closer to him and for a second Robert thought she was about to embrace him. He felt a rush of pleasure surge through his body. Every single part of him knew touching Louisa would be a bad idea, but still he desired it.

The disappointment he felt when Louisa merely smiled at him was acute, but he forced himself to smile back.

'We'll take this dress as it is,' Robert called to Mrs Willow. 'It seems to fit her well. I'll send someone to pick up the others in a couple of days.'

'Very good, sir.'

Robert did not want to examine his reaction to Louisa in detail. He knew his newfound attraction towards her was wrong on so many levels. Maybe it was natural, he told himself. She was a good-looking woman who had been transformed into a beautiful butterfly in front of his eyes. And he was a man who had denied himself any sort of female companionship for so long. Perhaps his attraction towards her was to be expected. After all, she was the first woman he'd spent any sort of time with in the last two years.

Robert could only hope that was all it was. The last thing he needed was to desire any woman, let alone the one he was legally bound to until she came of age.

Chapter Seven

Louisa felt transformed. It was amazing how something as insignificant as a dress could make her feel like a real woman, not some crazy orphan who had been stuck in an asylum for the last year.

She glanced at Robert. He hadn't said a word whilst the last few adjustments were being made to her dress, but she'd felt his eyes on her.

She couldn't quite work out what his motivations were. He'd just spent rather a lot of money on making her look respectable and, more importantly, making her happy.

Louisa had been well loved by her parents. She had fond memories of shopping trips with her mother and indulgent presents from her father, but since their deaths she hadn't received a single gift. Christmas had been a spartan affair with Mr Craven and she hadn't even known what day it was to celebrate her birthday whilst she was locked in the asylum. Now here was Robert, a man she'd known for only a day, willing to spend money on making her happy.

'Thank you,' she said again as they left the shop, Louisa feeling like a new woman in her emerald-green dress.

Her gratitude was genuine, but she couldn't shake the feeling that she was missing something. She didn't understand why Robert was being so kind to her.

'Why are you being so nice?' she asked as they reached the carriage.

He paused before he turned to face her. 'Nice?' he asked, as if confused by her choice of word.

'Yes, nice. How else would you describe how you've acted towards me?'

'I've done what any man in my position would.'

Louisa shook her head. 'My last guardian kept me prisoner in his house and stole all my inheritance.' She shuddered. He'd done more than that, worse things, things she didn't want to remember.

'It's what any decent man in my position would do.'

Maybe that was it, Louisa thought. Maybe he was a decent man. She hadn't known many in her life.

'You've taken me into your home, welcomed me into your life,' she said. 'That's above the call of duty.'

'After everything you've been through I could hardly send you off to live with some dreary relative in the country,' Robert said.

'I must have disrupted your entire life.'

He didn't say anything. Once again Louisa wondered about his past. He hadn't really told her anything about himself. Not that he had to, Louisa was just curious.

'I'm sure I can take a few days out of my normal schedule until we get you settled.'

Louisa nodded. She hadn't really thought much about the future. Only a few hours ago she'd been determined to set out on her own, disappear into the anonymous streets of London. After their talk Louisa had decided to give Robert and the life he was offering her a chance. If something went wrong, he'd promised he would let her leave and even help her with her independence. She hadn't thought much past that.

The problem was Louisa still couldn't quite believe she wouldn't soon wake up from a dream and find herself back in the asylum. Her life had changed so much in such a short time.

'Can we go for a stroll?' Louisa asked.

Robert looked from her to the carriage, then nodded in agreement.

They set off down the street arm in arm and Louisa felt like a normal young woman out for a walk with her guardian. She wanted this moment to last for ever.

'I know we have a lot to discuss,' she said, 'but can we pretend to be normal just for a little while?'

'You don't need to pretend, Louisa,' he said. 'Where would you like to go?'

She contemplated for a couple of seconds. 'It's a beautiful day—maybe a walk in the park? If there's anywhere suitable nearby.'

Robert took his pocket watch from his jacket and glanced at the time. Louisa wondered if he had somewhere else to be and almost told him she didn't mind going back to the house, not if he had other engagements.

'How about a stroll through Hyde Park?' Robert asked.

Louisa smiled. She couldn't think of anything more appealing.

'I've never been to a park in London before,' she said as they walked arm in arm down the wide pavement. 'I've never really been anywhere in London before, apart from the asylum.'

'Your parents didn't bring you here when you were young?'

Louisa shrugged. 'I suppose we must have visited once or twice, but I don't really remember.' She felt the pang of sadness she always did when thinking of her parents. 'You don't realise at the time that every moment is to be treasured, do you?' she said quietly. 'Otherwise you'd make an effort to remember more.'

Robert stayed silent, but she felt the empathy emanating from him.

'What *do* you recall about them?' he asked after a couple of minutes.

Louisa hadn't talked about her parents for so long. No one had been interested for so many years and if someone did bring up the subject she normally felt too upset to say much. Today, however, she wanted to talk. She wanted to tell Robert how she remembered her mother's laugh and her father's compassion. How her mother used to read to her before tucking her into bed and her father would whisk her up in front of him and teach her to ride on the back of his trusty horse.

'They were happy,' Louisa said. 'Every day was filled with laughter and sunshine and smiles.'

'It must have been a wonderful childhood.'

'It was.' Louisa knew she'd been lucky in her early years. Too many of her peers had absent fathers and downtrodden mothers. But Louisa had seen what true love could bring to a marriage. 'I can't ever remember being unhappy whilst my parents were alive.'

Robert remained quiet, allowing her to remember the happiness she'd felt for just a few moments longer.

'It was some mysterious illness that killed them,' Louisa said, surprising herself at how easy it was to open up to Robert. 'The doctors didn't know how they'd caught it or what it was, but one day they were both happy, healthy people in the prime of their lives and the next they were fighting a deadly illness.'

'You didn't get it?' Robert asked.

Louisa shook her head and felt the tears welling in her eyes. 'My father fell ill first of all, but when my mother succumbed she forbade my nanny from taking me to see her, knowing I would be in danger if I spent even a few moments in her room.'

'So you didn't see them before they passed away?'

Louisa paused. She'd seen them, and sometimes she saw them still in those quiet moments just before she dropped off to sleep.

'I sneaked into their bedroom in the middle of the night. I couldn't understand why they'd kept me away.' To this day Louisa could still remember the hideously sweet smell of the sickroom. 'My father was quiet, I think he was very close to the end, but my mother was writhing and moaning.'

Louisa had screamed, thinking someone was torturing her mother, not understanding she was in the grip of a fever making her delirious.

'I was bundled out, but I screamed and screamed until they let me back in the room. By that time my mother had settled and was sleeping fitfully.'

'That was the last time you saw them?' Robert asked softly.

Louisa nodded. 'I kissed them both on the cheek and told them I would see them at breakfast. They were dead by the next morning.'

'It must have been the end of your world.'

Louisa nodded. Robert seemed to understand her distress. She didn't know what it was about him that made him so easy to talk to. She hadn't told anyone about the last time she'd seen her parents before. Partly because no one had been interested, but also because she didn't want anyone to see her so vulnerable. Even though she'd only known Robert for a short while Louisa had known he wouldn't belittle her memory of her parents or the last time she'd seen them. He'd understand why it had been quite so harrowing.

'When you lose someone you're close to it leaves a gulf,' he said slowly, 'that never heals. In time we learn to bury that gulf, but it's always there, under the surface.'

He said it with such compassion Louisa knew he was talking from personal experience.

She hoped he might elaborate. She desperately wanted to know more about this man who had saved her from a lifetime of misery, but at the moment she didn't feel as though she could just come out and ask him. She knew he had been in the army, and that he'd lost a friend in the war, that much he'd let slip earlier on in the carriage, but other than that Louisa was pretty much in the dark as to Robert's past.

'So how did Thomas Craven become your guardian?' he asked.

Louisa grimaced as she thought back to the first time her old guardian had shown up in her life.

'I didn't have any other relatives,' Louisa said, trying not to think about how different her life would have been if she'd had a kindly aunt or grandparent left alive. 'Mr Craven was my father's business partner.'

Robert nodded, encouraging her to go on.

'I hardly knew him. He came into our lives about six months before my parents died and convinced my father to invest in some scheme or another.'

'But why did your parents make this man they hardly knew your guardian?'

Louisa shrugged. In truth she didn't really know. She'd been so young at the time.

'In the few months before my parents died he was around the house a lot. He stayed with us on numerous occasions. And he always made a show of fussing over me.'

'Your parents trusted him?'

She nodded. 'From what Mr Craven let slip over the years when he was inebriated, he'd worked hard to gain their trust. He thought they would leave him money in their will. He never even considered they would put me into his care.'

'But your parents were so young, much younger than Craven. He shouldn't even have thought about inheriting from them.'

Tears sprung to Louisa's eyes. It was something she'd not been able to ignore over the years, but a question she knew she would never know the answer to.

'Sometimes, when I've been particularly low, I've wondered how much of a role Mr Craven played in my parents' deaths,' she said slowly, wondering if Robert would think her crazy.

He didn't laugh or roll his eyes. Instead he seemed to consider the idea carefully.

'It does seem suspicious,' he agreed. 'It sounds as though Thomas Craven ingratiated himself with your parents, but with his death we'll probably never know whether that was purely to get money out of them whilst they were alive or whether he had a more sinister motive.'

Louisa found herself nodding in agreement. It felt reassuring to have Robert beside her, supporting her and agreeing with her. For years she'd wondered what exactly had transpired between her parents and Mr Craven. She'd known she had no other relatives, but Mr Craven must have been a good actor to convince her parents he was a suitable guardian for their only child.

'I just wish I had had an hour with him,' Louisa said quietly, 'to confront him and to force him to answer my questions.'

Robert squeezed her arm gently and Louisa felt his strength flowing into her. She had to accept she would never have answers. She would never know why her parents chose Mr Craven as her guardian and she would never know whether he had been involved in their deaths. In the past the uncertainty had upset her immeasurably, but today, with Robert beside her, Louisa felt herself letting go a little. Now was the time to look forward, not back. She might never have the answers to her questions, but she had her freedom and she had her entire life stretching out in front of her.

They walked in silence for a few minutes. Louisa glanced sideways at Robert every few seconds. She wanted to know more about him.

Just as she was plucking up the courage to ask Robert a little about himself, he paused and pointed to a gateway.

'Hyde Park, Miss Turnhill. The first of many London parks I promise to take you to.'

The park was quiet at this time, only a few young children with their nannies running around on the grass and one or two groups of young ladies strolling under parasols.

'We shouldn't meet anyone at this time,' Robert said as he guided her into the park.

Louisa realised that was why he'd checked his pocket watch earlier; he hadn't wanted them to bump into anyone. She wondered if he were ashamed of her, but quickly dismissed the thought. It would have been easy to send her off to some far-flung corner of England, far away from the prying eyes and wagging tongues of society, but instead he'd kept her here in London. No, Robert Fleetwood wasn't ashamed of her, she thought it more likely he wanted to protect her from having to answer any awkward questions.

It felt strange to Louisa to have someone looking out for her. For years she'd only been able to depend upon herself. She didn't think she would ever get used to someone else worrying about her welfare.

'You have a very tough decision to make now,

Miss Turnhill.' Robert turned to her with a grave expression on his face.

Louisa's heart dropped. She'd been enjoying not thinking about her circumstances for a few minutes.

'You need to choose whether you'd like to go and take a stroll around the Serpentine or sample the delicious new delicacy all society are talking about: flavoured ices.'

Louisa pretended to consider her decision very carefully. 'Are you sure I have to decide?' she asked.

'This is your outing, Miss Turnhill, your wish is my command.'

'Then I wish to do both.'

Robert smiled one of his rare smiles and Louisa caught a glimpse of the carefree young man he must have once been. Again she wondered what had happened during the war to make him quite so serious and withdrawn, but she knew now wasn't the right time to ask. They were having an enjoyable morning in the park and she didn't want to do anything to jeopardise that.

They strolled arm in arm around the Serpentine. Every few minutes Robert would impart some bit of knowledge about the park or London, and Louisa would listen with interest. She loved the way he spoke, he seemed so knowledgeable about so many things. Louisa's own education had been cut short—Mr Craven hadn't thought it necessary to continue her lessons after her parents had died. Although she'd read hundreds of the dusty books in the old man's library, it wasn't the same as a formal education.

She realised she must seem completely uneducated to Robert.

He'd stopped at the water's edge and together they stared out across the still water.

'It's beautiful,' Louisa said, glancing at Robert. 'I feel so lucky, being here with you.'

She turned to face him and felt the emotion welling up inside her.

'Thank you,' she said. 'Thank you for giving me a chance to experience the world for myself. Even if I was taken back to the asylum today I'd never forget the time we've spent together.'

Robert slowly turned to look at her and Louisa felt her breath catch in her throat at the intensity of his gaze.

'This is your right, Louisa. Every experience and every new sight is something you deserve to have.'

Louisa felt her tongue dart out to moisten her lips. She couldn't tear her eyes away from his. His words were said so passionately she understood how he had led troops into battle; she would follow him anywhere in this instant.

For seconds their eyes remained locked together. Louisa felt her body sway instinctively towards his and the gap between them closed.

She could see the desire in his eyes. He wanted to kiss her, just as much as she wanted to kiss him, but he didn't move.

Louisa felt the confusion wash over her. She wanted him so much, she wanted him to devour her with his mouth, to lay her down on the grass and cover her body with his own. Never before had she known such a strong physical attraction to someone. Yet at odds with the primal urge she had whenever she looked at him was the small voice in the back of her head telling her to run, to get as far away from the generous man with the serious eyes as possible. Falling for him could only bring trouble. He would hurt her just like everyone else, no matter how kind and caring he seemed now.

Despite a myriad of doubts Louisa still wanted him to kiss her. She wanted to feel his lips on her skin and shudder as he ran his fingers all over her body.

For a second she thought he was going to do just that. His eyes darkened and his breathing became a little heavier. Louisa held her breath.

'Lord Fleetwood.'

Both Louisa and Robert jumped and took a step back.

'I'm not interrupting anything, am I?'

Chapter Eight

Robert couldn't answer immediately; his brain had gone on an unscheduled holiday and left a mindless idiot in charge. He'd almost kissed Louisa. Again. Once was bad enough, but twice was unforgivable. And in a public park for anyone to see.

He forced himself to drag his eyes away from Louisa's delectable mouth and turned to face the woman who was addressing him.

'Mrs Knapwell,' Robert said, his heart growing heavy as he realised who had interrupted them.

'It's delightful to see you, Lord Fleetwood, it's been so long.'

Robert nodded, not able to find his voice.

'And you're looking so well.'

He grimaced. He didn't feel well at all.

'I don't think we've had the pleasure of being introduced,' Mrs Knapwell said, turning to Louisa.

'This is Miss Louisa Turnhill, my ward,' Robert said stiffly.

'Your ward?' It was said with such incredulity that Robert had to suppress a smile. 'I didn't realise you had a ward.'

'Lord Fleetwood has only been my guardian for a short while,' Louisa said, coming to his rescue. 'After my old guardian passed away.'

'It is lovely to meet you, Miss Turnhill, and my sympathies for your loss.'

Louisa smiled at Mrs Knapwell. 'There's no need,' she said. 'My old guardian was a beast. Lord Fleetwood is much kinder.'

Robert almost choked. Mrs Knapwell had to hide a smile.

'How have you been keeping, Mrs Knapwell?' Robert asked before Louisa could say any more.

She gave a brave little smile. 'Keeping busy. I've been staying with friends over the winter. I only came back to London to do some work with one of my charities. An appeal for the orphans of south London.'

Robert didn't know what to say. The guilt he felt every time he saw Mrs Knapwell wasn't getting any less after over two years. He was responsible for this kind woman's loneliness. He'd taken her son away from her.

What made it worse was Mrs Knapwell had been nothing but kind and sympathetic towards him. After Robert's father had died whilst he was still at school, Robert had spent most of his holidays with the Knapwells. In a way Mrs Knapwell had become the mother he'd never known, since his own had died when he was just an infant. And then Robert had taken her own son away from her.

'But enough about me. I want to hear how you've been doing. You looked so happy when I spied you from the other side of the park.'

Robert felt the bottom drop out of his world. She'd seen him looking happy, moving on with his life, when her son was dead and buried in an unmarked grave. He had no right to be happy.

The silence stretched out before them, but Robert couldn't find anything to say. Louisa looked at him strangely, but after a few seconds she linked arms with Mrs Knapwell as if they were old friends and soon had her chatting away.

They ambled along, the two women arm in arm with their heads bent together and Robert stumbling along behind. He felt as though he was in one of his nightmares.

'So where were you living before you came to stay with dear Lord Fleetwood?' he heard Mrs Knapwell ask. He didn't even have the presence of mind to jump into the conversation and stop Louisa blurting out the truth.

'My guardian, Mr Craven, had a house in

Norfolk,' Louisa said, avoiding the question artfully.

'And how are you enjoying your time with Lord Fleetwood?'

'He's so kind,' Louisa said. 'I'm sure he never would have asked for a ward, but he's been a perfect gentleman.'

A perfect gentleman who had nearly ravished her in the middle of the park.

Robert grimaced. He didn't deserve kind words from Louisa or Mrs Knapwell. For a while he'd forgotten his place in the world. After Greg Knapwell had been killed and half of Robert's men slaughtered alongside him, Robert had vowed he would never get himself into a position to hurt people again. The only way he could do that was to withdraw, to watch life go by from the sidelines. That way he couldn't hurt anyone else. He owed that to his friend.

He couldn't believe he'd almost kissed Louisa. A few more seconds and he would have compromised her in front of multiple witnesses. She'd looked so innocent and radiant, gazing out over the Serpentine, he'd felt his heart pounding in his chest and a primal urge to possess her had taken over him. He'd forgotten she was his ward and he'd forgotten his oath to avoid romantic involvement with women. In that moment it was just him and Louisa and an overwhelming attraction.

Maybe it was a good thing Mrs Knapwell had come along when she did and reminded him of all the reasons why kissing Louisa was a bad idea.

He glanced ahead. The two women were still deep in conversation. He thought he heard his name a couple of times and strained his ears. Mrs Knapwell was a kind woman and Robert knew she had never expressed any blame towards him for the death of her son, but deep down he also knew she must hold him at least partially responsible. He felt an unexpected pang of loneliness. For a little while he had allowed himself to remember what it was like to enjoy someone's company, to bask in Louisa's affection and happiness. But it was for the best that he'd been given a reminder of why it could never be, he reasoned, he couldn't allow himself to grow too attached to Louisa.

A few feet in front of him Louisa and Mrs Knapwell had paused and stood waiting for Robert to catch up.

'It has been lovely seeing you again,' Mrs Knapwell said, 'and delightful meeting you, Miss Turnhill, but I really must go, otherwise I'll be dreadfully late for my charity meeting.'

She paused and patted Louisa on the hand.

'You look after Lord Fleetwood, my dear, he deserves a bit of happiness.'

Robert felt his throat constricting with guilt and emotion.

'And I hope you will both be able to make my dinner party on Thursday. It'll just be a small affair, a couple of close friends.'

'We'd love to,' Louisa said.

Robert could hardly refuse the invitation, but already he was dreading it. A whole evening of sitting across from the woman who was still mourning the son he'd taken away from her. It would be torture, but it was nothing less than he deserved.

'It was lovely meeting you,' Louisa said as Mrs Knapwell gave her arm one last squeeze before walking off down the path.

For a minute Robert didn't say anything. Louisa stepped towards him and turned her lovely innocent face upwards. Even after what had just happened Robert still had the urge to kiss her. Her lips were so pink and inviting and her cheeks were just slightly flushed from the sun. She was beautiful, but he didn't deserve her. He couldn't taint her innocence.

'Mrs Knapwell seemed very nice,' Louisa said as she linked her arm back through his as if nothing had just passed between them.

'Mmm-hmm,' Robert murmured, not trusting himself to speak.

'She was telling me about her work with the orphans.'

At least she hadn't been talking about Greg. Robert didn't know if he could bear Louisa finding out what he was responsible for—not yet.

'She cares so much about them,' Louisa said. She paused before continuing, as if suspecting her next words might be delicate. 'She also told me about her son.'

Robert froze. Greg's face flashed before his eyes. The happy, smiling man he'd shared so much with. Their hopes and dreams, and their fears of the battlefield.

'What did she say?' he forced himself to ask.

'She said you'd been best friends and that after your father died you used to spend all your holidays at their house. You went to university together and then you went to fight in the war together.'

He could feel her eyes on his face, but he couldn't lift his gaze to meet hers.

'She said her son died on the battlefield.'

Robert could still remember the exact instant he'd realised his best friend was dead.

'And she said you blame yourself for his death.'

Robert couldn't take any more. He didn't want Louisa to know what had happened. He knew she would start looking at him differently, as if he were a monster, and he couldn't bear the thought of that.

'We need to go home,' he said abruptly.

Louisa's face fell, but she nodded and allowed him to lead her back the way they had come, retracing their steps through the park.

'I'm sorry,' she said quietly.

Robert wanted to reach out to her and explain, but he couldn't. That would mean admitting how he was responsible for Greg Knapwell's death and he wasn't ready for Louisa to know that. That was a secret he'd kept inside for a very long time and he wasn't going to air it now.

She looked hurt, as if he'd physically slapped her. He knew she was vulnerable, but he just couldn't explain it all to her.

So they walked on in silence, Robert hating himself more with every step they took.

Chapter Nine

Louisa skipped down the stairs, humming to herself. It was a beautiful sunny morning and she was a free woman. And she was wearing the second of her new dresses. She couldn't help being happy.

Robert had been in a strange mood all of yesterday afternoon after their encounter with Mrs Knapwell in the park. He'd barely spoken to her at dinner and had disappeared off immediately afterwards, leaving Louisa to her own devices.

At first she'd been hurt by his refusal to speak to her, but slowly she'd realised he was still mourning his friend and she'd probably been a bit insensitive in the way she'd brought it up.

Today she was determined to make a fresh start with him. They'd been having such a good time in the park before they'd met Mrs Knapwell. She felt Robert had finally let her see some of his true self. Then there had been that moment by the lake.

Louisa paused for a minute and thought back to it. She was sure Robert had looked as though he was going to kiss her. And she'd allowed herself to sway towards him, inviting him in.

She couldn't deny she was attracted to him. He was a handsome man, but more than that he was kind and good. He was the first person in a long time to treat her like a human being and not an animal. No wonder she was attracted to him. It was a bad idea and she knew it couldn't go any further, but it was quite flattering that he obviously found her at least a little attractive, too.

Louisa paused outside Robert's study. After she'd eaten breakfast on her own, she'd been determined to seek Robert out and make her peace with him. She would somehow communicate that she wouldn't go prying into his past any more than he wanted her to. She would respect his privacy and they could go back to how it had been before they'd met Mrs Knapwell.

There were low voices coming from the study. One was Robert's—even after just a couple of days Louisa thought she'd be able to pick his serious voice out from a crowd. The other she didn't recognise, but from her position outside the door she could tell it was a man.

She stepped closer, knowing all the time she

should just walk away and allow Robert privacy to conduct his business in.

'You want me to assess her?' she heard the stranger ask.

'I think it would be helpful. She spent so long in the asylum.'

Louisa felt her heart pound in her chest. They were talking about her, and Robert was asking someone to assess her. Surely he didn't mean to send her back to the asylum. Over the last couple of days Louisa hadn't once regretted her decision to stay. She'd even started to trust Robert a little. Now here he was talking to someone in private about getting her assessed.

Louisa had the urge to flee. Just to walk out of the house and never look back. She might be on her own, but at least no one would be able to send her back to the madhouse.

She glanced at the front door. The streets of London would be better than the asylum any day.

She hesitated and realised she didn't like the idea of leaving and never seeing Robert again. Over the last couple of days she'd grown to like and respect him. He'd opened his home and his life to her, and he'd been the first person to care about her since her parents had died. She couldn't quite believe he was getting ready to send her back to the asylum.

Louisa glanced one last time at the front door,

decided she would give Robert the benefit of the doubt, then raised her hand to knock on the study door.

The voices inside fell silent.

'Come in.'

Louisa opened the door, her heart pounding in her chest. She stood awkwardly in the doorway as she surveyed the two men in the room.

'Just the person,' Robert said with a smile. He didn't look like a man who was just about to condemn someone to a lifetime of misery.

He rose from his seat and crossed the room towards her.

'Trust me,' he whispered in her ear, so the other man didn't hear.

Louisa found herself nodding, unconsciously replying to his request.

'This is Dr Wade. Dr Wade, this is my ward, Miss Turnhill.'

Louisa forced herself to smile and wondered if her efforts made her look mad.

'Good to meet you, Miss Turnhill,' the doctor said, rising from his seat.

Louisa was suspicious of doctors. Her previous encounters with men of the medical profession hadn't gone well. The first time she'd met a doctor had been when her parents died. The second time was when she'd been declared insane.

Robert must have sensed her uneasiness. He

slipped a protective arm around her waist and led her to the sofa. Louisa felt the comfort of his touch and allowed herself to relax a little.

'Dr Wade has come at my request,' Robert said.

'To see me?' Louisa could feel her anxiety levels building.

'To see you,' Robert confirmed.

She glanced nervously at Robert, who smiled serenely down at her. She loved his smile. He didn't smile enough in her opinion, but when he did he looked carefree and young.

Focus, she told herself, she could sort out her inappropriate feelings for Robert later. Now she had to appear completely sane in front of this man who had come to assess her.

'I thought I would ask Dr Wade here to see you,' Robert said, removing his hand from around her waist. Louisa suddenly felt lonely. 'Doctor Wade is going to ask you some questions and assess you.'

Louisa glanced at the door and wondered if she could make a run for it.

'A year ago when the doctor pronounced you insane, he did something unethical and unforgivable,' Robert said. 'We're going to rectify that today.'

'So you're here to certify I'm not mad?' Louisa asked the doctor.

'I'm here just to ask you a few questions, Miss Turnhill.' So Dr Wade would be making up his own mind.

Louisa suddenly felt very hot. What if he thought she was mad? What if she actually *was* mad and she'd just been fooling herself all this time?

'You're going to do just fine,' Robert murmured very close to her ear.

Louisa felt Robert's confidence in her boost her own.

'Tell me a little about yourself, Miss Turnhill.'

She didn't know where to start.

'Just some basic facts: who you are, your age, your family,' Dr Wade prompted.

'Well, I'm nineteen years old and I'm an orphan. My parents died of a fever when I was ten.' Louisa paused and felt Robert silently willing her on. 'After that I lived with Mr Craven for eight years before I spent just over a year in the Lewisham Asylum.'

'Can you remember what your guardian said was wrong with you? Why he had you sent to the asylum?'

Louisa looked uncomfortably at Robert. She didn't want him believing any of Thomas Craven's lies.

'We can do this in private if you would prefer.'

She glanced at Robert. 'No, I would feel happier with Lord Fleetwood here.'

Louisa realised it was true. He would stop the interview if he thought the doctor was getting the wrong impression. And as her guardian he had the right to know these things.

'He said I was prone to fits of melancholia, followed by episodes of mania and hyperactivity. He said I had tried to hurt myself on multiple occasions and had even tried to kill myself. And he said I heard voices that weren't there.'

'That's quite a collection of mental illnesses he thought you had.'

Louisa smiled. 'I think he thought the madder the better.'

'Tell me a little about your time in the asylum, Miss Turnhill.'

Louisa shuddered as she thought back, but Robert's hand tightened its grip on hers and she found the courage to remember.

'When I first arrived it was horrible,' Louisa said, remembering the dark days when she'd first been sent to the asylum, 'They stripped me down and immersed me in cold water multiple times a day. They said it would purge the madness from me.'

The doctor nodded sympathetically.

'Some of the wardens beat me. they would all

throw me around or slap me if I wasn't quick to respond.'

Louisa could feel Robert stiffen next to her.

'But after a few weeks things got better. I was moved to my cell and it felt as though I was almost forgotten about.'

Louisa had wept with relief once the cold baths and beatings had stopped.

'They kept me restrained, chained to the wall, but apart from that they left me alone.'

Dr Wade nodded sympathetically. 'It must have been very lonely for you.'

It had been. At first Louisa had cherished being left alone, but as the days turned to weeks she craved human contact. The only people she saw were those delivering her meals and even they didn't interact with her.

'At one point I started to provoke the wardens, doing anything to make them interact with me. I got beaten more, but it seemed worth it to hear them speak, to realise I wasn't the only person left in the world.'

Louisa felt the tears brimming in her eyes and worked hard to gain control of herself. She'd survived over a year in the asylum, she could cope with a few memories.

'Sometimes loneliness can be worse than physical pain,' Robert said quietly.

Louisa nodded.

'Have you ever tried to hurt yourself, Miss Turnhill?'

Louisa could tell Robert was surprised by the directness of the question. He shifted in his seat beside her and opened his mouth as if to object.

'Never.'

'And have you ever tried to kill yourself?'

'No. For a while after I was first put into the asylum I used to wake up thinking it would be better if I just wasn't here any more. But I've never tried to hurt myself in any way.'

'Given your circumstances I think many people would rather not exist than wake up in a mental institution every morning,' Dr Wade said reassuringly.

Louisa felt Robert relax a little beside her. She was still unused to anyone wanting to protect her in the way he did. He was sitting there poised, ready to spring to her defence as soon as she needed it.

'Do you ever hear voices only you can hear?'

'No.' That one was simple to answer.

'And do you have any special powers, things other people can't do?

Louisa felt herself raising her eyebrows. 'That's a new one. You mean like being able to fly or walk through walls?'

'Exactly.'

'Just answer the question, Louisa,' Robert said

quietly in her ear. She liked it when he called her
Louisa, rather than the formal Miss Turnhill.

He was nervous, she realised. He was nervous
for her. He realised how important this was for
her and he wanted everything to go smoothly.

'I don't have any special powers,' Louisa said,
'except having survived over a year in a madhouse.'

'That is quite a remarkable feat,' Dr Wade
said. 'Just a few more questions, Miss Turnhill,
then I'll have all the information I need.'

'Certainly.' Louisa's nerves had settled now
and she was confident she was coming across
well.

'Do you ever feel low in your mood, or as if
you don't feel able to enjoy things in life?'

Louisa laughed, 'No.'

'And do you ever have problems sleeping or
eating?'

It was Robert's turn to laugh, 'She has the
healthiest appetite I've ever known.'

'And I don't have any problems sleeping.'

'Wonderful. Thank you for being so open and
honest with me, Miss Turnhill. I know it can't
have been easy for you.'

Louisa leant forward ever so slightly and realised she was holding her breath, waiting for his
verdict. Beside her Robert was doing the same.

'I'm pleased to say I agree with Lord Fleetwood, Miss Turnhill. I do not think you display any signs of melancholy or mania. You seem to be a well-adjusted young woman who cruelly had her freedom taken from her.'

Louisa felt the relief seep through her. She'd known she wasn't mad. All along she'd known, but it was hard to quieten that little doubt that sometimes crept in. Now she had the reassurance from a medical man that she wasn't insane.

'I can only apologise for the wrong one of my colleagues must have done to have you committed to the asylum. I will be writing up my notes of our conversation today and will of course let you have a copy of my conclusions.'

'Thank you, Dr Wade.'

'It was a pleasure to meet you, Miss Turnhill.'

Robert stood and showed Dr Wade out. Louisa felt herself sag into the sofa. She felt relieved and ecstatic at the same time.

She was still slumped into the sofa when Robert returned.

'I'm sorry to spring that on you, Miss Turnhill,' Robert said.

'You called me Louisa earlier.'

He hesitated. 'Just in private,' he said.

That was good enough for her.

'I thought you might worry if I told you about it beforehand.'

'When I knew there was a doctor in here I

did wonder if you were going to send me back to the asylum,' Louisa said, 'but then I realised you wouldn't do that.'

Their eyes met and Louisa gave him a tentative smile.

He'd sat down again on the sofa beside her. He was too close for propriety and he was making Louisa feel a little breathless.

'You realised I wouldn't do that?' he asked, his voice low.

Louisa nodded, not trusting herself to speak.

'So you trust me?'

'A little.' She was surprised to find she spoke the truth.

'Just a little?'

'A little is a lot for me.'

He contemplated her words for a few seconds. 'I suppose I'll take a little bit of trust.'

She could feel the strong muscles of his leg pushing against the material of her dress. There must have been at least four layers of fabric between them, but Louisa could feel the heat emanating off him as though his bare skin was pressing against hers.

She felt her heart pounding in her chest and Louisa realised she wanted Robert to kiss her. She wanted him to take her in his arms and lay her down on the sofa and kiss her all over her body.

She didn't understand the attraction she felt towards this man she'd known for just a couple of days. He was handsome, that much was true, and he was kind, but if she thought about it she barely knew him. What was more, she knew she didn't want to allow him to get too close to her. If she let him in, then he would be able to hurt her. Despite all this she still wanted him to kiss her. Just once, she reasoned, just so that she would know what it was like.

'You're an incredible woman, Louisa,' Robert murmured.

She didn't know how to respond. Robert didn't seem to notice. Instead he bent his neck and brushed his lips against hers. For a second Louisa stiffened, unsure how to react, then her primal instincts took over and she started to kiss him back.

His lips moved unhurriedly across her, tender and passionate at the same time. Louisa felt a fire building from her toes and rising up through her body. She was burning with desire all for this man.

Robert grazed his fingers across her cheek, sending shivers down her spine. Louisa tentatively reached up and ran her hands through his hair, pulling him closer to her and deepening their kiss.

'Oh, Louisa,' Robert murmured as he broke away.

They looked at each other for a few seconds, both only just realising the implications of what they'd done.

'I'm so sorry,' Robert said. 'That was unforgivable.' His voice was still low and husky and Louisa had the urge to pull him towards her for another kiss.

'Yes, unforgivable,' she murmured.

Their eyes locked together and once again Robert's lips were on hers. This time he kissed her fervently, as if he were afraid she'd disappear at any moment. Louisa returned his kiss with the same urgency, knowing any second he would wake up and realise it was her, Louisa Turnhill, he was kissing, and not the woman of his dreams.

His hands gripped her upper arms firmly, holding her against him.

Louisa hoped the kiss would never end. Robert made her feel like a woman, something no other man had ever done.

'We have to stop,' Robert said, pulling away. Regret and hope mixed on his face. 'We can't do this.'

He was still looking at her as though he wanted to ravish her right there on the sofa.

This time it was Louisa who leant forward

and pulled his mouth back to hers. He groaned in submission and kissed her deeply. Louisa felt his hands run down the length of her spine and cup her bottom. Gently he laid her back on to the sofa, not once breaking their kiss.

'You're beautiful, Louisa,' he murmured as he kissed her neck.

Louisa could only shudder as his lips flew over her skin. Slowly his head dipped lower and he was kissing the base of her throat, her collarbones and finally the skin of her chest.

Louisa felt a rush of anticipation as his lips moved towards the swell of her breasts. She pushed her chest up towards him, urging him to go lower.

He'd just started to push the material of her dress lower when there was a knock on the door.

Guiltily they sprang apart. Louisa felt the rush of blood to her head and knew her cheeks would be a deep crimson colour.

Robert leapt off the sofa and stalked over to the window, facing outwards so she couldn't see his expression.

As Louisa hurriedly straightened her dress and manoeuvred herself into a more ladylike position she darted a glance at Robert. It was hard to tell what he was thinking with his back towards her, but the stiffness of his posture and stillness of his body gave her a very good idea.

He was regretting their kiss already. Only twenty seconds ago he'd been kissing her as though she was the most precious thing in the world and now he couldn't even look at her.

Louisa took the pain and hurt that realisation caused and told herself to remember that feeling. This was why she couldn't trust anyone. Even a man like Robert, a good man, would just end up hurting her.

Chapter Ten

Robert felt his heart pounding in his chest and fought to control himself. He couldn't believe how he'd just behaved. He'd kissed Louisa, almost ravished her on the sofa in his study. Louisa, his ward. The young woman he was meant to protect from these sorts of ungentlemanly advances.

'Come in,' he said brusquely, still not able to turn from the window.

A footman opened the door.

'There's a Mrs Hempshaw here to see you, my lord.'

One of the companions he'd invited for an interview.

'Put her in the drawing room, I shall be there shortly.'

The footman withdrew, closing the door behind him.

Robert glanced at Louisa sitting on the couch.

She'd straightened her dress and had fixed her expression to one of indifference. There was no indication he'd almost kissed her senseless. Maybe she hadn't been as affected by the kiss as he had.

'I'm sorry, Louisa,' he said, taking a step towards her. 'I shouldn't have kissed you. It was unforgivable.'

She looked at him blandly, even gave a small, emotionless smile.

'I promise it won't happen again. I lost control and I won't allow that to be repeated.'

She nodded, still not meeting his eye.

Robert could feel the muscles in his arms tensing as he clenched his fists. He couldn't believe what he'd just done. Louisa was his ward, an innocent young woman he was supposed to protect, and he'd just done the unthinkable.

He stood awkwardly for half a minute, trying to figure out exactly what she was thinking. He couldn't tell if she was angry at him for kissing her or annoyed they'd been interrupted.

She had seemed to enjoy it when he was kissing her. She'd responded to his lips and to his touch, she'd moaned and gasped underneath him and worked him up into a frenzy. But now she was sitting there as though they'd just been having a banal conversation about something insignificant.

Stop it, he told himself. *Just because Louisa has more self-control than you.*

'Louisa…' he said, trailing off as he realised he didn't know what to say, he just wanted to say something.

'Shall we go and interview this companion?' she asked breezily.

And that drew a line under their amorous moment.

Robert knew he should feel relieved. Louisa was giving him an out, an escape route, but he had to make sure she understood it had been a mistake.

'Louisa,' he said, catching her arm and spinning her gently round to face him, 'I need to be sure you understand.' He paused as he waited for her to meet his eye. 'That was a mistake, one that I deeply regret. It won't happen again.'

Robert saw a flash of pain in Louisa's eyes before her mask was back in place and her serene visage stared back at him.

'Of course it was a mistake,' she repeated, her voice devoid of emotion. 'Of course you regret it.'

Robert nodded, glad she understood, but concerned at her lack of emotional response. Louisa pulled away from him, refusing to meet his eye any longer, and walked out into the hallway.

He followed Louisa out of the room, trying

not to watch the hypnotic sway of her softly rounded backside.

He couldn't believe what he'd just done. Not only had he nearly ruined his already fragile relationship with Louisa, he'd abandoned all his principles as well. For two years he hadn't touched a woman, hadn't even allowed himself to think about a woman. Then Louisa had entered his life and turned his whole world upside down. No matter how much he tried to deny it, she enthralled him. Her resilience and her humour and how she was just starting to allow herself to trust him—all of it was endearing. Added to that the fact she was beautiful, how could a man resist?

He would resist, he told himself. One moment of weakness was forgivable, but it wouldn't happen again. Louisa deserved to be able to live in peace, not wondering when her guardian would launch himself at her next, and he would keep his vow and spend his life alone and companionless, otherwise he wouldn't be able to look at himself in the mirror.

'Good morning, Mrs Hempshaw,' Louisa said as they entered the drawing room. Her voice was cheerful and she had a smile on her face. Robert felt a stab of annoyance that their kiss hadn't affected her more. He must have lost his touch.

'Good morning,' the severe-looking woman said, rising from the armchair she was perched on.

'Thank you for coming today,' Robert said, pushing thoughts of Louisa to the back of his mind, which was difficult when she was standing so close to him. So close he could just reach out and she'd be back in his arms.

'I understand you wish to employ an experienced companion,' Mrs Hempshaw said. 'I have good references and an impeccable reputation.'

Robert disliked the woman already.

'There will not be a single word of scandal voiced about Miss Turnhill whilst I am her companion.'

Robert thought that was probably because Louisa wouldn't be able to have any fun whilst Mrs Hempshaw was around.

'Have you been the companion of a young lady before?' Robert asked, wondering how anyone had put up with the old bat.

'My employers have by and large been older women,' Mrs Hempshaw said, 'but recently I was employed by Lord Huntley to chaperone his daughter to social events and ensure none of the young gentlemen overstepped the boundaries of propriety.'

He doubted any young gentlemen had come

close when they'd seen Mrs Hempshaw escorting the poor young girl.

'Do you have any questions for Mrs Hempshaw, Louisa?'

The older woman frowned at his overfamiliar use of Louisa's first name.

'Do you like dogs, Mrs Hempshaw?' Louisa asked sweetly.

Robert wondered where she was going with this.

'I can tolerate them.'

'And cats?'

'I hate the disease-spreading creatures. No real purpose. They disgust me.'

'What a shame,' Louisa murmured. 'I have four cats, they go with me everywhere.'

Mrs Hempshaw frowned as if unsure whether Louisa was speaking the truth.

'Unfortunately I don't think this is the right job for you,' Louisa continued. 'But thank you very much for coming.'

Mrs Hempshaw looked at Robert incredulously, as if she couldn't believe she was being dismissed by Louisa.

'Yes, thank you for coming,' Robert said, playing along, 'but Miss Turnhill is right, we do love our cats in this house. I'll make sure I mention your name to anyone else I know looking for a companion.'

He stood and ushered her out of the room, waiting until she was in the hands of his capable footman, then closed the door firmly.

'Cats?'

'Well, I could have told her she was a miserable old crone and I'd rather spend my days chained to a wall in a straitjacket than with her.'

'Don't joke about it, Louisa,' Robert said, with more force than hc'd intended.

He crossed the room in a couple of long strides, stopping when she was only two feet away. She was half-turned away from him and gently he grasped her by the upper arms and turned her towards him.

'I'm sorry about what happened in the study,' Robert said, knowing they had to get rid of this awkwardness between them. 'It was unforgivable of me to take advantage of you.'

'You didn't take advantage of me,' Louisa said, looking down at her feet.

She looked so vulnerable, standing there in front of him, her arms crossed across her chest stubbornly.

'I'm your guardian, Louisa, and I kissed you. I shouldn't have allowed it to happen. Especially not after what happened with Mr Craven.'

'It was nothing like the same situation,' she said quietly. 'You didn't force yourself upon me, I didn't have to fight you off.'

Robert felt the rage mounting as he realised what Louisa's life must have been like before his great-uncle had sent her to Lewisham Asylum. It made kissing her even worse.

He reached out and gently tilted her chin up with one finger. With great resolve he stopped himself from caressing the skin of her face and instead dropped his hand back to his side. Louisa was now staring at him from under her long, dark eyelashes.

Robert swallowed. She looked so beautiful and so vulnerable. He wanted to sweep her into his arms and protect her from the cruel world and at the same time ravish her on the spot. Maybe it was he whom she needed protecting from.

'Every night at dinner Mr Craven would drink far too much wine and afterwards he'd invite me to join him in the drawing room. If I refused, he would grow violent. If I agreed, the evening would always end the same: with him chasing me through the house in a drunken stupor.'

'Did he…?' Robert trailed off, not knowing if he wanted to know the answer to the question.

'Did he succeed in taking advantage of me?' Louisa asked, looking him directly in the eye. 'No. He was always too drunk to catch me. And in the cold light of day he would apologise for his behaviour and hint it was my fault for refusing to marry him.'

Robert stepped forwards and took her gently in his arms, pulling her towards him in an embrace.

'I promise you will never have to be afraid again,' he said quietly.

She was stiff against his chest. Her arms were still hanging down by her side and she wasn't moving a single muscle.

He'd lost her, he realised. All the trust and openness they'd built over the last couple of days had been ruined by him kissing her. It wasn't that he'd forced himself on her—he might not have been with a woman for a long time, but he knew how one responded when she was enjoying his attentions—but she'd withdrawn into herself afterwards. The woman who stood before him was more like the untrusting young woman he'd rescued from the asylum than the one who'd answered Dr Wade's questions so openly.

Robert stepped away, trying not to let the fact her coldness hurt him show. He knew he would have to work to regain the trust he had lost and that would take time. There could be no more stolen kisses either.

He glanced at her lips. That was a mistake. Her tongue was just darting out to moisten her lower lip, something he'd noticed her doing when she was nervous. It was surprisingly erotic and Robert felt a stirring in his loins. Inwardly he groaned. How did such an innocent young thing know how to arouse him in a way no experienced woman could?

'There are two more companions coming to be interviewed today. I think it would be a good idea if you sat in and helped me interview them,' Robert said. 'That way if you don't like them you can let me know.'

He needed to get her a companion, Robert realised. Every second they were alone together was too much of a temptation.

Chapter Eleven

'It's a delight to be cooking for someone who actually enjoys their food,' Mrs Rust said. She was gently folding flour into a cake mix, working with the practised ease of an expert. 'Lord Fleetwood is the best employer you could wish for, but sometimes I think he wouldn't notice if I served him tadpoles and donkey rather than salmon and beef.'

'Why do you think he's so unfussy?' Louisa asked, absent-mindedly drawing patterns with her finger in the flour on the worktop.

'He never used to be this way,' Mrs Rust said. 'Quite a fussy eater when he was a child.'

'You've known him since he was a child?'

'Been with the family for thirty-one years,' the cook said proudly.

'So what changed?' Louisa asked. 'When did he stop caring about his food?'

Mrs Rust slowly started to pour the mixture into a tin, levelling the top with a flat spoon.

'The war. Changed Lord Fleetwood in so many ways. He was a carefree boy when he left and a shadow of his former self when he returned.'

Louisa had to stop herself from leaning forwards. She wanted to understand what it was that haunted Robert. Why he was so serious and so distant. Maybe Mrs Rust could give her even a little information.

'I don't know what happened on that battlefield, but I do know it robbed more than young Master Knapwell of his life.'

Louisa stayed silent, hoping the cook would continue.

'Took his friend's death hard, Lord Fleetwood did, hasn't been the same since.' She leant in closer to Louisa and dropped her voice to a whisper. 'There was talk Lord Fleetwood blamed himself for Master Knapwell's death. All nonsense, of course, he loved that man as though they were brothers. But the guilt has been eating him up ever since.

'You hear of it, of course, people returning from war, feeling guilty to have survived when their friends have perished, but you don't really understand until you see it first hand. Lord Fleetwood hasn't allowed himself to live, to enjoy life, ever since he returned.'

Louisa wondered what had happened to make Robert blame himself for Greg Knapwell's death. Even after only knowing him for a few days Louisa knew he wouldn't have intentionally done anything to harm his friend, but something awful must have happened for him to be still blaming himself after so long.

'When Lord Fleetwood returned we were hopeful that slowly he would heal, but for two years he's kept himself separate from society...' Mrs Rust paused. 'But maybe now...'

Louisa looked up sharply.

'Well, he's got you to think about now, dear.'

She supposed it was true. Sometimes the best way to move forwards was to focus on something or someone else.

'Already you've been good for him.'

Louisa pictured his stiff posture after they'd kissed and the way he couldn't look at her. She wasn't too sure she was all that good for him.

'Miss Turnhill.'

Louisa jumped at the sound of Robert's voice. 'Louisa,' she reminded him as he descended the stairs into the kitchen. Mrs Rust had turned a deep crimson colour and was looking guiltily at Robert as if trying to ascertain how much of their conversation he'd overheard.

'Lord Fleetwood.' Mrs Rust bobbed into a curtsy. 'What an unexpected delight.'

Robert looked around the kitchen as though he hadn't been down there for a very long time.

'I've been discussing the dinner menus with Mrs Rust,' Louisa said, wondering why Robert had come looking for her himself, rather than sending a footman.

'Good,' he said with a smile. 'I hope you've come up with some good ideas between you.'

'Mrs Rust has an excellent recipe for donkey,' Louisa said, keeping her voice serious, 'with a side of tadpole.'

He looked at her for a couple of seconds before smiling. 'Donkey I've eaten before, very chewy and tough, but I don't think I've ever had the pleasure of sampling tadpoles.'

'You've actually eaten a donkey?' Louisa asked, incredulous.

'Not a whole one,' he reassured her.

'Why on earth did you eat part of a donkey?'

'I was hungry,' Robert said with a shrug.

Louisa couldn't help herself, she burst out laughing.

'Donkey was actually one of the finer animals I sampled during my time in the army.'

Louisa leant forward, oblivious to the fact her elbows were in the flour spread over the work surface. He was revealing just a few more details about his life.

'So what was the worst?' she asked.

He contemplated her question for a few seconds before answering. 'Mouse. No meat on them whatsoever.'

'Strike dormouse from the menu, Mrs Rust,' Louisa said, grinning.

'We have more companions to interview, Louisa,' Robert said, getting back to business.

She stood. Robert took a step towards her and Louisa felt her pulse start to quicken. She wished he didn't make her feel quite so out of control. After his reaction to their kiss upstairs Louisa had vowed she would not allow herself to act like a simpering fool. She was determined to stay aloof and distant, but when Robert looked at her as though she was the only one in the room and stepped towards her, all of her resolve went out the window.

She held her breath as he reached out towards her. Gently he brushed the flour off her elbows. Louisa slowly exhaled. He was making her look presentable, nothing more. The contact was completely innocent. He wasn't touching her in any special or intimate way. She scolded herself at the disappointment she felt as his hand dropped back to his side and the contact between them ceased.

'Who is there this time?' Louisa asked, hoping her voice didn't come out as a high-pitched squeak.

'There's two of them. Hopefully one will suit.'

'I promise not to be too picky,' Louisa said.

Robert seemed very keen to get someone who could act as a buffer between them installed into the house.

He shrugged. 'We've got to live with her. I'd rather we got it right.'

She followed him up the stairs, promising to return to Mrs Rust later to continue their discussions about food.

'If you don't like someone, I want you to let me know,' Robert said as they paused outside the door to his study. 'I want you to be happy, Louisa.'

Louisa nodded, a lump forming in her throat. She had such conflicting emotions about this man. One minute he was kissing her, the next acting as if there had been no connection between them. Now he was worried about her happiness. No wonder she was in turmoil when he acted so differently towards her all the time.

They entered the study and Louisa sat down on the sofa she'd occupied earlier during their kiss. This time Robert didn't sit next to her. She wondered if he didn't trust her to keep her hands off him.

After a few minutes of silence the first woman was shown in by one of the footmen.

'Miss Carter,' Robert said, looking down at a sheaf of papers, probably her references, 'thank you for coming. This is Miss Turnhill, my ward.'

Louisa smiled at the young woman. She was the complete opposite to Mrs Hempshaw. Miss Carter was young, attractive and smiled a lot. Louisa's eyes flicked towards Robert. He was smiling, too.

'It's a pleasure to meet you both.'

'Why don't you tell us a little about yourself?' Robert prompted.

He was being ever so nice. Louisa glanced at Miss Carter again. She was very pretty.

'My family are originally from Yorkshire,' Miss Carter started, 'but for the last few years I've been working as a companion for Lady Sheldon.'

Robert nodded encouragingly.

'Lady Sheldon unfortunately passed away last month so I've been looking for a new position ever since.'

'What do you like doing, Miss Carter?' Louisa asked.

'Oh, most things,' she said with a smile. 'I like going for walks and reading and music.'

She sounded like the perfect woman. Louisa glanced once again at Robert. He was still smiling at Miss Carter. Louisa thought this was the longest time she'd ever seen him smile for.

Louisa wasn't a naturally jealous person. She'd never really had anyone to be jealous of. But in that instant she felt undeniable jealousy for the way Robert was looking at Miss Carter.

'Miss Carter has excellent references,' Robert said, motioning to the sheets of paper in his hands.

'I'm sure,' Louisa murmured. 'Have you lived in London before, Miss Carter?'

The young woman shook her head. 'I've always resided in the country, but I need to find work and I don't mind the city too much.'

Louisa suddenly felt very ashamed of herself. Miss Carter was just a young woman looking to work for her living. It wasn't her fault she was attractive and personable. It wasn't her fault if Robert found her attractive.

Not that Louisa should even care that Robert found her attractive. He'd made it perfectly clear earlier on that their kiss had been a mistake, and in any case, she most certainly didn't want a relationship with him or anyone else.

Still, having him lust after her companion might be a little hard to stomach.

'Thank you for coming along, Miss Carter, we'll be in touch soon,' Robert said.

He rang for a footman, who showed the attractive Miss Carter out.

'What did you think?' Robert asked.

'She seemed very nice,' Louisa said, trying to be a good person and not let her petty jealousy live on.

'She did. And she has very good references.' He paused as if hesitating. 'But she's probably a little too distracting for the male members of staff.'

Louisa nodded, trying not to be too pleased.

'Seems a shame to eliminate her just because she's pretty,' Louisa said.

'We'll keep her as a maybe.'

The door opened and the third of the prospective companions was shown in.

'Good morning, Mrs Crawshaw,' Robert said. 'Please have a seat.'

This woman was more what Louisa expected a companion and chaperone to look like. She was well past middle age, heavy around the middle and had a kindly face.

'Would you tell us a little about yourself?' Robert asked.

'Pardon?' Mrs Crawshaw said.

'Would you tell us a little about yourself?' Robert repeated, much louder.

'Until recently I was companion to Lady James, living in Chelsea. I'd been with her ladyship for many, many years.'

Louisa thought she saw Mrs Crawshaw's eyes starting to water at the memory of her late employer.

'I have no family,' Mrs Crawshaw continued, 'and I'm always completely dedicated to my employer.'

'What do you like to do, Mrs Crawshaw?' Louisa asked.

'Pardon, my dear, I'm a little hard of hearing.'

'What do you like to do?'

'Well, I used to like to embroider before my eyesight started to deteriorate and I love to go to social events, to watch all the vibrant young people dancing and having fun.'

Louisa felt a little sorry for this woman who had no family and it sounded as though no real life outside her job. If she was her companion, Louisa had no doubts she would be able to get away with anything. The older woman had atrocious hearing and it didn't look as though her eyesight was much good either. Mrs Crawshaw would be easy to evade. A chaperone for appearances' sake only.

Louisa wondered why it was quite so important to her to have a companion she could evade easily. The main reason they were searching for someone was to avoid any scandal around her living with Robert alone in his house. She told herself it was in case she decided she wanted to leave in a hurry. She still hadn't decided what to do in the long term. The last couple of days spent in the safety of Robert's house had been wonderful, but she knew it couldn't last for ever. Already she'd allowed herself to get caught up in the fantasy and already she'd been hurt. She was the only person she could rely on and eventually she would have to leave and make her own way in the world, otherwise she risked growing too close to Robert. If that happened, the eventual betrayal, in whatever form it came in, would be all the much harder to recover from.

'What did you think?' Robert asked once Mrs Crawshaw had left.

'I liked her,' Louisa said. The older woman had seemed harmless enough and Louisa had no doubt she would get all the freedom she desired with Mrs Crawshaw as her chaperone.

Chapter Twelve

Robert took a deep breath before getting down from the carriage. Since returning from the war he'd attended only a handful of social events. There had been one or two dinner parties he'd been unable to get out of and one very disastrous ball he'd spent a grand total of thirty-five minutes at.

Tonight was going to be difficult. Actually, difficult was an understatement. It was going to be close to impossible. He glanced at Louisa as she took his hand and stepped from the carriage and reminded himself why he was doing this—for her.

She was nervous, too, he told himself. Once again she'd been twisting her hands together throughout the entire carriage ride to Mrs Knapwell's house. He'd tried to put her at ease, but his own misgivings about the evening hadn't helped him to be reassuring.

'What if I say something wrong?' Louisa asked, her fingers digging into his arm.

'You won't,' he said.

She pulled a face at his lack of advice.

'It's only a small gathering,' he tried to reassure her, 'and Mrs Knapwell will ensure you are not overwhelmed. She knows you have not come out into society so she will not seat you with anyone but the most pleasant.'

Louisa turned her face towards him, panic in her eyes.

'I won't be sitting with you?'

Momentarily Robert felt a surge of happiness that she felt so much more at ease with him than anyone else.

'Normally at these events the seating is decided beforehand by the hostess. Most likely we won't be sitting together.'

'What if I let slip where I've been all this time?' Louisa asked. 'Or if everyone thinks I'm mad?'

Robert could see she was working herself up into a state.

'One little mistake and everyone will know I've been in an asylum for the last year.'

Robert knew how catastrophic that would be. One slip and Louisa would be a social outcast. People would talk about her behind her back, exclude her from balls and dinner-party guest lists and make her life a misery. He knew this, but he also knew Louisa. She would be just fine. She was a strong, confident woman who had overcome so much already; she could deal with a few members of the *ton* looking at her inquisitively.

He stopped at the bottom of the steps, turned to face her and gripped her gently by the upper arms. He could feel the warmth of her skin on his hands through the thin silk of the dress and had to resist the urge to run his palms down the entire length of her arm until he met the bare skin at her wrists.

Focus, he told himself.

'No one will think you're mad because you're not mad Louisa,' he said firmly.

She looked as though she were about to protest.

'You're not mad,' he said. 'We even have the paperwork to prove it.'

He relaxed a little as Louisa smiled at his comment.

'You're going to be absolutely fine. You're a beautiful, charming woman who everyone is going to adore.'

'Really?' She said it with such innocence and lack of guile Robert wanted to sweep her into his arms and carry her back home.

'Really.'

Louisa gave him an uncertain smile and took

a deep breath. She was ready. Now all he had to do was give himself the same sort of pep talk.

They ascended the steps and the door was opened immediately by a smart-looking footman. Robert felt Louisa tighten her grip on his arm as they stepped over the threshold, but she maintained her poise and her sunny smile. To everyone else she looked like a confident debutante, not a scared young woman who'd spent the last year languishing in the Lewisham Asylum.

'Lord Fleetwood, Miss Turnhill, I'm so pleased you could make it,' Mrs Knapwell said.

She was standing in the hallway, ready to greet her guests as they arrived.

'You look lovely tonight, Miss Turnhill,' Mrs Knapwell said.

Robert felt Louisa relax a little beside him and silently thanked the older woman for knowing how to put Louisa at ease.

'You're the last of my guests to arrive,' she continued, 'so why don't I take you into the drawing room and introduce you to everyone.'

Mrs Knapwell linked her arm through Louisa's and led her into the drawing room. Robert felt surprisingly bereft as she left his side. The feeling was soon forgotten as he followed the two women into the room.

It was only a small gathering. Robert counted

ten other people besides himself and Louisa, but already he felt out of place.

He scanned the faces in the room and realised he knew most of the assembled people. The *ton* was a small, intimate group with very few additions over the years. Most of the people here he knew from his short time attending social events before he'd left for the war.

'Fleetwood, been an age, old chap,' a familiar voice said from behind him.

Robert turned and found himself looking into the face of Harry Baldwin, a man he'd been at school with. Suddenly his throat felt dry. Baldwin had known him when Greg was alive. In fact, the three boys had often played sports together.

'How the devil have you been?'

Baldwin had spoken in unnecessarily elaborate language even as a boy.

'Not bad,' Robert replied.

He hated making small talk.

'I hear you've acquired a ward.'

Both men turned to look at Louisa, who was currently being introduced to a woman Robert knew to be Lady Grey and a younger woman he assumed was her daughter.

'Delightful young thing,' Baldwin murmured appreciatively.

'She's off limits,' Robert growled immediately.

'Earmarked her for yourself, have you?' Baldwin asked. 'Sensible chap. She'll be ever so grateful to you for taking care of her.'

Robert remembered why he and Baldwin had never really been friends.

'I haven't earmarked her. She's just off limits.'

Baldwin looked at him appraisingly for ten seconds, then shrugged.

'I'm on the hunt for a gal myself. Need to settle down and start producing heirs. Keep the old man happy.'

Robert thought this was a ridiculous reason to get married, but didn't say anything.

'Need a docile mare, though, don't want to tie myself to a harridan.'

Robert grunted. His attention was still fixed on Louisa. She looked happy enough. Mrs Knapwell was keeping her moving around the room, staying close to her side.

'See you haven't become any more articulate with age, Fleetwood. The war can't have changed you much.'

'Good catching up, Baldwin,' Robert said, clapping the other man on the arm before striding away, leaving Baldwin staring after him with an open mouth.

Robert knew he should feel remorse at leaving the man in the middle of the conversation, but if he'd stayed a moment longer he knew the conversation would have turned to the war and he didn't know how he would respond to any insensitive questions. He might have ended up punching Baldwin, something he couldn't allow himself to do at Mrs Knapwell's dinner party.

'Lord Fleetwood, as I live and breathe. I haven't seen you for an age.'

Robert tried not to let frustration show on his face as a woman in her midtwenties stepped into his path. He glanced again at Louisa. At the present moment she looked as though she was coping. He had a few seconds to exchange pleasantries with this woman, whoever she was.

'You don't remember me, do you?' she asked.

Robert peered at her face, trying to recall exactly who she was.

'You cut me deep, Lord Fleetwood,' she said with a coy smile. 'but it was a few years ago now, and I think I could forgive a man like you anything.'

Still Robert couldn't place her. Her face looked familiar, but he didn't have a clue who she was.

'It's Emilia Ruddock, or Lady Gillingham as I am now.'

Emilia Ruddock. Of course, how could he have forgot. She had been a coy debutante during the Season he'd actually attended a few balls. She had been a flirt then, toying with all the young men. So she'd gone ahead and married Lord Gillingham.

'I'm sorry for your loss,' he said.

She shrugged. 'Dear Gillingham left me well provided for. So now I'm able to have fun with whomever I choose.'

Robert didn't think any woman had ever been so obvious in her attentions before.

'You're looking well, Lord Fleetwood.'

He opened his mouth to return the compliment, but closed it again promptly. He didn't want this woman getting the wrong idea. The last thing in the world he wanted was an affair with a merry widow.

'This is the point where you tell me I look well, too,' she prompted him.

'I'm sure you have plenty of suitors to pay you compliments, Lady Gillingham.'

She threw her head back and laughed loudly, drawing stares from the other guests.

'Indeed I do, Lord Fleetwood, but a lady can never have too many compliments. Especially from a man such as yourself.'

Robert wondered how he could extract himself from Lady Gillingham's company.

She reached forwards and dusted an imaginary speck of dust from his jacket, allowing her hand to linger on his chest.

'I've always had a penchant for military men, Lord Fleetwood. It's something about the way they hold themselves. And the feeling that although they're so controlled and rigid on the outside, once you strip away the layers they might just lose control.'

'I'll be sure to tell any military men I meet of your admiration.'

'You tease me,' she said, pouting ever so slightly. 'But I warn you, Lord Fleetwood, I'm a lady who knows what she wants.'

He raised an eyebrow.

'And tonight I want you.'

'I do hate to disappoint,' Robert said, stepping back out of arm's reach, 'but tonight my only role is to chaperone my ward, Miss Turnhill.'

Robert gestured towards Louisa.

'Good looks, a brooding manner and a kind heart,' Lady Gillingham said. 'You're not making yourself any less appealing.'

'It was nice to see you again, Lady Gillingham,' Robert said blandly, then quickly bowed and stepped away before she could say anything else.

He wondered who else was going to corner him before he could reach Louisa. Already he'd been propositioned by a merry widow and had nearly punched an insensitive twit from his school days. Surely the other guests couldn't be quite so awful.

'Fleetwood.'

Robert froze.

'It's good to see you.'

Robert turned to look at the young man who was addressing him.

'It's been too long.'

'Dunton.'

Robert stood completely still, trying to compose himself. This was what he'd been dreading. It was bad enough having to face Mrs Knapwell, but Dunton was probably worse. This man knew exactly what had happened. He knew just how foolish and neglectful Robert had been. He'd seen everything.

'How have you been?'

Robert shrugged. 'You know.'

Dunton looked him in the eye and nodded. 'I know.'

'What have you been doing with yourself?' Robert asked.

'Spend most of my time running the estate.'

'I thought your brother inherited.'

'He did,' Dunton said, 'but he's useless with money. Nearly ran the place into the ground with all his schemes whilst I was away. I run it for him now.'

'I bet it's prospering.'

Dunton shrugged modestly. 'It's getting back up to full strength.'

They stood silently for a few moments.

'I've often looked for you at social events,' Dunton said eventually.

'I don't go to many.' That was an understatement.

'And this is Major Dunton,' Mrs Knapwell said, coming up beside them.

'Major Dunton, this is Miss Turnhill. She's Lord Fleetwood's ward.'

Robert's old comrade turned and gave him such a look of incredulity Robert almost smiled.

'Major Dunton served in the army with Lord Fleetwood and my son.'

Louisa bobbed into a quick curtsy and looked at Dunton curiously. Robert made a mental note to keep the pair of them as far apart as possible.

'Have you met everyone?' he asked Louisa.

'I think so,' she said. 'Mrs Knapwell's been ever so kind introducing me.'

'Nonsense, my dear, it's my job as your hostess.'

Mrs Knapwell patted Louisa on the arm in a motherly fashion, then slipped away.

'You've got a ward?' Dunton asked, turning back to Robert.

'Why does everyone react like that?' Louisa asked, laughing.

'I'm not exactly the kindly guardian type,' Robert said gruffly.

'You're the best guardian a girl could wish for.'

Robert glanced at Dunton and saw his old friend was grinning.

'Fleetwood as a guardian. You must tell me all about it.'

Robert stepped forward, ready to do anything to keep Louisa from chatting to Dunton.

'If you would like to make your way to the dining room,' Mrs Knapwell announced, 'dinner is ready to be served.'

Robert silently thanked her for her perfect timing. He stepped forwards to take Louisa's arm, ready to escort her into the dining room, but already Louisa had placed her hand at Dunton's elbow. He felt a surge of anxiety mixed with the unfamiliar tang of jealousy.

He was just about to follow them closely into the dining room when a voice said by his ear, 'It looks as though you have the pleasure of escorting me in to dinner.'

Robert suppressed a groan. Louisa had been whisked away by the one person he didn't want her to talk to and now he'd been cornered by Lady Gillingham. The night was a disaster and it had only just started.

Chapter Thirteen

Louisa felt slightly more at ease as she walked into the dining room on Major Dunton's arm. Mrs Knapwell had spent the last quarter of an hour introducing her to the other guests and Louisa didn't think she'd made a fool of herself or said anything she shouldn't have. All the time she'd been conscious of her secret bubbling under the surface. If she let slip even the slightest hint of where she'd been this last year, she would be a social outcast.

'How long have you been living with Fleetwood?' Dunton asked as he pulled out her chair for her.

'Less than a week,' Louisa said, wondering who would be sitting either side of her.

She hadn't really liked the predatory-looking Lady Gillingham, but everyone else had seemed perfectly pleasant. She was pleased when Major Dunton sat down to her right. He had known

Robert during the war and might tell her a little about it.

Robert was always very quiet if she ever brought the subject up. He didn't want to talk about it. Something had happened that made him want to block out all memories of that time. Louisa hadn't pushed him on the subject. She knew well enough what it was like to want to forget large chunks of your life.

Nevertheless she was curious about the war and what had happened to make Robert so serious and withdrawn from some of the pleasures of everyday life.

'And how are you finding it?'

'Living with Lord Fleetwood is wonderful,' Louisa said. 'He is very kind and thoughtful. My last guardian was not the nicest man in the world and Robert—' she paused and corrected herself '—Lord Fleetwood has done so much to make me feel welcome in his home.'

'Fleetwood always did have a tendency to try to look after other people,' Dunton said quietly.

'I would like to know a little about the war,' Louisa said, glancing round for Robert. He was just sitting down opposite her. Lady Gillingham was whispering something in his ear and he was looking at her distractedly. 'If it's not too painful for you.'

'Fleetwood hasn't told you much?' Dunton asked.

'He doesn't seem to like to talk about it,' Louisa said, 'which is completely understandable, it's just I feel as though I would understand him so much better if I knew a little about what went on.'

Robert caught her eye and gave her a reassuring smile. Suddenly Louisa felt guilty about asking his friend to tell her about the war. Maybe she should just wait and let him tell her in his own time.

'We were just boys when we left to join the army,' Dunton said, leaning back slightly so the footman could place the first course in front of him. 'We had just finished university, Fleetwood, Knapwell and I, and we wanted adventure,' he scoffed at his own naivety.

Louisa could picture younger versions of Robert and Dunton setting off for their grand adventure, not knowing what was really in store for them.

'We were all patriotic and so idealistic. We thought we'd join up and make a difference. That within months we would have defeated the French and return home heroes.'

Louisa glanced across at Robert. He was scowling and trying to catch Dunton's eye, no doubt wondering what his old friend was saying to her.

'That's what all young men want, isn't it? To be heroes.'

Robert's eyes flitted to her and Louisa gave him a reassuring smile. His frown deepened.

'The first few months were tough. We went through some basic training, then met up with the men we'd be leading. At first there was some resentment between the officers and the recruits.'

'But surely you were all fighting for the same cause.'

Dunton grimaced. 'To the common foot soldiers we were overprivileged toffs playing at war whilst they were doing the dirty work. Many of the men had families back at home and this was the only way to support them. They would have fought for anything if it kept their loved ones clothed and fed.'

Louisa nodded thoughtfully. She could imagine the tension between the officers and the other soldiers, but surely when they started fighting side by side that would have all passed.

'The three of us were sent to the Peninsula. We were lucky all to stay together, but we made a good team and the higher powers realised that. It wasn't long before Fleetwood was promoted and was asked to head up a light infantry squad.'

'And what about you and Mr Knapwell?' Louisa asked.

'We stayed around as his seconds-in-command to make sure Fleetwood didn't go and get himself killed doing something awfully patriotic.'

Louisa took a bite of her first course. She was so engrossed in Dunton's account she had barely noticed when the dish was placed in front of her. She felt as though she understood so much more about the war already. It wasn't something that had been spoken of much. She hadn't received any news whilst she was in the asylum and Mr Craven had been of the opinion the less she knew about the wider world, the less trouble she would cause. Dunton's account was fascinating and gave her a glimpse of what it must have been like for Robert.

'Dunton,' Robert said loudly from the other side of the table.

Everyone stopped eating and looked at him.

'I hope you're not boring Louisa with war stories,' he said.

To the casual observer his words were light and joking, but Louisa knew he was issuing a warning to his friend to stop whatever he was saying.

Louisa opened her mouth to protest. She needed to hear more of what Major Dunton had to say. She felt as though he had the knowledge that would help her to understand Robert more, to unlock the mysteries of his past.

'Not at all, old chap,' Dunton said back across the table.

He glanced at Louisa and gave a small shrug. It seemed their conversation was at an end.

Louisa frowned as she took a few more bites of her first course. What could truly be so terrible in his past that Robert would actively seek to keep it from her?

'How are you enjoying London, Miss Turnhill?' the small man on her left asked, taking advantage of the lull in conversation.

Louisa racked her memory. She thought this man was called Baldwin, but she could not for the life of her remember if he was a Lord or a Mister.

'Very well, thank you,' she answered politely.

'Has Lord Fleetwood made any plans for your coming out?' Baldwin asked.

He leant in towards her as he spoke and Louisa had to stop herself from shifting in her seat to get farther away from him. She wasn't sure what it was about the man, but she felt uncomfortable when his attention was fixed on her.

'My coming out?' Louisa asked.

'You must be of age and a beautiful young woman like yourself would have no shortage of suitors. Lord Fleetwood will find you a match in no time.'

Louisa felt sick. She put her fork down on to her plate and forced herself to take a couple of deep breaths. Robert wasn't going to force her to marry anybody. She'd only just got her freedom, he wouldn't take that away from her already.

'You'll probably get a proposal within a week or two,' Baldwin continued, oblivious to Louisa's discomfort.

She didn't want a proposal. She didn't want to marry anyone. And she didn't even want to have a coming out. She was perfectly content with spending her days with Robert and having intimate dinners, just the two of then, each evening.

Louisa glanced across the table to find Robert glowering at her. She smiled weakly, wondering what he was upset about. Maybe he did want to get her off his hands, get rid of his responsibility.

As soon as she thought it, Louisa felt guilty. Robert had been nothing but kind to her. He'd taken her into his home and welcomed her into his life. Over the last few days he'd done everything he could to make her feel comfortable and safe.

He wasn't trying to get rid of her. He wasn't going to try to marry her off to anyone. Louisa felt some of her confidence returning and she turned back to Baldwin, ready to face the irritating man.

'Of course it does depend what sort of dowry Fleetwood decides to settle on you,' Baldwin said.

'I'm in mourning,' Louisa said bluntly, 'for my old guardian.' Finally Mr Craven was being useful. 'I doubt Lord Fleetwood will want to go against propriety and have my coming out whilst I am still in mourning.'

Baldwin looked at Louisa's sapphire-blue dress as if searching for the black mourning gown.

'My guardian expressly asked that no one wear mourning clothes for him,' Louisa said, starting to enjoy herself. 'In fact, he asked that his family and friends celebrated his life by wearing brightly coloured clothes.'

'How unusual,' Baldwin murmured, unconvinced.

'He was a most unusual man,' Louisa confirmed.

An unusual man who was finally being useful to her. He was a perfect reason for her not to have to worry about social events and marriage proposals. She was in mourning for the lecherous old fiend.

Feeling pleased with herself, Louisa resolutely turned back to her meal. The main course had just been placed down in front of them and Louisa tucked in, discouraging Baldwin from talking to her again.

When she was halfway through her pork and confident Baldwin had started to engage Lady Grey in conversation on his other side, she took the chance to glance over at Robert. He'd momentarily stopped glaring at her and had just the slightest of frowns on his face; for Robert he looked positively happy. He was still engaged in conversation with Lady Gillingham, the young widow who had seemed rather familiar with him earlier in the evening.

Louisa felt an unfamiliar pang of jealousy towards the older woman. She was poised and confident and looked as though she knew how to get exactly what she wanted. And, if Louisa wasn't mistaken, Lady Gillingham wanted Robert.

She wondered if they had been close before. The intimate way Lady Gillingham brushed her hand against Robert's as she reached for her fork made Louisa think maybe they had. Suddenly Louisa felt awfully young and inexperienced. No wonder Robert had seemed unmoved by their kiss, he'd probably kissed hundreds of women. Real women like Lady Gillingham, not silly young girls like Louisa.

She tried to tell herself it didn't matter. Robert could have a dalliance with whomever he chose. He was a grown man who could make his own choices. And it wasn't as if she wanted him for herself. She might have given in to her desire for him once, but it wouldn't happen again. She wasn't about to tie herself to someone so intimately, that would just be begging for pain and heartache when it all went wrong.

No, she was resolute she would never marry or allow herself to fall in love. She might get lonely, but at least she wouldn't get hurt. She glanced again at Robert and Lady Gillingham, knowing she should be pleased if he found pleasure and intimacy with this woman. Just because she had decided to spend her life alone and independent didn't mean Robert had to.

A little bit of love would be good for him, Louisa realised. He was still hurting from whatever awful things had happened to him in the war. Love could heal that. She saw him look in her direction and smiled encouragingly. He'd been so good to her, the very least she could do was wish him happiness and companionship.

Louisa felt a lump forming in her throat. She might have known him for not quite a week, but Robert was the kindest man she'd ever met.

If she did ever decide to give up her freedom and spend her life with someone, she just hoped it would be with someone as loving and perfect as him.

Chapter Fourteen

'How are you doing?' Robert murmured in Louisa's ear.

She seemed to be coping incredibly well, but he didn't want her to overdo it at her first social event.

She gave him a sunny smile. 'I'm enjoying myself,' she said genuinely.

Robert wished he could say the same. He'd been cornered by Lady Gillingham at dinner and politeness had kept him from turning his back on her. Once the meal had finished Robert had been one of the first to stand and leave the table, eager to get away from her overt flirting.

'You look as though you've got yourself an admirer,' Louisa said airily.

He grimaced. 'An unwanted admirer,' he corrected her.

She smiled again and Robert felt his pulse quicken. He had a sudden urge to reach out and run his fingers through her hair, pull it from its elegant coiffure and tousle it around her shoulders.

He gave himself a mental slap; he shouldn't be thinking thoughts like that about Louisa at all, let alone whilst at the dinner party of the woman whose son he had as good as killed.

Louisa was looking up at him innocently, her wide brown eyes unaware of the turmoil he was feeling inside. Every time he looked at her he wanted to sweep her into his arms, lay her down beneath him and do very wicked things to her. It was inappropriate to the extreme. She was a vulnerable young woman who was also his ward. He needed to stop these thoughts as soon as possible.

Unaware of how much she had unsettled him, Louisa reached up and took his arm, her hand seeming to burn through his layers of clothes and make the nerve endings in his skin tingle.

'It was lovely talking to Major Dunton,' she said as they took a slow walk around the room.

Robert grimaced. He wondered how much his old friend had revealed to Louisa.

'Shall we get a breath of fresh air?' he asked, motioning to the open doors that led to the small terrace outside.

They stepped outside. The weather was balmy, almost tropical, and the skies overcast. The garden was in almost complete darkness, but there were a few flickering candles placed on the terrace area, casting small pools of light and illuminating the immediate surroundings.

They were the only people outside, the rest of the small dinner-party guests were only a few feet away, but their voices had quietened to a background hum and Robert had Louisa to himself.

He realised how easy it would be to press her up against the stone columns and steal a kiss. Easy, but disastrous. Robert reminded himself why he had brought Louisa out here; it was to find out what Dunton had told her, not to compromise her.

'I wish we could see the stars tonight,' Louisa said dreamily. 'When I lived in Norfolk I used to love gazing out of my window at the night sky. It made me feel as though I wasn't alone, that I was part of something much bigger.'

She gazed wistfully at the sky for a few moments, then turned back to him.

'You've done very well this evening, Louisa,' Robert said, his voice low.

'I was nervous,' she admitted. 'Very nervous. But everyone has been so kind and welcoming. Mrs Knapwell is a lovely hostess.'

Robert felt himself grimace at the mention of

Mrs Knapwell. Every time someone even mentioned her name he felt guilty.

'You seemed deep in conversation with Major Dunton at dinner,' he said casually.

Louisa looked at him intently for a few seconds, studying his face.

'Are you annoyed with me?' she asked.

'Annoyed? Why would I be annoyed?'

'You didn't want me talking to him about the war.'

Louisa had a knack of getting to the point quickly. Most people would sidestep around the subject for a few minutes before bringing it up. Louisa was much more direct than that. He supposed it was all those years with just herself for company.

'It's not that I didn't want you talking to him about the war,' he said slowly.

It was exactly that. He didn't want Louisa knowing anything about what had happened in those awful few years, and especially not what had happened to Knapwell and half the rest of his company.

'You basically told him to stop talking to me in front of the whole dining room.'

He couldn't deny it.

'Louisa,' he started, not sure how to explain things to her without revealing what had happened, 'war is terrible. When people talk about it they make it sound incredibly romantic and idealised. It's not.'

He thought of the men screaming as they slowly bled to death from internal wounds, or dragging themselves across a muddy battlefield, one of their legs missing and the other hanging off. War most certainly was not romantic. It was hell on earth.

Louisa was looking at him intently, hanging off his every word. He realised she wanted to know more about what had been such a big part of his life and suddenly he wondered if telling her would be quite so bad. She was kind and understanding, maybe she wouldn't judge, but the thought of her shying away from him, looking at him with disgust, stopped him from going ahead and telling her anything more personal.

'Every day you're faced with death. Death of your men, men who have become like brothers, and death of the enemy.'

'It must be hard having to kill,' Louisa said.

Robert nodded. He'd found it incredibly difficult the first time he'd killed a man, but Knapwell and Dunton had been there. They'd supported each other, and the next time was, if not easier, at least bearable.

'The worst thing is knowing that most of them are just ordinary men, following orders. They don't care about this piece of territory or that piece of land. They just want to stay alive so they can go home to their loved ones.'

Louisa stepped towards him so they were almost touching.

'But if you didn't kill them they would have killed you.'

Robert nodded. And they had. The French had killed the British in the thousands. Thousands of young men cut down in their prime, never returning to their wives or children or mothers and fathers again. Just left to rot in an unmarked field, forgotten almost immediately.

'The worst thing is you get hardened to it. Over the months and years fighting and killing becomes the norm and you forget it is an aberration.'

Louisa reached up and cupped his cheek with her hand. Robert grasped her wrist with his fingers and held her in place, taking comfort from the warmth of her touch.

'It was never the norm for you,' she said quietly. 'I can see it in your eyes. Every death, every man you killed and every soldier you lost, you remember each and every one, don't you?'

He nodded silently. He could still see the faces of each of the soldiers who had died under his command.

'It haunts you, doesn't it?'

Robert wasn't used to being this vulnerable.

He was the strong one, the one who was meant to protect people.

'Every night in my dreams I go back to the battlefield,' he said quietly.

He'd never told anyone that before. His nightmares were his penance, he believed, his punishment for surviving whilst his friends and comrades did not.

'Every night?' Louisa asked.

He nodded. He couldn't remember the last time he hadn't woken up in a cold sweat, his heart pounding and his body ready to fight, as if he were back on the Peninsula.

His hand that was grasping her wrist moved slowly up her arm until he cupped her shoulder, pulling her even closer towards him. Robert knew kissing her was a bad idea, but he needed the comfort she was offering. A few seconds of her lips on his and he would be able to forget the pain that was piercing his heart.

He felt her breathing become shallower as she realised his intentions, but she did not pull away. Robert gave in. He brushed his lips against hers, savouring the velvety soft feel of mouth underneath his and the sweet taste of her lips. She was heavenly.

He allowed his hand to run down her back, caressing the bare skin of her neck before dropping to cup her buttocks through the multiple layers of her dress.

She was kissing him back. Her lips moved against his and he felt her body soften against him as if they were melting together. Her hand that had been on his cheek snaked round the back of his head and he felt her fingers run through his hair.

All the time he was kissing her Robert knew he should stop. Someone could come outside and discover them at any minute and then there would be a momentous scandal. Not only that, but he was Louisa's guardian, he was meant to protect her from advances like this, not inflict them upon her.

Slowly, reluctantly, he pulled away. Louisa's eyes were glazed over and her cheeks were flushed.

'I'm sorry,' he murmured. 'I just couldn't help myself.'

She smiled at him, almost nervously, and allowed her hand to drop from the back of his head.

They stood facing each other for a few minutes, neither wanting to be the first one to move away. There was no awkwardness as there had been after their previous kiss. Robert felt surprisingly content. He supposed the guilt would come later.

'I'd like to know more about the war,' Louisa said quietly. 'It's such an important part of your life.'

Before Robert could answer they were bathed in light as the curtain was held aside and someone stepped out on to the terrace.

'Isn't it a beautiful evening?' Mrs Knapwell said as she came to join them. 'I thought I might find you two out here.'

Robert looked at her sharply. Did that mean she expected them to be alone in the darkness, with him taking advantage of sweet, innocent Louisa?

'I do love warm summer nights,' Mrs Knapwell continued, looking up at the sky wistfully, 'but I always wish the London skies weren't so hazy. It would be lovely to see the stars.'

'I was just saying the same thing, Mrs Knapwell,' Louisa said.

'I'm so pleased you could come this evening.'

Robert nodded. His words always seemed to desert him when faced with Greg Knapwell's mother's kindness.

'I don't see enough of you these days, Lord Fleetwood.' She turned to Louisa. 'Lord Fleetwood was always in and out of our house as a boy. He and my son Greg were friends from the very first day at Eton.'

Robert found himself smiling at the memory.

They actually hadn't been friends from the first day. On the first day Knapwell had punched him and Robert had blackened Knapwell's left eye. All over some supposed family-themed insult. They'd become friends the day after, a mutual respect blossoming from admiration of each other's fighting skills.

'I know you miss him nearly as much as I do,' Mrs Knapwell said quietly.

Robert felt a lump forming in his throat. He did miss Knapwell. They'd been best friends for twelve years by the time he died. They'd survived school and university and four years of war together.

'Why don't you rejoin the other guests, my dear?' Mrs Knapwell said to Louisa. 'I just want to have a few words with Lord Fleetwood.'

Louisa looked at him questioningly, the concern she had for him etched on her face.

He nodded. He didn't want Louisa to hear whatever it was Mrs Knapwell was about to say.

Reluctantly Louisa stepped back inside the house. Mrs Knapwell moved closer to him.

'She's a lovely girl,' she said.

Robert nodded again, not trusting himself to speak.

They stood in silence for a few minutes.

'I know what happened,' Mrs Knapwell said

eventually, 'and I know you blame yourself for Greg's death.'

Robert opened his mouth to speak, but found the words wouldn't come out.

'You weren't to blame,' she said sincerely. 'Major Dunton told me everything. He told me how you looked after the two of them, protected them time and time again, put your life on the line for them.'

Robert tried to protest. He'd done what any good commander would have, but in the end he was the reason Knapwell had died.

Mrs Knapwell held up her hand to stop him. 'He told me what happened on the day my son died and why you blame yourself.'

Robert raised his head and looked her in the eye, knowing he needed to see the hatred and disgust she had for him as she confronted him about the part he played in her son's death.

Instead he only saw warmth and compassion.

'It wasn't your fault,' she said sincerely. 'You couldn't have known you were going to be betrayed, no one could have known. Greg went away to war knowing exactly what could happen. You were not responsible for him and you were not responsible for his death.'

Robert wanted to take her by the arms and shake her, make her understand it *was* his fault. Greg would still be alive if it wasn't for him.

'You need to stop blaming yourself,' Mrs Knapwell continued. 'Greg died on the battle-field, but you didn't. You need to start living your life for the two of you, not building a barricade of guilt and distance between you and the world.'

She patted him on the arm in a motherly fashion. 'I don't blame you for Greg's death,' she repeated again, 'but I do thank you for being such a good friend to him whilst he was alive.'

Robert couldn't even begin to make sense of what she was saying. He'd been convinced she would blame him for her son's death. He was responsible, no matter what she said. If it wasn't for him, Knapwell probably wouldn't even have joined up, let alone be dead. He'd be out enjoying himself, flirting with young women or playing cards at a club.

'I know you aren't going to be able to start living again overnight,' Mrs Knapwell said, 'but I can't stand to see you wasting your life, cutting yourself off from the world. It's not what Greg would have wanted for you.'

Robert thought of his friend's happy demeanour and knew Knapwell wouldn't have held any resentment towards him. He would have forgiven him in an instant, but even so, that didn't mean Robert could forgive himself.

'Miss Turnhill is a lovely young woman and

she cares a lot about you. Why don't you talk to her about it?'

She gave him another motherly pat on the arm, then turned to walk inside. Just before she pulled back the curtain she turned back to him.

'My husband and I were only blessed with one child,' she said softly, 'but when Greg brought you home with him for the holidays I felt as though we had gained another. I lost one son in the war, I don't want to have lost two.'

Chapter Fifteen

They travelled home in silence. Louisa wasn't sure what Mrs Knapwell had said to Robert, but whatever it was it had affected him deeply. Their hostess had reentered the lounge a good fifteen minutes before Robert. When he'd stepped back into the room he looked stunned and troubled, but not overly upset. Louisa had excused herself immediately from the conversation she was having with Lady Grey and had gone straight to his side.

'We should leave,' he'd said gruffly.

Louisa hadn't argued. She'd quickly made her way over to their hostess, thanked her for a lovely evening and then joined Robert out in the hall. Within minutes they were seated in his carriage and speeding through the streets of London.

She glanced at Robert for what felt like the hundredth time. He was frowning deeply, as if trying to think something troubling through in his head. She wished she could help. She wished he would share what he was worrying about with her, but she knew what he needed now was time and space to think.

So instead of saying anything Louisa sat back and relived the moment on the terrace when Robert had kissed her. She'd been more prepared for it than before, it had seemed natural, right somehow. He'd run his hand up her arm and pulled her towards him. Then he'd lowered his mouth onto hers and kissed her tenderly. It had been a kiss filled with warmth and gentleness, but with an underlying thrum of desire and passion.

It confused her more than their kiss the day before. That had been heated and almost animalistic. It was the kiss of two people who desired each other. Today Robert had kissed her as though he loved her.

Louisa quashed the thought immediately. He didn't love her. Of that she was sure. What did she know about love? No one had shown any sort of love towards her for nine years. Thinking Robert kissed her with love was just wishful thinking, nothing more.

She glanced across at him. He was still frowning, lost in his own world. She wondered again what Mrs Knapwell had said on the terrace, what had triggered his desire to escape so suddenly and why he was so quiet and withdrawn now.

They pulled up outside Robert's house. As the carriage came to a halt Robert looked up at her, his eyes meeting hers with such an intensity Louisa felt a shiver run through her body.

Wordlessly he helped her down from the carriage and followed her inside. Once they were alone in the hallway he seemed to hesitate, as if unsure what to do next. Louisa stood still, not wanting to interrupt his decision making.

'Will you have a drink with me in my study?' Robert asked, almost formally.

Louisa nodded. She followed him into her favourite room of the house. She supposed she liked it because it had Robert's personality stamped all over it, from the comfortable leather chairs to the books that lined the walls.

Silently Robert poured two glasses of whisky. He handed one to Louisa and motioned for her to sit down. He remained standing.

'Do you want to talk?' Louisa asked gently.

She took a sip of the whisky and grimaced. The fiery liquid burned her throat and sat heavily in her stomach. She set the glass down on the small table by her side and turned back to Robert. He still hadn't answered her.

'Or we can just sit together?' she suggested, patting the space on the sofa next to her.

He sank down on to the cushion, still looking distractedly around him. Louisa wondered what he was thinking about.

'Would you like to hear about the war?' he asked quietly.

Louisa nodded. 'Only if you would like to tell me about it.'

'I think maybe I should,' he said. 'Mrs Knapwell said something to me this evening that made me realise that keeping everything inside maybe wasn't the best idea.'

Louisa reached out and took his hand firmly in hers.

'I think Mrs Knapwell is a very wise woman.'

'By the time I've finished you might hate me,' Robert said, 'but please promise me you won't leave because of what I've done.'

'I promise,' Louisa said simply.

Now wasn't about her. She had to forget her fears and her worries. Right now she had to be strong for the man who had rescued her from a life of misery. It was the least she could do.

'I met Knapwell on our first day at Eton,' Robert stated. 'He punched me, I gave him a black eye.'

Louisa frowned. She was sure Mrs Knapwell had said they'd been friends from the very first at Eton.

Robert saw her frown and explained, 'After

that we developed a mutual respect that blossomed into friendship. By the end of the first term we were inseparable.'

Louisa tried to picture Robert as a child, going to school for the first time. She wondered if he was quite so serious back then.

'My mother had died when I was very young and when I was fourteen my father passed away. That Christmas, Knapwell took me home to his family and they treated me like one of their own.'

Louisa could imagine the kindly Mrs Knapwell taking a mourning orphan boy into her family fold. She would try to help ease the pain of spending his first Christmas without a family.

'He became more of a brother than a friend. When we left Eton we both went to Cambridge to study—that was where we met Dunton.'

He paused for a second, and Louisa smiled at him encouragingly. She knew he had a long story to tell her and it would be cathartic to finally confide what had happened in someone, but soon it was going to get harder for him, more painful.

'When we were all in our final year at Cambridge we started hearing more and more about the war. We went to a few political discussions, but it was mainly undergraduates giving their opinions on what was happening miles away.' He looked away for a second. 'I didn't like what

Napoleon was trying to do. Every country has the right to independence, not to be ruled by some foreign dictator, sitting in a decadent palace thousands of miles away whilst the people starve.'

Louisa could see the passion and conviction in his eyes and knew if the situation arose again he would make the same decision; he would go off to war.

'I decided to join the army, went along and bought my commission the day I graduated. I didn't have a father to talk me out of it, no one to tell me I was being selfish leaving the estate to fend for itself.'

'And the others?' Louisa asked.

'Knapwell joined immediately; as soon as he found out I was going to fight he wanted to come with me. Said I'd get myself killed if he wasn't there to keep an eye on me.'

'And Dunton?'

'He bought his commission a few days later. He was always more level-headed than Knapwell, thought everything through thoroughly. But as a second son he knew he'd have to either join the army or find himself a profession. He decided to join us.'

Robert lapsed into silence. Louisa wondered if he was remembering the time when the three friends had been together, before their ideals had been crushed by the realities of war.

'We had some basic training, nothing much more than how to hold a sword and fire a musket, and then we were sent to Portugal. We travelled with the men we'd be fighting with, those under our command. By the time we reached our destination we knew them all well enough.'

Louisa leant forwards ever so slightly. Robert was getting into the flow of telling his story and was less hesitant now. She could already tell it was good for him, sharing the memories.

'We fought a few battles, lost some men. Suddenly it was all rather real. It wasn't an academic debate over whether Napoleon should be forced out of Portugal. It was a fight to the death in a muddy field.'

Louisa couldn't even begin to imagine how awful it must have been. For three young men used to all the luxuries of life to be thrown into such a scenario must have been a shock. No wonder so many came home from the war mere shells of their former selves.

'After a few months we started having some success. We implemented a new way of fighting, drilled the men in the importance of keeping in formation, that breaking rank meant the breakdown of order and losing the battle.'

She smiled at the thought of Robert going

in and improving the age-old ways of warfare. His analytical brain and ordered way of thinking would have served him well in that situation.

'A few of the high-ranking officers thought they might be able to use me and my men in one of the light infantry units. We would scout ahead of the main body of the army, find and exploit any weaknesses in the enemy's lines. Often we would engage much larger forces than ours, but our men were well trained and we'd selected the best fighters. Normally we came out on top.'

Louisa could hear the note of pride in his voice. Robert would have been proud to lead such brave and talented men. He'd served his country and looked after the men in his unit.

Robert fell silent. Louisa could tell they had reached the difficult part of the story. Everything he'd told her so far was just the setting, the background information to some terrible event that had changed Robert for ever.

'On the fifteenth of September we came across a village,' Robert said, seeming to change the direction of his story suddenly. 'St Mamede. A few locals hadn't fled the village and seemed welcoming, supplying us with food and beds for the night.'

Louisa felt his grip tighten on her hand and squeezed back reassuringly.

'Ana Mendez was the daughter of a farmer.

She showed us around the village, helped us find beds for all our men, encouraged the other residents to give us food.'

Louisa knew as soon as Robert had said her name they had been lovers. She felt jealous of this foreign woman who had held Robert's heart, even if it was only for a brief period of time.

'She persuaded us to stay in the village for a few days, recuperating. We'd been marching and fighting for two months solidly and the men needed a rest.'

Louisa knew Robert wouldn't have made the decision to stay based on his own desires for this woman. He'd have considered what was best for all his men, putting his own needs to one side, and then decided.

'By that time we'd become quite famous amongst the enemy. We were known for our lightning-speed attacks and our ability to take on much bigger forces than our own and still win. We didn't know it at the time, but the enemy had offered a reward for anyone who helped to destroy us.'

Louisa felt the first dawning of realisation. They'd been betrayed.

'We spent two weeks in St Mamede. The men were well rested and by that point we were almost ready to move on. We had new orders and the plan was to march east at dawn the next morning.'

Louisa could feel the pain and guilt emanating from Robert. She wished she could take away all the hurt and regrets and make him realise what a wonderful, caring man he as.

'Ana and I were…' he trailed off, as if aware he shouldn't be talking to Louisa about his lover '…intimate. The last night before we left Knapwell said he'd gather the men together for one last talk. He told me to go enjoy myself for once and let him speak to the men.'

Louisa could imagine Robert giving in to his friend's insistence he spend one last evening with his lover.

'I spent the evening alone with Ana, unaware of what was unfolding only half a mile away.'

Louisa felt sick. She knew what he was going to say. They'd been betrayed and his men, the brave and talented light infantry unit, had been slaughtered whilst he was oblivious.

'I lay in bed whilst French troops crept up to the village. They knew exactly where the men would be, how many there were and what they were armed with.'

His voice had become flat and emotionless. Louisa supposed he had to distance himself from the memory or he'd go mad.

'What happened?' Louisa asked, unable to keep quiet any longer.

Robert chuckled, but it was a humourless sound.

'Ana made a mistake,' he said. 'She pulled a knife on me whilst she thought I was sleeping. I opened my eyes to see the woman I loved, the woman who I thought had loved me, about to stab me through the heart.'

Louisa couldn't even begin to imagine the betrayal and hurt he must have felt all in that instant.

'What did you do?' she asked, her eyes wide with anticipation.

'I wanted to kill her,' Robert said simply. 'I wonder sometimes if I hadn't had my men to think about whether I might have.' The anguish on his face told her there was so much more depth to his emotions than he was letting on. 'I pushed her away from me, across the room. She fell and hurt herself against the wardrobe, dropped the knife. I picked it up, got it away from her. In that moment I could have killed her.'

'But you didn't.'

Robert shook his head. 'It was a split-second decision. I could either kill her or go to my men. In the end saving my men was more important than meting out my own form of justice.'

'So she was a spy?' Louisa asked.

Robert grimaced. 'They all were, all the so-called residents left in the village. We found out afterwards they'd slaughtered the inhabitants before we'd arrived and set themselves up as the few remaining villagers, the ones who hadn't fled before Napoleon's troops.'

'Why?' Louisa asked.

'To stop us.'

Louisa realised then just how effective Robert's unit must have been. It was a lot of trouble to go to for one group of soldiers, but if they were really that deadly she supposed a trap like the one they'd fallen into in St Mamede was the only way to stop them.

'What happened to your men?' Louisa asked, knowing this was what Robert felt guilty about.

'I sprinted to where Knapwell had been speaking to the men, explaining our orders, where we were heading to next, but I was too late. The slaughter had already begun.'

'But you didn't all die,' Louisa said. 'You and Dunton got away at least.'

Robert nodded, looking as though he wished he hadn't survived.

'I told you my men were well trained. Those who were killed were the ones closest to the forest where the French troops attacked from. As soon as the true fighting began my men fell into formation and fought back as best they could.'

Even now Louisa could tell he was proud of his troops.

'When I arrived about half were dead. We fought the French for our lives that evening, and eventually, even though they outnumbered us four to one, they retreated.'

Louisa gripped Robert's hand even tighter, trying to convey sympathy and love all through that one simple touch.

'And Knapwell?' Louisa asked gently.

'He'd been run through with a sword,' Robert said. 'He was still alive, but he didn't last long.'

Robert's face contorted with the pain of remembering his friend's death.

'Did he say anything to you before he died?' Louisa asked.

Robert nodded. 'He told me to live for the both of us.'

They both fell silent. Louisa felt shocked. She knew something awful had happened to Robert during the war, but she hadn't imagined anything like this. What she couldn't understand was why he seemed so ashamed and guilty. He was a hero. He hadn't done a single thing wrong. Even she could tell that and she hadn't been there.

'And have you?' she asked after a couple of minutes of silence.

He looked at her questioningly.

'Have you lived for the both of you?'

Slowly Robert shook his head.

* * *

Robert sat completely still. He felt as though he was being swept out to sea and the only thing anchoring him to shore was Louisa's hand. He gripped on to her as if his life depended on it. Never before had he told anyone exactly what had happened, not like he'd confided in Louisa. When he'd had to explain the loss of three-quarters of his men to the senior officers he'd talked in military terms. He'd described the trap they'd been caught in and how the fighting had developed. He hadn't once mentioned Ana.

'You do realise it's not your fault?' Louisa asked suddenly.

He looked at her for a few seconds, not saying anything.

'None of it was your fault.'

Of course it was. The whole awful affair was his fault. If he hadn't been deceived by the trap, if he hadn't been seduced by Ana, if he'd realised what was going on, his men, his friends, would be alive.

'None of it was your fault,' Louisa repeated resolutely.

'I was their commanding officer,' Robert said. 'I should have protected them.'

'You can't protect everyone. And you can't foresee everything.' She was speaking calmly, rationally, but Robert knew she was wrong.

'You've told me everything that happened?' Louisa asked.

He nodded. He had. Louisa was the first person he'd told this story to and he'd told her everything.

'From outside the situation, as someone who is not emotionally involved, I can say with confidence there was no way you were responsible for Greg Knapwell's death.'

'If I'd been there...' Robert trailed off.

'Is it a prerequisite that the senior officer takes all briefings?' Louisa asked.

Robert shook his head.

'So sometimes the second-in-command can address the troops?'

He nodded.

'So why should you have been there?' she asked.

'I should have realised it was a trap.'

Louisa shifted towards him and raised her hands up to touch each side of his face. She held his eyes as her fingers stroked the skin of his cheeks, grazing over closely shaved stubble.

'Why should you?' she asked softly. 'You are only human, Robert. You may be a very intelligent and capable human, but you're human all the same. You can't expect to get everything right. You can't expect to make perfect judgements about people's characters all the time.'

He wondered if she was right. Her earnest eyes staring into his were persuasive as well as beautiful.

'But this lack of judgement lost my men their lives.'

'And it was your judgement, your leadership, that got them through so many other tough situations and difficult fights. Without you many would have died much sooner.'

Robert thought back to the skirmishes they'd been in. He supposed she had a point—soldiers could die at any time. It was a hazard of the job.

'You can't go on blaming yourself for something that was not your fault,' Louisa said, her thumb grazing his cheek rhythmically. 'You led your men as best you could through difficult and dangerous times. Yes, many died, but in war that is not surprising.'

He found himself nodding. When did this young woman get so wise? he wondered. She'd spent half her life locked away from the world by a lecherous old man or shut in isolation in the asylum, but still she spoke with authority and conviction.

'You have to forgive yourself,' Louisa said quietly, 'otherwise there was no point in coming home from the war.'

Forgive himself? Robert mused, he hadn't ever even contemplated that. For so long he'd carried the guilt of what had happened in St Mamede everywhere he went. He'd continued to fight in the army after the incident, knowing he had to see the war to the end. He'd owed Knapwell that much. Then he'd come home and lived this half life, not a real existence, plagued by guilt. Guilt at surviving and guilt at being responsible for his friend's death.

He couldn't imagine what life would be like if he actually forgave himself, if he didn't spend each and every day hating himself for the mistakes he'd made.

'You're a good man, Robert,' Louisa said quietly. 'You deserve happiness.'

Robert looked at Louisa intently. She was beautiful, this little waif he'd spirited from the asylum less than a week ago. She'd listened to his account of what had happened in Portugal and she still thought he was a good man. Maybe she was right. Maybe he needed to forgive himself just a little.

She dropped her hands from his face and immediately he missed the touch. His body cried out for him to kiss her, to lay her back on the sofa and make her his, but Robert knew that was a step too far. He might be able to forgive himself a little, but he knew he could never deserve a woman like Louisa. She was kind and caring and the most understanding woman he'd ever met. She deserved only the best.

So instead of kissing her, Robert sat back and closed his eyes, trying to control his desire, pushing the thought of Louisa's soft lips and pliant body far from his mind.

Chapter Sixteen

Louisa had barely slept. All through the night Robert's story kept running through her mind. She understood him so much better now, could grasp where the pain and anguish came from. He was a good man, that much was clear, and a brave man. A man who had led his troops successfully through peril time and time again, only to be tricked by a woman. She supposed she understood why he blamed himself—not that it was his fault at all, but Robert was the kind of man who took his responsibilities very seriously.

She entered the dining room and stopped short. Each morning since she'd arrived at Fleetwood House Robert had been up and ready for the day far earlier than she. When she came down for breakfast he had normally already finished his and was sitting drinking coffee and reading the paper. Today he was nowhere to be seen.

Louisa looked around for signs he had been and gone. There wasn't a stray crumb or evidence of disturbance. She knew with certainty no one had been in to breakfast yet. Although where Robert was remained a mystery, she wasn't surprised Mrs Crawshaw was nowhere to be seen. Louisa's elderly companion had been a good choice. The woman could barely see anything, couldn't hear what was being said unless it was directed solely at her and seemed to sleep half the day. She was a companion for propriety's sake only, and hadn't got in the way of Louisa enjoying Robert's company one little bit.

A footman entered and Louisa spun round.

'Shall I tell cook you're ready for breakfast, miss?'

'Has Lord Fleetwood gone somewhere?' she asked.

The footman hid a grin; Robert's punctuality was well known around the house.

'No, miss. He only rose ten minutes ago.' The footman leant in closer. 'It's the first time he's slept in past seven for two years.'

Louisa didn't know what to make of this piece of news.

'I'll bring breakfast up for you and his lordship,' the footman said.

Louisa perched on the edge of a dining-room chair, every few seconds looking over her

shoulder, wondering when Robert would make
an entrance. She supposed his nightmares had
probably got worse, after dragging up all the
memories last night.

'Good morning, Louisa,' Robert said, coming in and taking his normal seat at the head of
the table.

He looked refreshed, not like a man who had
been tossing and turning all night.

'Did you sleep?' Louisa asked, looking for
signs of exhaustion on his face.

'Like a baby,' he said with a frown. 'No, better than a baby.'

Louisa looked at him questioningly. Robert
never slept well.

'And the nightmares?' she asked.

'Didn't have a single one.' His frown deepened and he looked puzzled, as if he couldn't
quite believe what he was saying. Then he
shrugged and smiled at her and Louisa found
herself smiling back. He looked younger than
normal, more carefree. She liked this version
of Robert.

'What's for breakfast?' Robert asked, looking
around just as the footman reentered with a tray.

'Scrambled eggs, my lord,' the footman said.

'I'm ravenous.'

Louisa watched as Robert tucked into his
plate of scrambled eggs. He was eating it with

the same level of enjoyment as she had as she approached each meal.

'This coffee is delicious,' he commented, taking a break from his breakfast to drain the cup. The footman immediately stepped forwards and refilled it. 'Is it new?'

'Just the same coffee you've had for two years, my lord.'

Robert shrugged and turned back to his plate of eggs.

'What do you fancy doing today?' Robert asked.

Louisa tore her eyes away from the man who yesterday hadn't even glanced at the food on his plate with any amount of interest.

'Something outdoorsy,' she said. 'It's going to be a beautiful sunny day.'

Robert nodded with enthusiasm.

'Maybe a trip to the park,' she suggested. She'd enjoyed their first walk around the park just a week ago. She couldn't believe it was only a week since they'd first met. Sometimes she felt as though she'd known Robert for a lifetime, especially now he'd opened up to her and shared such intimate details about his past.

'Or how about I take you riding?,' he suggested.

Louisa looked at him sceptically. 'You do realise I haven't been on a horse for nine years,' she said, 'and before that I wasn't exactly an expert horsewoman.'

'Did you enjoy it?'

She nodded. She'd enjoyed the freedom, the knowledge that she could gallop off through the fields and be the only one for miles. She'd missed that once her parents had died. It was another bit of her former life Mr Craven had stripped from her.

'Would you like to learn how to do it properly?' he asked.

'Will you be the one teaching me?'

'Of course.' He said it as if she were mad to think he'd let anyone else teach her.

'Then I'd love to.'

Louisa watched him as he finished his scrambled eggs and savoured the second cup of coffee. He'd bared his soul to her last night, told her things he hadn't ever told anyone else. She felt privileged, special, and she wondered why he had chosen her to tell it all to.

For the past week Louisa had known her feelings for Robert were growing into something more than gratitude. At first she'd just been thankful he'd rescued her from the asylum. Then had come the friendship. She hadn't really had a friend before, not as an adult at least, but she enjoyed the feeling of someone looking out for her, caring for her.

Then as well as the friendship was desire, for Louisa couldn't deny she was attracted to Robert. He was a good-looking man and every time they were alone Louisa had the urge to press her body up against his and invite him to do very wicked things to her. It wasn't the way a well-brought-up young lady was meant to behave, but she couldn't seem to stop the wanton thoughts.

Her body had responded to his kisses instinctively, as if she'd been born to be kissed by Robert Fleetwood.

Louisa felt the heat rising through her body and realised these were dangerous thoughts for the breakfast table. She told herself to get back to the subject and figure out exactly what it was she felt for Robert Fleetwood.

Did she trust him? Louisa asked herself. She hadn't trusted anyone since her parents had died. But Robert was a hard man to ignore. Every day he did something that made her feel more and more comfortable in his presence. And he was the one she turned to if she was afraid or unsure of something.

'You have a visitor, Lord Fleetwood,' Smith, the footman, said as he came in to collect the empty plates. 'Mrs Knapwell. I've put her in the drawing room.'

Robert glanced at her, shrugged and stood to leave.

'Shall I come with you?' Louisa asked.

He nodded, some of the tension back in his shoulders already. Louisa hoped seeing Mrs Knapwell wasn't enough to send him back into a guilty frame of mind.

'I'm so sorry to call so early,' Mrs Knapwell said as soon as they both entered the drawing room. 'I know it's extremely uncivilised of me.'

'Not at all. You're always welcome here no matter what time of day.'

'I was meaning to mention it last night,' she continued. 'I wanted to ask if Miss Turnhill would like to accompany me to the Southwark Orphanage today.'

Louisa glanced at Robert. He shrugged as if leaving it up to her.

'We're having a bit of a gala,' Mrs Knapwell explained. 'It's a fund-raising event, an open house really. The girls are putting on a little exhibition about their daily lives.'

Louisa couldn't imagine that the general public would want to know the grim realities of the orphans' daily lives.

'I'd love to,' Louisa said.

She wanted to support Mrs Knapwell's cause. The older lady had been so kind to her over the last few days and she wanted to do something in return. Plus, it would do her good to stop mulling over her own problems for a change and think about other people.

'Is there space for one more?' Robert asked.

Louisa watched him as he waited for Mrs Knapwell's reply, knowing how much courage it had taken him to ask to spend the day with his friend's mother.

'I'd be delighted and honoured if you would accompany us, Lord Fleetwood,' Mrs Knapwell said sincerely.

'You don't mind postponing our riding lesson?' Robert asked.

Louisa shook her head. The idea of a riding lesson with Robert was tempting, but there would be plenty of other opportunities. It wasn't as if she was going anywhere.

It was only a few seconds later that Louisa realised what she had just thought. She wasn't going anywhere. Only a week ago she'd been so set on striking out on her own she'd risked her life and her safety by sneaking off into the deserted streets of London in the middle of the night. Now she was unconsciously planning ahead, thinking of the future, a future that involved Robert.

'We can do it another time. I'm not going anywhere,' she said softly.

Robert grinned at her. 'You're not going anywhere,' he repeated.

If Mrs Knapwell thought their exchange strange, she didn't comment. She smiled at them both.

'I'm on my way to the orphanage now, but if it's too early for you I can give you the address and you can follow later.'

'Can you wait for ten minutes whilst we gather everything together?' Robert asked.

Louisa nodded. This was encouraging. Robert wasn't taking the opportunity to spend less time with Mrs Knapwell as he would have not twenty-four hours ago. She'd given him a very easy way out and he'd chosen to spend more time in her company.

'Of course.'

Louisa followed Robert out of the room

'Thank you,' Louisa said.

'What for?'

'For putting me first.'

Robert looked at her oddly. 'I will always put you first, Louisa,' he said, before striding up the stairs, taking them two at a time.

Louisa stared after him and wondered exactly what he meant by it. It sounded almost like a declaration of love. Louisa chided herself. It was nothing of the sort. It was the words of a diligent guardian looking out for his ward. She told herself to stop reading so much into his innocent words. He didn't love her, he cared for her.

She couldn't ask for anything more. She didn't want anything more. Or at least that's what she told herself. Love would complicate matters. She was just learning to trust again. She needed to take things slowly and not get ahead of herself.

Chapter Seventeen

Robert leant against the wall and watched Louisa bend forwards and exchange a few words with one of the orphans. She was a natural in this situation; her past experiences meant she could interact easily with people from all different social classes without even thinking about it. Before they'd left his town house Robert had warned Louisa again not to let anything slip about her past. They were mainly among friends here, but you never knew who was listening. One wrong word and Louisa's past could be exposed and with it her future ruined.

'Twice in two days, Fleetwood,' Dunton's familiar voice called as he came up beside Robert. 'Didn't expect to see you here after your rapid departure last night.'

So it had been noted. Dunton must have seen his face for he continued. 'Don't worry, I made sure you weren't missed too much. I have to say it was your ward everyone was asking about, not you.'

Robert grunted.

'As eloquent as ever, I see.'

'What are you doing here?' Robert asked.

The Southwark Orphanage for Girls was a worthy cause, but apart from Robert and one or two elderly gentlemen, the gathering was mainly female.

'Mrs Knapwell asked me to come,' Dunton said.

'I didn't know you two were acquainted.'

They certainly hadn't been before the three of them had left for war. Although Robert and Knapwell had been good friends with Dunton it wasn't the sort of friendship you took home to meet your parents. They'd spent their evenings drinking and debating as most students did.

'I went to see her after we got home,' Dunton said. 'Thought she might like to know what had happened to her son.' There was no reproach in his voice. 'I went to see her a few times after that. She was grieving, but she appreciated the chance to talk about Knapwell.'

'I should have gone,' Robert said.

He had been to see her once. It had been terrible. Mrs Knapwell had hugged him and cried. She'd thanked him for being such a good friend to her son and all the time Robert had just stood there, unable to say anything, unable to offer any words of comfort, knowing he was the reason her son was dead.

'You're here now,' Dunton said simply. 'You don't know how much that means to Mrs Knapwell.'

Robert nodded. The older woman had been positively beaming throughout the carriage ride south of the river and she'd proudly introduced him to each of her friends once they'd arrived at the orphanage.

'I talked to Louisa about it last night,' Robert said quietly.

'About the war?'

'And about Ana.'

He felt Dunton go completely still beside him. Robert never talked about Ana. Even when Dunton had tried to bring up the issue he dodged the subject.

'What did she say?'

Robert shrugged. 'She told me it wasn't my fault and that I had to start forgiving myself.'

'Sensible girl.'

They stood in silence for a few minutes, watching the upper-class guests interact with the shy orphan girls.

'You should marry her,' Dunton said suddenly.

Robert spun to face him, unsure whether he was joking.

'I'm being serious. She's good for you.' Dunton laughed at the expression on his face. 'Why not?'

'I've only known her a week.'

'Exactly. You've only known her a week and look what a change she's brought about already. You're out in public, you're interacting with people. And I swear I've actually seen you smile.'

Robert deepened his glower just to prove his friend wrong.

'Admit it, for the first time in years you're actually happy.'

He remained silent. Glancing over at Louisa, he felt the familiar tightening inside his stomach as she smiled. He loved her smiles.

'I'm never going to marry.'

'Poppycock.'

Robert turned back to his friend and said seriously, 'I'm not exactly a good judge of character when it comes to women.'

Dunton laughed. 'You made one mistake. You were exhausted after months of guerilla warfare and Ana offered rest and recuperation in her arms. Any man would have fallen for it. Plus she was a professional spy.'

He made good points, but Robert still knew marriage just was not for him.

'She was trained in deception and treachery.

You can't swear off women just because one deceives you.'

'Deceives me and in the process kills my men and my best friend.'

Dunton fell silent for a few seconds. 'Miss Turnhill could be good for you,' he said eventually. 'I only spoke to her for a short while, but that was enough to know she is sweet and kind and doesn't have a deceitful bone in her body.'

That much was true at least. Robert knew Louisa would never betray him the way Ana had.

'So your plan is to spend your life alone and miserable?' Dunton asked.

He had to admit it didn't sound appealing when put like that.

'She won't wait for you for ever, Fleetwood. Look at her with those orphans.'

Robert glanced over again at Louisa. She was smiling and laughing with a small child. The little girl reached up and took Louisa'a hand and proceeded to lead her to the next table in the room, pointing things out as she went. He couldn't hear what Louisa was saying, but it must have been something complimentary as the girl beamed up at her in response.

'She'll want children, a home of her own.'

He thought Dunton was getting a bit ahead of himself here. Just over a week ago Louisa was locked in a cell all day with only her imagination for company. Surely she'd be content with spending her time with just him for a little longer.

'She's what, eighteen? Nineteen?' Dunton asked.

'Nineteen.'

'Already most young women have had their coming out by this point. Half are married by her age.'

Robert realised his friend had a point.

'A beautiful young woman like Louisa isn't going to struggle to find a husband, but people will wonder why she waited so long if she doesn't have her debut soon.'

Robert felt slightly sick at the thought of Louisa marrying another man. He recalled their kiss and felt the same flood of desire crashing over him as it always did when he pictured her lips brushing against his. He couldn't deny he wanted her, desired her. Every time she flashed him a smile he imagined her underneath him, writhing in ecstasy, his hands and lips exploring her naked body.

Yes, he desired her, but he knew he couldn't have her. She deserved so much better. After nine years of misery and loneliness she deserved only the best. And Robert was far from the best. She deserved someone who could devote every waking minute to making her happy, someone who could make her laugh and smile, not someone who was still half living on a battlefield in Portugal.

He wondered for a second what life would be like if he did marry her. Waking up to her smile every morning, kissing her as she banished the last remnants of sleep from her body, but he knew he had to stop himself. It was just too painful otherwise.

'She'd say yes if you asked,' Dunton said quietly before clapping Robert on the shoulder and walking away.

Robert watched as Louisa was introduced to two of the other patronesses by Mrs Knapwell. She listened intently to whatever they were saying to her, nodding in all the right places. She was blossoming before his eyes into a confident young woman.

Would she say yes? Robert asked himself. She'd responded instinctively to his kisses, even if she had seemed unaffected after the first. And she had heard the very worst things about him, the secrets he had vowed never to tell another living person, and she'd still stuck around.

It didn't matter if she would say yes, Robert chided himself, he wasn't going to ask her to marry him. He might have decided to start the process of forgiving himself for what had happened in St Mamede, but he wasn't going to allow himself to get romantically involved with any woman, let alone his ward.

'I'm so pleased you could come, Lord Fleetwood,' Mrs Knapwell said as she bustled over to him. Louisa was still listening intently to what the other patronesses were saying, holding the little girl's hand at the same time.

'It's my pleasure,' Robert said. Surprisingly it was the truth. It felt good to be out in public, supporting a good cause.

'Miss Turnhill seems to be enjoying herself.'

Robert's eyes had never left Louisa. 'Thank you for thinking to invite her,' he said. 'I fear having a grouchy man as her guardian that perhaps she's missing out.'

'Don't put yourself down, Lord Fleetwood. You're doing a wonderful job as her guardian,' Mrs Knapwell chided.

Robert thought of the stolen kiss on Mrs Knapwell's terrace the night before and knew he was not safeguarding Louisa's reputation as well as he should.

'And it's clear she adores being with you.'

'I think she has done much more for me than I for her,' Robert said quietly.

Mrs Knapwell looked at him astutely, nodding her head. 'I'd probably have to agree.'

'I want to apologise,' Robert said, taking a deep breath and tearing his eyes away from

Louisa, instead focusing them on Mrs Knapwell's face.

'Whatever for?'

'I should have been there for you,' Robert said, 'when we returned from the war.'

Mrs Knapwell shook her head and patted him kindly on the arm.

'No,' Robert insisted, 'Greg was my best friend and you were like a mother to me all those years we were at school together. You deserved better.'

'You were hurting,' Mrs Knapwell said. 'We all mourn in our own way. I'm just glad you're here now. I couldn't bear it if you shut yourself away your whole life. Guilt isn't a reason for living.'

They stood side by side for a few minutes, taking comfort in each other's company.

Robert glanced back at Louisa. She had been led off by her young guide and was now on the other side of the hall. He saw Mrs Knapwell follow his gaze.

'I need your help with something,' Robert said, somewhat reluctantly.

'Of course, anything.'

'Miss Turnhill is a lovely young woman, but it has been pointed out she isn't getting any younger and if she doesn't make her debut into society soon she may not make a good match.'

'You want her to get married?' Mrs Knapwell asked, sounding a little shocked.

'I want her to be happy.'

The older woman looked at him strangely for a few seconds, then nodded.

'Of course you do, my dear.'

'She'll want children, a house of her own,' Robert repeated Dunton's words.

'With a man she loves,' she added.

'Of course.'

'And you think she needs to be launched into society to find these things.' It was said as a statement more than a question.

'Well, she's hardly going to find someone suitable cooped up in my study all day.'

Mrs Knapwell gave him a long, hard look, then let out a sharp little exhalation of breath.

'I would really appreciate your help and guidance on the matter.'

'Of course I'll help, if that's what you think is best for her.'

Robert nodded.

'I always wanted a daughter to launch into society. She'll be a success, you know.' It was phrased rather like a warning.

'I know,' Robert said grimly, trying to block out the picture of Louisa being surrounded by a flock of admiring gentlemen.

Chapter Eighteen

'Would you like to see my favourite place on earth?' asked Gertie, the little orphan who had taken a shine to Louisa.

'I'd love to.'

Gertie tugged Louisa through the crowd of people and out the door into the main hallway.

'You won't get into trouble, will you?' Louisa asked, not wanting to be the reason this sweet little girl was punished.

Gertie pulled a face. 'No one will even notice I'm gone.'

Louisa thought this was a sad state of affairs, but the young orphan didn't seem to mind too much.

'I'll show you my room first,' Gertie announced.

Louisa followed the child up the wide staircase and on to the first-floor landing. The orphanage was rather grey and dreary. It reminded

Louisa of the Lewisham Asylum in its colour scheme. She supposed all of these institutions where they shut the unwanted away from the rest of the world were decorated in greys and browns.

'This is my bed,' Gertie said as they entered a large dormitory. There must have been at least twenty metal cots lining the walls. There was just space to squeeze between them. Each of the beds was identical and there were no personal items to identify the inhabitants.

'So is this your favourite place, Gertie?' Louisa asked.

The little girl pulled a face and looked at Louisa as though she were mad.

'No. This is my least favourite place. I even prefer the laundry room to here. In here I'm the youngest and the other girls are always telling me I won't understand their conversations or that I'm too young to be included.' Gertie pulled a face and muttered, 'I'm not too young. And I'm cleverer than most of those halfwits.'

She spun around suddenly and grabbed Louisa's hand. Quickly they left the dormitory and dashed along the corridor. They stopped outside a narrow wooden door. Gertie looked carefully from the left to the right, then turned the handle and slipped inside. Louisa followed her.

'I showed you the dormitory so you'd understand why I liked it up here so much,' Gertie explained as they climbed a rickety staircase.

They seemed to climb for a good few storeys and Louisa wondered where the young girl was taking her.

When they reached the very top of the building Gertie flung open another door and light flooded into the stairwell. Louisa had to squint whilst her eyes adjusted to the brightness.

'Come on,' Gertie instructed as she stepped onto the roof.

Louisa followed her into the fresh air, picking her way over discarded tiles and pieces of guttering. She realised they were on the flat ledge that ran around the top of the building. To one side was the slanted roof and to the other was a long drop to the street.

Gertie stopped suddenly and sighed contentedly.

'Isn't it wonderful?' she said.

Louisa followed her gaze out over the rooftops of London. She had to admit it was rather impressive. The sky was hazy, but she felt as though she could see for miles. Off to the right and over the river she could see the awe-inspiring dome of St Paul's Cathedral. Farther away was the tall tower that commemorated the awful fire of 1666. Over to the left was the impressive sight of Westminster Abbey, towering over everything else in awe-inspiring splendour. And between the unmistakable grand buildings of London the River Thames snaked across the landscape, a murky grey slash dividing the rich and the poor.

'I feel like I'm on top of the world when I'm up here,' Gertie said quietly.

The young girl had sat down with her feet dangling over the edge fearlessly. Louisa looked down to the street a long way below and felt her stomach lurch.

'It's all right,' Gertie said. 'I've been up here hundreds of times, thousands, even, and I've never fallen.'

Louisa envied the fearlessness of childhood. Carefully she sat down beside Gertie and looked out over the city.

'How long have you lived here, Gertie?' Louisa asked.

'All my life…' She paused, then corrected herself. 'At least it feels like all my life. Apparently I lived with my grandmother when I was a baby.'

'You don't remember?'

Gertie shook her head. 'I don't remember my parents or my grandmother. It's as though I've always lived here. What's it like, having parents?'

Louisa looked at the young girl and saw the curiosity in her eyes.

'I'm an orphan, too,' Louisa said, 'but I do remember my parents. I was ten when they died.'

Gertie took her hand and patted it comfortingly. Louisa thought it was sad this young girl knew how to behave in such an adult way. She should be playing with dolls and spinning fairy tales, not talking about death.

'Having a mother and father was wonderful,' Louisa said as Gertie looked at her expectantly. 'My mother would kiss me goodnight every evening and my father would read me stories. When they were alive I always felt safe and loved.'

Gertie looked wistful.

'One day I'm going to leave here,' Gertie said with conviction.

'Where will you go?'

Gertie grinned. 'My Prince Charming is going to come and rescue me from this rooftop on his white horse and we'll gallop off into the sunset together.'

So *someone* was reading fairy tales to these orphans.

'You carry on dreaming, Gertie, it does happen.'

The young girl kicked her feet against the bricks.

'Can you keep a secret?' Louisa asked.

Gertie nodded, her eyes lighting up at the prospect of a confidence. Louisa knew she shouldn't tell anyone where she had spent the last year of her life, but Gertie wasn't going to tell anyone who could do her any damage. One little slip in front of any members of the *ton* and she would become a social pariah, but Gertie was a safe confidante.

'Not long ago I was in a place a little like this, but it was worse, much worse.'

'Worse than this?' Gertie scrunched up her nose as if she didn't believe it was possible.

'Much worse than this. I was locked in a tiny room all day and chained to the wall. I only ate porridge and gruel for one year.'

'That does sound worse,' Gertie conceded.

'Then one day, out of the blue, my very own brave knight came and rescued me.'

Gertie's eyes were wide with disbelief.

'He swept me out of that horrible place and took me into his home.'

'Did you marry him?' Gertie asked.

Louisa laughed.

'Everyone knows the girl always marries her Prince Charming,' Gertie insisted.

Louisa looked out into the distance and contemplated the young girl's words. In fairy tales the girl always did marry Prince Charming, but life wasn't a fairy tale. She allowed her imagination to wander, thinking about what life could be like if she were married to Robert. She pictured them strolling arm in arm around his country estate, broods of children skipping by their sides, and in the evening, when it was just the two of them, he would whisk her off to their bedroom where he'd do very wicked things to her.

Louisa felt the colour start to rise in her cheeks and hastily turned back to Gertie to distract herself.

'After my parents died I lived with a very horrible old man,' Louisa said. 'Eventually he sent me to the place where they locked me in my room and chained me to the wall.'

'He does sound horrible,' Gertie agreed.

'After that I told myself I would never rely on anyone else again. I would trust in myself and no one else.'

Gertie pulled a face. 'That's silly,' she said. 'Everyone has to trust someone else. We can't live our lives alone.'

Louisa wondered how this eight-year-old girl who had spent her entire life in an orphanage was so wise.

'Every time I'd trusted someone they'd hurt me,' Louisa tried to explain.

'Then maybe you trusted the wrong people.'

Louisa thought of Robert. She remembered his supportive presence when he'd invited the doctor to certify she wasn't mad and she thought of his encouraging smile every time her confidence wavered. Suddenly Louisa knew Robert wouldn't hurt her. She knew it as well as she knew her own name.

'Maybe you're right,' Louisa said.

'So you'll marry him?' Gertie insisted.

Louisa laughed. 'It's not quite as simple as that.'

The young girl rolled her eyes with exasperation.

'You love him and he loves you. That's how it always works in fairy tales.'

Louisa thought of their kiss on the terrace the night before. It had been filled with passion and desire, but more than that it had been tender and almost loving. For a second she dared to wonder if Gertie was right.

'You do love him, don't you?' Gertie asked, suddenly suspicious.

Louisa felt her throat go dry and her heart start to pound in her chest. How could she love a man she'd only known for a week?

Gertie shrugged. 'You love him,' she said with certainty.

She got to her feet, leant down and gave Louisa a quick kiss on the cheek.

'I think I believe in fairy tales now,' she said, before walking back to the door and disappearing inside the orphanage.

Louisa remained where she was for a while.

She found it peaceful up on this rooftop, away from everyone else.

She contemplated Gertie's words and wondered if she did love Robert. She'd been so preoccupied by not getting too attached she hadn't paid much attention to what she actually felt. All she did know was that the idea of leaving Robert, even if it was to strike out on her own, was now unbearable. She couldn't begin to imagine waking up each morning and not seeing Robert's face at the breakfast table. Or sitting reading a book if she wasn't seated on her favourite sofa in Robert's study with his comforting presence close by.

She felt her pulse quicken as she realised Gertie was right. She loved Robert Fleetwood. She loved him so much she would break every promise she'd made to herself about not relying on anyone else. For Robert she would learn to trust again. she'd learn to do anything.

'I was told I'd find you up here.' Robert's voice came from the doorway.

Louisa looked around. Gertie must have sent him up to the rooftop, the little minx.

'Come and sit.' Louisa indicated a spot beside her. 'The view is wonderful.'

Robert strode over to where she was perched and sat down beside her. He showed none of her earlier hesitation or fear. Louisa supposed that once you'd faced angry French troops in battle, everyday fears didn't really bother you that much.

'That is wonderful,' Robert said, looking out over the rooftops.

Louisa regarded him from the corner of her eye. He was a handsome man, a man many women would swoon over. She felt her pulse quicken and she remembered Gertie's words. Maybe Robert *was* her Prince Charming.

'What are you thinking about?' Robert asked, as he turned to find her studying his face.

Louisa swallowed, wondering if she was brave enough to put her feelings into words. The last thing she wanted was to spoil what they had already. She was so happy. These last few days had been the best of her life. She didn't want to tell Robert that she loved him only for him to reject her and push her away.

She told herself to stop being a coward.

Louisa rocked ever so slightly towards Robert. She felt her arm brush up against his chest. This was what happened in fairy tales, she told herself. Everyone lives happily ever after once they've shared true love's kiss.

Louisa felt her lips suddenly go dry and she nervously rubbed them together to moisten them. She'd kissed him before, but never had she been the one to initiate the kiss.

Slowly, Louisa reached up, placed a hand on the back of Robert's neck and pulled him towards her. Just before their lips met Louisa hesitated. She could see the confusion in Robert's eyes, but in an instant that was overpowered by a flash of desire and his lips were on hers.

She kissed him as if the world were ending. Frantically she pulled him closer to her, afraid every second he might pull away and chastise her for her lack of propriety.

'Louisa,' Robert groaned in between kisses, 'you don't know what you do to me.'

Spurred on by his reaction Louisa ran her hand down his chest, feeling the firmness of the muscles beneath the layers of clothes. She paused as she reached his taut abdomen, not bold enough to continue lower.

She loved him, she realised. All her doubts had now been banished. She loved this man.

Robert started to pepper kisses down her neck, starting just below her earlobe. Louisa shuddered with pleasure as a shiver ran through her entire body. She held her breath in anticipation as his mouth journeyed even lower. He kissed along the length of her left collarbone and into the hollow of her throat. Then his head dipped even lower.

Louisa's body screamed with impatience as

his mouth caressed the skin of her chest, moving so slowly towards the swell of her breasts.

Suddenly Robert froze. He lifted his head and looked at Louisa with an expression of horror.

'I'm so sorry,' he whispered, sounding haunted. 'I can't believe what I've just done.'

He pushed himself away from her, looking as though he couldn't quite believe what had just happened.

'It's all right,' Louisa said, reaching out for his hand. She wanted to tell him it was what she desired. She wanted to be kissed by him, ravished by him, and she wanted it to happen every day for the rest of their lives.

'No, Louisa,' Robert said, 'it's not all right. It's unforgivable. I'm your guardian. I'm in a position of trust. I should be looking out for your welfare, not doing…' He trailed off and waved his hand to signify what they'd just been doing. 'It can't happen again.'

Louisa took a deep breath and steadied herself. She knew he was only saying it because he thought that was what was right. He didn't know she loved him, that she wanted to spend the rest of her life with him. Once he knew that he'd understand. He'd realise kissing her wasn't the wrong thing to do.

Only a few days ago she'd told him she was only staying with him for a short time. Of course he didn't know she wanted to spend the rest of her life with him.

'I came out here to tell you something, Louisa,' Robert said seriously.

This didn't sound good.

'I've spoken to Mrs Knapwell and she's agreed to help launch you. I know you're a little late for the start of the Season, but it won't matter too much.'

'Launch me?' Louisa asked.

'Into society.'

'So I can find a husband?'

Robert nodded. 'Amongst other things.'

Louisa felt sick. She looked down and immediatcly regretted it. The ground seemed miles below and the world seemed to be tilting dangerously to one side.

He wanted to get her off his hands. She couldn't believe she'd misjudged the situation so completely. He wasn't in love with her, he wanted to get rid of her. Louisa scrambled to her feet, holding one hand against the slanted tiles for support.

She turned to face him, but found no words would come out. Instead she fled back to the stairway and down into the orphanage, wondering how she could have been so stupid.

Chapter Nineteen

Robert stared into his glass of whisky and swirled it around absent-mindedly. Every few minutes he saw the look of pure betrayal on Louisa's face when he'd rejected her on the rooftop of the orphanage. For that was what it had been: a rejection. She'd kissed him with passion and intensity and he'd pushed her away. Then he'd told her she was going to have to marry someone else.

The last few days they'd barely spoken to each other. Louisa was withdrawn and had gone out of her way to avoid him. At first Robert had tried to explain, but over time he'd realised the damage was done. Maybe it was better this way.

When they'd kissed on the rooftop Robert had lost control of himself. He'd known it was a bad idea, downright irresponsible, but he hadn't been able to stop. Just one last kiss, he'd told himself. The problem was that it was a kiss of love. Louisa had given herself to him with that kiss and he'd rejected her.

He tried to convince himself it was for the best. It wasn't as though they could have any future together. Louisa shouldn't have to settle for a man who was living in the past, unable to forget his demons. He didn't deserve her. And after how he'd behaved, he very much doubted he deserved anyone at all.

There was a knock on the door and Robert set down his glass before calling, 'Come in.'

Mrs Knapwell entered, followed by Mrs Crawshaw.

'It is my pleasure to present Miss Louisa Turnhill,' Mrs Knapwell said grandly.

Louisa entered the room, looking stunning. Robert frowned. The gentlemen of the *ton* would be all over her.

'Doesn't she look wonderful?' Mrs Knapwell said with a full smile.

Robert nodded. She was dressed in pale green, a shade that complemented her colouring to perfection. Her hair was pulled back with a few curled strands delicately framing her face. Her neck was exposed and suddenly Robert had the urge to run his fingers over her soft skin until she shuddered with anticipation.

Louisa gave a cursory smile, but it didn't reach her eyes.

'We're going to have such fun tonight,' Mrs Knapwell said. 'Everyone will be so thrilled to meet you.'

Robert frowned again. He wasn't so keen on Louisa being thrust into the slavering jaws of society with only Mrs Knapwell and Mrs Crawshaw to keep her safe.

'I've changed my mind,' Robert said quickly. 'I'll accompany you.'

'Oh, how wonderful,' Mrs Knapwell said. 'Isn't that good news, Miss Turnhill?'

'Don't trouble yourself, Lord Fleetwood,' Louisa said coolly. 'I'm sure we'll be fine without you.'

'I insist,' he growled. He wasn't going to let Louisa be fawned over by unsuitable men. He'd be right there beside her making sure only the very best were allowed near.

'You can't come out looking like that,' Louisa said sharply.

He supposed he deserved that. Glancing down at his crumpled shirt, Robert knew he didn't look like a guardian should when proudly introducing his ward into society.

'I can get changed.'

'Then we'll be late.'

'It'll take only five minutes.'

Louisa sighed. Robert rose to his feet and strode out of the room. He didn't want to go to whatever ball it was they were attending, but Mrs Crawshaw was hardly a reliable chaperone and Mrs Knapwell couldn't be expected to fend off all the disreputable men that would surely try to seduce Louisa. He would have to be there.

Just to watch over her, Robert assured himself, nothing more. At least he knew which of the young men of the *ton* had reputations for gambling or drinking. He would be able to guide Louisa away from the most unsuitable. It was what a good guardian should do after all.

Robert changed quickly, hurrying his valet along and reemerging downstairs only a few minutes later. For a second he thought the women had gone ahead and left without him. He cursed silently until his footman motioned to the waiting carriage outside.

'Miss Turnhill suggested they wait in the carriage, my lord. If I could be so bold as to recommend you move quickly—Miss Turnhill was mumbling something about giving you ten minutes, then leaving whether you were there or not.'

Robert strode out of the door and pulled himself up into the carriage. The three women were already seated. Louisa was sitting next to Mrs Crawshaw, refusing to meet his eye.

'Swap with me, Mrs Crawshaw,' Robert said in a tone that brooked no argument. 'I feel sick travelling backwards.'

Louisa rolled her eyes.

'I'd be happy to move, Lord Fleetwood,' Louisa said sweetly. 'I wouldn't want you feeling unwell on my account.'

'You stay where you are.'

Robert looked at Mrs Crawshaw with his steely gaze until she shuffled to the other side of the carriage and took her seat next to Mrs Knapwell.

Robert sat. It wasn't a small carriage, but it wasn't that large either. Normally when two people sat side by side their legs would brush up against one another. This evening it felt as though there was a gulf between him and Louisa. He peered at her. The silly girl was scrunched up into the corner as if she were trying to get as far away from him as possible.

Robert spread out, ignoring her irritated huff as his leg pressed against hers.

'You really shouldn't have bothered, Lord Fleetwood,' Louisa said as the carriage moved off. 'I'm sure I'm quite capable of having fun without you.'

'That's what I'm worried about,' Robert murmured.

Louisa raised her eyebrows, but didn't say any more.

'It will be a great honour for you to dance the

first dance with Miss Turnhill,' Mrs Knapwell said. 'Launch her properly into society.'

'I'm sure that's not necessary,' Louisa said before Robert could reply.

Dance with Louisa—could there be a more exquisite torture? Her body pressed against his, so close he'd be able to smell her unique scent, feel the beat of her heart, but be unable to do anything under the watchful eyes of society.

'It's necessary,' Robert and Mrs Knapwell said in unison.

'If he doesn't, all the guests will be asking why.'

'You'll dance with me first and last,' Robert said in a tone that brooked no argument. 'The rest of the time you'll be free to choose whomever you like to dance with.'

'Good.'

'Good,' Robert repeated.

They lapsed into silence. The carriage slowed as it emerged on to a larger street and met with the queue of other carriages heading for the ball.

Robert glanced down and saw Louisa was wringing her hands together. She was nervous. He wanted to reach out and still her fingers, let her know everything was going to be all right. She would be a success, Mrs Knapwell was right. She was beautiful and interesting and men would be fools not to fall at her feet.

Louisa noticed him watching her and glanced down at her hands. Immediately she stopped moving them, straightened her back and resolutely looked out the window.

'You must keep well hydrated tonight, my dear,' Mrs Knapwell said as they crawled closer to their destination. 'It is thirsty work talking and dancing your way through a ball.'

Louisa nodded obediently.

'And no alcohol,' Robert growled.

She didn't respond.

'Lord Fleetwood is right. It will be a long night for you and you don't want a sore head stopping you from talking to as many people as possible.'

Louisa smiled at Mrs Knapwell. Robert wished she would smile at him.

'Don't talk to strange men,' Robert commanded.

'Surely that is the whole point of this evening,' Louisa said sweetly, finally turning to face him.

Robert was pleased to get some sort of reaction from her at last.

'You wish for me to get married. If I'm not mistaken, that requires a gentleman for me to marry. At the moment I do not know any gentlemen so they will all be strangers. So, if I don't talk to any strangers I won't talk to anyone and I won't ever get married.'

Robert grunted.

'Unless you wish to turn this carriage round and take me back home, I suggest you allow me to talk to strange men tonight.'

He was sorely tempted. Louisa looked beautiful even when she was angry. The colour flooded to her cheeks and her eyes flashed with passion. Robert nearly reached up to bang on the roof and command they be taken back home. Home where it was just he and Louisa and a long, long night together.

Robert restrained himself. He'd been over this time and time again. Ultimately he wanted Louisa to be happy. He knew he couldn't make her happy, so he had to allow someone else the chance.

'You're not going to be standing over me all night, are you?' Louisa asked suspiciously.

'Why?'

'You'll scare everyone off. You glower a lot.'

'If they're scared by a bit of a frown, they're not exactly prime specimens of men, are they? You deserve better than that.'

'Surely it's up to me to decide what I deserve.'

'You sell yourself short,' Robert said bluntly.

'I'm not the only one,' Louisa murmured so quietly he only just heard her. Then she turned her back to him and stared out the window.

'I'm sure Lord Fleetwood will find the right

balance between protective guardian and enjoying the ball. You are here to enjoy yourself as well, remember,' Mrs Knapwell said, turning to him.

Robert stopped himself from scoffing. Attending a ball to watch Louisa get pawed at by unworthy pups was not his idea of a good night out.

'You might even start to think of marriage yourself one day soon.'

Louisa laughed, but there was no humour in the sound.

'I think that's unlikely, Mrs Knapwell. Lord Fleetwood has sworn off women.'

Mrs Knapwell looked shocked. 'Surely not completely, Lord Fleetwood.'

Robert grimaced. He didn't want to have to explain himself.

Louisa and Mrs Knapwell looked at him expectantly.

'Completely,' he confirmed eventually. 'I will never marry.'

Instead of triumph he saw desolation in Louisa's eyes. Again he wanted to reach out to her, pull her body close to him. He hated that he was the one hurting her, but he couldn't do anything about it.

'Oh, look, how pretty,' Mrs Crawshaw said, oblivious to the conversation and the tension inside the carriage. 'I do love lanterns.'

They had pulled to a stop outside the Impington town house and there were signs of the festivities everywhere. Lanterns decorated the staircase leading up to the front door and footmen lined the street, ready to assist the guests from their carriages and welcome them to the ball.

'Last chance to back out,' Louisa whispered as Robert took her hand to help her down from the carriage.

'I don't back out of anything,' Robert said.

Chapter Twenty

They entered the crush. Despite her coolness in the carriage Louisa was secretly glad to have Robert with them. She still hated him for how he'd treated her, giving her hope, then snatching it away, but nevertheless there was something about his presence that calmed her and gave her confidence.

Louisa made sure her touch on Robert's arm was feather-light. She didn't want him to realise how nervous she was. She needed to seem aloof, unaffected. Only by maintaining an icy demeanour did she stand a chance of getting through the evening without breaking down in tears and telling anyone who would listen that she loved Robert Fleetwood, but he did not love her in return.

'The dancing will start in about ten minutes,' Mrs Knapwell explained, leaning in close so Louisa could hear her. 'Lord Fleetwood will take the first dance, then after that, gentlemen will ask you to dance with them.'

Louisa nodded. They'd been through this so many times before, but still she worried she was about to do something monstrously wrong and offend the entire *ton* on her first real outing.

'You have your dance card?' Mrs Knapwell asked.

Louisa held up her wrist obediently where the card was tied on with a green ribbon.

Robert leant over and carefully untied the card. Louisa had to stop herself from shivering as his fingers met her skin. Even the slightest touch made her feel wanton.

After a couple of seconds his touch was gone. Carefully he pencilled his name into the spaces for the first and last dance.

'You don't have to dance with Miss Turnhill twice, Lord Fleetwood,' Mrs Knapwell said quietly. 'I've no doubt Miss Turnhill will have gentlemen clamouring to fill her dance card.'

Robert continued to fill his name in the last slot. Unexpectedly Louisa felt a small bubble of pleasure at the idea that he wanted to dance with her. She told herself he was merely doing his duty, but deep down she hoped it was something more.

'Fleetwood, Miss Turnhill, Mrs Knapwell.' Dunton's familiar voice cut through the crowd as he made his way towards them. 'Good to see you.' He gave Robert a strange look. 'Thought you weren't coming tonight.'

'I changed my mind.'

'Clearly.' Dunton turned his attention to Louisa. 'Miss Turnhill, I rushed all the way over here before any other gentlemen could be introduced. Will you do me the honour of granting me a dance?'

Louisa smiled. 'Of course. It would be my pleasure.'

She handed her card to Dunton and watched as he picked a slot in the middle of the evening. She was pleased there would be at least one familiar face.

'You look quite ravishing tonight, Miss Turnhill,' Dunton said. 'But I'm sure you've been told that hundreds of times already.'

'Thank you, a girl can never receive too many compliments.'

'After tonight you might disagree. You're turning heads already.'

Louisa blushed. She knew he was just being kind, but she surreptitiously glanced around the room.

'Oh, look, there's Lord Frinton,' Mrs Knapwell said.

All heads turned in the direction she was

looking in. A good-looking young man was making his way over to their group.

'Lord Frinton's sister is a patroness of the orphanage,' Mrs Knapwell told Louisa quietly. 'Lord Frinton has been a most generous benefactor.'

'Mrs Knapwell.' Lord Frinton bowed over her hand before murmuring greetings to the rest of the group.

'This is Miss Turnhill,' Mrs Knapwell said with a smile.

'It is a pleasure to meet you, Miss Turnhill. Might I say you've caused a bit of a stir.'

Lord Frinton took her hand and placed a feather-light kiss on her knuckles.

From the corner of her eye Louisa could see Robert glowering at Lord Frinton.

'Everyone was dying to meet Lord Fleetwood's ward even before they caught a glimpse of you. Now I fear you'll be besieged with eager young gentlemen and jealous young ladies.'

'You're flattering me, Lord Frinton,' Louisa said, 'and that's not good for a lady's modesty.'

Robert stepped forward as if to plant himself between the pair, but Louisa turned slightly, excluding him from the conversation. She didn't understand him. One minute he was telling her in no uncertain terms that he would never marry, that there was no future for them, but insisting she marry some man she did not love. The next he was glowering at any man who dared to come close, trying to scare them off before they even had the chance to get to know her.

He was infuriating. Well, if Robert wanted her to find a husband that was what she would do. Or at the very least she would show him she could do just that if she wanted to. Louisa was still not convinced she wanted to spend her life relying on anyone else, but for now she was happy to go along with everyone's expectations and enjoy the balls and parties.

'Can I claim a dance?' Lord Frinton asked. From behind her Louisa could sense Robert about to step forward and intervene. She wondered if he would actually say no. That would be terribly rude, and although Robert wasn't the kind of man who put much stock in polite conversation she didn't think he would normally go out of his way to offend someone.

'That would be lovely,' Louisa said hurriedly before Robert could say anything.

Lord Frinton pencilled in his name on her card.

'I hear the band striking up for the first dance,' Robert said, stepping in between Louisa and Lord Frinton. 'Shall we?' He offered his arm to Louisa and after a few long seconds Louisa placed her hand on his jacket and allowed him to lead her off.

She strained her ears. She couldn't hear anything from the band and she suspected it would be a few minutes before they started to play.

'That was rude,' Louisa muttered.

Robert said nothing.

'You're going to have to remember your manners,' she tried again. 'You'll never get me married off if you scare all the eligible young gentlemen away.'

'Frinton's not suitable,' was all Robert said in response.

'Why?'

Robert took a few seconds to answer and Louisa suspected he was racking his brain for any small reason the charming man wasn't suitable.

'He's a womaniser,' Robert said eventually. 'He wouldn't be faithful.'

'And you're telling me most men don't have mistresses? I'm not naive. I know I can't expect my future husband to be faithful.'

Louisa expected exactly that, but she wasn't about to let on to Robert. If she ever did get married, it would be for love and it would have to be a mutual all-encompassing love like her parents had shared. Her husband wouldn't want to be unfaithful to her.

'Your husband will be faithful,' Robert growled.

'Don't try and pretend you haven't had a mistress before,' Louisa said, knowing she was baiting him, but unable to stop herself.

Robert remained silent.

'So why is it one rule for Lord Frinton and another for you?'

Still no response.

'You can't tell me a man is unsuitable if he has a character flaw all men share.'

'Lord Frinton is not suitable,' Robert said, his voice low and dangerous. Louisa felt a thrum of anticipation slice through her body as Robert turned to face her, his attention entirely focused on her. 'If I were married to you, I would be faithful. I would never even look at another woman. Any man who would rather spend time with his mistress than with you is a fool.'

Louisa looked back at him with an open mouth. She didn't know what to say. Robert had spoken so passionately and so forcefully that she knew he'd spoken from the heart. If they were married, he'd be faithful to her to the very end.

She felt the tears start to build in her eyes and swallowed a few times in quick succession, adamant she wouldn't make a fool of herself in the middle of her first ball by sobbing like a little girl.

Robert held her gaze for a long minute, then eventually looked away.

'Let's dance,' he said gruffly.

The band had struck up the introduction to the first dance and people were slowly filing on to the dance floor. Louisa allowed Robert to lead her forward, walking as if she were in a trance. She didn't understand this man who looked at her as though he wanted to ravish her, but coolly told her she was to marry somebody else. Then to tell her he would be faithful to the last if they were married! Louisa felt the anger building inside her, replacing the sadness. It wasn't fair. He shouldn't treat her like this. She never knew where she stood. All she wanted was for him to tell her once and for all how he felt, not say one thing, then contradict his words with every action.

Louisa felt Robert slip his arms around her and she tried to hold on to her anger. It was so hard to be angry when she was in his arms, everything felt right with the world. Silently he took her hand in his and started to guide her through the steps.

Louisa had been practising her dance steps all week, knowing she was going to have to dance at a ball where everyone else had been dancing for years. But with Robert's hand in the small of her back Louisa didn't even have to think of the steps. He guided her through them effortlessly and she felt as though she were floating rather than dancing.

As her body brushed against his she felt the now-familiar stirrings of desire deep inside. She wanted this man. Even though he had rejected her, even though he had told her quite categorically she should marry someone else, she wanted this man.

Louisa knew the attraction was a physical response, an age-old instinct implanted in the human species to ensure they did not go extinct. She struggled to overcome it, knowing deep down that Robert would never be hers, not in the way she wanted it.

Robert spun her round and Louisa realised their dance was nearly at an end. Part of her wanted the band to continue playing so their dance could last for ever, but the other part just wanted it to be over. She needed to get away from Robert and his smouldering eyes. Every time she looked at him she felt drawn towards him.

As the dance finished and Robert bowed stiffly in front of her Louisa felt her smile harden. She had to protect herself now. He might desire her, but he wasn't going to marry her. She couldn't rely on him. It was just as she'd always known deep down—she couldn't rely on anyone but herself.

'Thank you for the dance, Lord Fleetwood.'

She could see her formal tone hurt him, but she resisted the urge to reach out and touch him, take his hand in her own. She had to protect herself now and the only way she could see to do that was by pushing Robert away.

Chapter Twenty-One

Robert watched Louisa laugh at some young gentleman's joke and felt his frown deepen. He hadn't spoken to her since their dance, first thing in the evening. When she'd been in his arms it had almost been as if they were floating through the air, but afterwards she had stiffened, curtsied, then stalked off through the crowds.

Robert had been watching her ever since. She was radiant. Men flocked to her. Her smile was inviting, her happy demeanour encouraging. So many times he'd nearly pushed his way through the crowds to pull some young man away from her, but he'd restrained himself, knowing this was all his own doing.

Louisa had been ready to give herself to him. Up on the rooftop of the orphanage she'd kissed him. She'd leant forwards, brushed her lips against his and given him her heart. And he'd been the fool who'd thrown it back at her.

This was his punishment: watching her encourage all the other young men in the room whilst steadfastly ignoring him.

Robert still knew he couldn't have Louisa. He was still living in the past, paying for his mistakes. She needed a better man than him.

The rebellious part of him asked him why he was still punishing himself. Everyone else had forgiven him, so why couldn't he? Robert's frown deepened. If he forgave himself, there was nothing stopping him from claiming Louisa as his own. He could marry her and whisk her away from all these other men, closeting her in his bedroom for many years to come.

The image of Louisa naked, sprawled beneath him, popped into Robert's mind and he groaned out loud, gaining him an odd look from a group of ladies standing nearby.

It was, oh, so tempting. The idea of Louisa as his wife, the mother of his children.

'Lord Fleetwood, how are you enjoying the evening?' Mrs Knapwell asked, coming to stand beside him.

Politeness stopped him from grunting in response. Instead Robert murmured something incomprehensible.

'Miss Turnhill is doing ever so well, isn't she?' Mrs Knapwell said.

'She's certainly a success with the gentlemen,'

Robert said, trying to keep the bitterness from his voice.

'She's beautiful, of course, but I think it's more her inner beauty that shines through. She makes even the shyest of the gentlemen feel at ease in her presence.'

'I hope they're noticing her inner beauty,' Robert said.

Mrs Knapwell smiled. 'I take it you don't approve of all the young men here tonight.'

'Louisa could do better.'

'She does deserve someone who loves her, someone who makes her happy.'

'She does,' Robert agreed.

'I'm sure you'll get a few marriage proposals for her before the month is out.'

The idea was unpalatable to say the least.

'She seemed a little withdrawn earlier,' Mrs Knapwell said after a minute's pause. 'Is everything all right?'

Robert didn't know how to answer. He knew his reaction to her kiss on the rooftop had crushed her. She'd started to trust him, a momentous thing for Louisa to be able to do, and with a few stupid words he'd destroyed that trust.

Robert had been amazed that Louisa hadn't left him in the last week. Every night he would lie awake thinking he was going to hear the soft click of the front door closing and look out his window to find Louisa slipping away into the night. All of the trust he'd managed to build was gone and Robert knew it was only a matter of time before Louisa was gone as well.

He watched her take the hand of her next dance partner and glide across the dance floor. It was a miracle she had stayed, really, after how he'd behaved, but maybe it was because Dunton was right. Maybe she wanted to find a husband, start a family of her own. Robert might have been her first choice of husband, but another man would do. She'd said earlier on she didn't expect her future husband to be faithful. If she was willing to compromise on that, she would be willing to compromise on other things, too. So maybe she'd stayed because Robert was going to help her find a husband. That hurt more than he could ever have imagined.

'I'm sure she was just nervous,' Robert said distractedly.

'And are you all right, Lord Fleetwood?' Mrs Knapwell asked quietly.

Robert nodded, not trusting himself to speak. He was far from all right. He'd been given a glimpse of what his life could be like and then he'd thrown it all away. It was nobody's fault but his own.

'It is nearly time for the last dance,' Mrs Knapwell reminded him quietly. 'Why don't you go and find Miss Turnhill after she finishes dancing with Mr Wilson?'

Robert watched as Louisa smiled at her dance partner and shared a few words as the music stopped. He felt his pulse quicken as he strode towards Louisa, ready to claim her for the last dance.

For an instant, when she first spotted him, Louisa smiled. It was a genuine smile, one of happiness and anticipation. Then suddenly her smile froze as she remembered everything that had passed between them. Reluctantly she bid farewell to Mr Wilson and took Robert's arm.

'How have you enjoyed the ball, Louisa?' Robert asked as they made their way back to the dance floor.

'It has been a most enjoyable night,' Louisa said.

Robert had the feeling she was lying. He'd caught a glimpse of her face in one of the rare moments she wasn't surrounded by gentlemen and she'd looked sad. It had almost broken his heart.

'You'll be pleased to know I've met plenty of eligible young gentlemen. I'm sure I'll be off your hands in no time.'

'That's not what I want, Louisa,' Robert said as he pulled her closer to him.

The music started and for a second Louisa didn't move.

'What *is* it you want, Robert?'

He didn't answer. Instead, he tightened his grip on her and started to lead her around the dance floor. Not once did his eyes leave hers. For five minutes they were one person, the energy flowing through their hands into each other's bodies. Robert felt his heart pounding, not from exertion, but from the exhilaration of holding Louisa close.

The other dancers melted away and to Robert it seemed as if they were the only two in the room. Every one of his senses felt heightened and stimulated by Louisa. He revelled in the softness of her skin against his fingers and the fluttering of her pulse beneath her skin. He breathed in her unique scent, a mixture of lavender and something he couldn't quite identify, but wished he could bottle and smell each and every morning. He listened to the rhythmic swish of her silk skirt, picturing her creamy white legs underneath picking out the steps with ease and grace. And he watched her as she stared up at him, pupils dilated, looking more beautiful than ever.

The only sense that was missing was taste. And Robert wanted to taste her so badly. He almost forgot where he was, wanting to press his lips against her skin, lick and nip every inch of her body, memorise the taste of her and make her his in every possible way.

The music stopped all too soon and Louisa and Robert were left standing on the dance floor staring at each other, neither wanting to be the first one to move and break the spell.

'Thank you for the dance, Robert,' Louisa said. This time there was no anger in her voice or rebellion in her eyes, just sadness, as if she realised they would not share many more moments like this. 'We should find Mrs Crawshaw and Mrs Knapwell.'

Robert nodded, unable to move. He just wanted to stay in this moment for ever, holding on to Louisa and never letting her go.

Eventually it was Louisa who moved and broke the spell.

Robert carefully tucked her hand into the crook of his elbow and started to lead her through the crush of people standing in groups, talking and enjoying the last few minutes of the ball. All he wanted to do was sweep Louisa into his arms, push through the crowd and disappear off into the night with her. Instead he politely sidestepped through the throng of people, all the while wondering what exactly was stopping him from making Louisa his own.

Chapter Twenty-Two

Louisa stirred to the sound of muffled voices downstairs. The sunlight was streaming in through a chink in the curtains and it looked to be a beautiful day. She stretched, realising she was aching from all the dancing from the night before.

Slowly she sat up in bed, wondering what time it was. They hadn't arrived home until the early hours of the morning, and before bidding her goodnight, Robert had gruffly instructed her to sleep in.

Louisa strained to hear who was downstairs. One of the voices was certainly Robert's, she'd know his deep tones anywhere. The other she thought she recognised, but couldn't quite place.

Curiosity won over comfort and Louisa threw off her covers and rose. She still hadn't got used to the idea of having someone help her to dress, but with the more intricate fastenings of her new

gowns she couldn't make herself look presentable on her own. She reached for the bell cord
and pulled.

A few minutes later a maid appeared, looking
flushed and excited.

'Good morning, Miss Turnhill,' Betty said,
looking eager to share her gossip.

'Who is downstairs with Lord Fleetwood?'
Louisa asked.

'You won't believe your eyes when you go
down, miss,' Betty said as she lifted Louisa's
dress over her head. 'There have been hundreds
of gentlemen callers for you.'

'The drawing room must have got a little
crowded with hundreds of gentlemen cramped
in,' Louisa said.

Betty was known to exaggerate at the best of
times. Louisa suspected there might have been
two, at most three.

'Lord Fleetwood is fighting to keep them out
of the house. He's like a bear with a sore head,
miss, if you don't mind me saying.'

Louisa couldn't help but smile at the thought
of Robert fighting to keep his house, his sanctuary, private.

Betty pulled the fastenings together at Louisa's back, working quickly as she talked.

'The ball must have been a success, miss,
that's what all the other servants are saying, for

you to get so many gentlemen callers after your first dance.'

Louisa tried to summon some enthusiasm. It was good news that she had been a success. It meant she hadn't made a fool of herself.

'Have you chosen someone to marry, miss?' Betty asked as the last of the fastenings was secured.

Louisa shook her head absent-mindedly. She didn't want to marry anyone. A week ago she would have jumped at the chance to marry Robert, have a life of safety and security and pleasure in his arms. Then he'd reminded her she couldn't trust anyone. He'd pushed her away and now Louisa knew she was the only one she could rely on and trust.

'Good idea,' Betty continued. 'If I had so many men chasing after me, I'd keep them all waiting for a while, enjoy the attention.' The young maid looked wistful, as if she knew she'd never have men pursuing her.

Louisa sat in front of the mirror whilst Betty expertly pulled her hair back from her face. All in all it had taken only ten minutes for Louisa to get dressed and be made presentable, but it had felt like an age.

'Good luck, miss,' Betty said as Louisa left the room.

She paused at the top of the stairs, her curiosity giving way to nervousness. She wasn't sure she wanted to see who had come to call. It wasn't as if she planned on marrying any of these men.

Slowly Louisa descended the stairs. She could hear Robert's voice getting louder as she neared the drawing room.

'Besieged in my own house,' he was grumbling.

'It is rather wonderful, isn't it?' Mrs Knapwell's familiar voice floated through the drawing room door. 'I knew dear Miss Turnhill would be a success, but this is better than I ever could have hoped.'

'It's like a plague,' Robert continued.

Louisa paused, not wanting to make her presence known just yet, eager to hear what else he had to say.

'It's not like a plague, Lord Fleetwood,' Mrs Knapwell said admonishingly. 'This is exactly what every debutante dreams of. And what their parents or guardians dream of.' The last part was said pointedly.

Robert remained silent. Louisa stepped forward and opened the door.

She gasped. Inside there was indeed a plague of flowers. Every surface had at least one bunch, beautiful arrangements that made the drawing room look like a tropical paradise.

'Isn't it wonderful, Miss Turnhill?' Mrs Knapwell gushed as she took Louisa by the hand. 'All of these gentlemen have sent their regards and have promised to call again later in the day.'

Robert mumbled something again about a plague. Louisa turned to him.

'It's strange,' she said. 'I don't remember reading anything about a plague of flowers in the Bible.'

Robert just frowned at her.

'You were a big success,' Mrs Knapwell continued. 'So many very eligible young gentlemen have expressed their interest in you.'

Louisa looked at the beautiful flower arrangements and felt slightly sick. She didn't want any of this. She didn't want to get married and she didn't want men bringing her flowers. She just wanted to be left alone.

She turned to find Robert staring at her. She looked at him beseechingly, willing him to understand. Suddenly his eyes softened and Louisa felt her heart skip a beat.

'You don't have to marry anyone you don't want to, Louisa,' he said quietly. 'You don't have to go to another ball or receive a single gentleman if you don't wish to.'

It felt as though the room had shrunk and they were the only two in it. For a second Louisa forgot Mrs Knapwell's presence; it was just her and

Robert. She found she was holding her breath, waiting for him to say more.

'This is your life Louisa, you can make all the decisions. I just want you to be happy.'

Louisa felt the dread lifting from her body, but it was replaced by sadness. Robert had just given her exactly what she'd wanted: freedom. He'd just told her she could make all the decisions in her life. She didn't have to do what he wanted or what anyone else wanted. It should have made her happy, but Louisa found herself unable to smile.

Robert had just given her a wonderful gift. He'd promised her he wouldn't force her to take a husband. He wouldn't stop her from doing what she wanted or making her own decisions. But Louisa wanted more from him. She loved him, despite not wanting to, despite trying so hard the last week to hate him. She loved him and she wanted him. She wanted to be married to him and spend her whole life with him. For him she would give up her independence, she would break her vow to only ever rely on herself. But that didn't matter because he didn't want her.

'Thank you,' she managed to say.

He smiled at her, then reached out and ran a finger down her cheek.

Mrs Knapwell coughed awkwardly and they

sprung apart. They'd both forgotten her presence for a few minutes.

'Lord Fleetwood,' Mrs Knapwell said quickly, 'would it be a terrible imposition if I took some refreshment with Miss Turnhill?'

Robert bowed and walked from the room, assumedly to arrange for some tea to be brought up.

'And something to eat,' Louisa called after him, aware of the growling in her stomach.

Mrs Knapwell waited for a few seconds, then crossed to the door and closed it.

'Shall we sit?'

Louisa sat down next to the older woman and waited for her to speak.

'It has come to my attention that you are in love with Lord Fleetwood,' Mrs Knapwell said without any further preamble.

Louisa gasped. She was about to deny it, but Mrs Knapwell flapped her hand and continued.

'It is obvious, my dear, to anyone who looks at the two of you. You're in love with him and he's in love with you.'

Louisa shook her head. She might not be able to deny her feelings for Robert, but she knew he didn't love her. She'd given him the opportunity to tell her up on the rooftop and he'd rejected her.

'Lord Fleetwood has been very kind to me, but he does not love me,' Louisa said.

Mrs Knapwell patted her hand. 'Trust me, my dear, he's in love with you. He can't take his eyes off you for a single second when you're in the room. He takes every opportunity to touch you and he's always by your side.'

'He's just being a good guardian,' Louisa said, not daring to hope.

'Lord Fleetwood has not gone to more than two balls or dinner parties in the two years since he's returned from the war. In the last week he's been out in society twice. For you.'

'To launch me,' Louisa insisted. 'To find me a husband.'

Mrs Knapwell sighed. 'Deep down you know that's not true. You know he loves you.'

Louisa thought back over the past couple of weeks. All of the moments they'd shared, the kisses, the touches, the smouldering looks. She was almost convinced, but then Robert's rejection of her on the rooftop came crashing back into her mind and she knew he couldn't love her.

'Lord Fleetwood is a complicated man,' Mrs Knapwell continued. 'He blames himself for my son's death and the deaths of the other men under his command.'

Louisa nodded.

'He thinks he doesn't deserve to be happy. He thinks he doesn't deserve you.'

'But he's the best man I've ever known.'

Mrs Knapwell nodded. 'I never said he was right. But that's what he thinks.'

Louisa swallowed hard and thought back to each time Robert had got close, only to push her away at the last minute. Was it because he didn't think he deserved her?

'I know I'm not privy to all of the events of your past,' Mrs Knapwell continued, 'but I think it's safe to say you have some problems trusting people.'

She looked at Louisa for confirmation. Louisa slowly nodded her head. She wondered if it was so obvious that everyone could see it about her.

'I know it is hard, my dear, but you're young, in the prime of your life. You'll want a home, a family. Don't consign yourself to a life alone. It will only make you miserable.'

Louisa didn't know what to say. She felt as if Mrs Knapwell had seen through all the protective layers Louisa covered herself with to her soul beneath.

'Don't throw away your chance of happiness because you're afraid.'

'Robert doesn't want me,' Louisa said quietly, 'and I don't think I could bear his rejection for a second time.'

Mrs Knapwell smiled kindly, 'Trust me, you won't have to. We just need to remind Lord

Fleetwood he deserves to live and he deserves to be happy.'

Louisa still wasn't sure. She'd opened herself up once, decided to let go of all her worries and concerns and trust someone else, then he'd hurt her. She wasn't sure she was strong enough to go through it all again.

'Think about it, my dear. You're miserable without him. Do you want to spend the rest of your life miserable?'

A few weeks ago Louisa's dream was of freedom. She would have given anything to be a free woman, living on her own terms, not relying on anyone else. Before she had met Robert she would have laughed at the idea that she might want to surrender her heart and her freedom to a man. But now, even after everything that had happened she wasn't so sure. Maybe Mrs Knapwell was right.

'Just say you're right,' Louisa said slowly, 'and I was in love with Lord Fleetwood. How would I go about convincing him he doesn't want me to marry some other man?'

Mrs Knapwell smiled. 'We're halfway there already. You saw how he looked at you last night. He hated you talking to other men. He hates that now they're bringing you flowers and wanting to court you.'

Louisa couldn't deny Robert had been in a

foul mood last night and it had been he who had
insisted he accompany them to the ball.

'All you need to do is encourage these other
men, let Robert see what he is missing out on.
And he will realise none of them are good
enough for you because they don't love you the
way he does.'

Louisa felt a flicker of hope. 'I'm not sure,'
she said.

Mrs Knapwell patted her on the hand again
and smiled.

'Why don't you have a think about what you
want, my dear? Think about what your life
would be like with Lord Fleetwood and what it
would be like on your own.' Mrs Knapwell stood
and walked to the door. 'It would be a shame for
you both to be unhappy just because you're too
scared to fight for what you want.'

Louisa was left alone in the drawing room,
surrounded by all of her flowers. Mrs Knapwell's words kept circling around in her head.
The problem was she didn't know what she
wanted.

No, Louisa thought, that was a lie. She wanted
Robert. She'd wanted him ever since the day he'd
strode into her cell at the Lewisham Asylum and
demanded her release. She'd wanted him every
time he'd kissed her and she'd wanted him even
when he'd rejected her.

Her difficulty was more that she didn't want to have to rely on anyone else. She knew if she gave her heart to Robert she was likely to get hurt and Louisa wasn't sure if she could bear to be hurt again.

A little voice piped up in her mind, asking whether she could bear living her whole life without him.

There was a soft knock on the door. Before Louisa could answer it swung open and Robert stepped into the room. He was frowning and he looked as though he hadn't slept a single wink.

'You've got another gentleman caller,' Robert said gruffly. 'I tried to throw him out, but Mrs Knapwell said you would want to receive him.'

In that instant Louisa's mind was made up. She was going to fight for this man. She would make him realise he was the man for her.

Chapter Twenty-Three

Robert wondered if he had died and gone to hell.

'I'm sure Mrs Crawshaw is chaperone enough if you have things you would rather be doing,' Louisa said sweetly.

An army of Frenchmen couldn't chase him away from Louisa whilst Lord Frinton was in the room.

'I'll stay,' Robert said abruptly.

Louisa smiled at him, then turned her attention back to Frinton.

'Did you enjoy your first ball, Miss Turnhill?' Frinton asked.

Robert leant forwards. He wondered if Frinton was sitting too close to Louisa for propriety. The man was only about four feet away. Maybe Robert should usher him farther across the room.

'I had a lovely time, thank you, my lord,' Louisa said.

My lord? Robert glared at her. She was flirting. The little minx had only been out in society for a day and she was flirting with one of London's most notorious rakes.

'The Season in London is quite diverting once you know which balls to attend,' Lord Frinton continued. 'I'm more of a country person myself, but I do enjoy the diversions of the city for a few months.'

'You have a country estate?' Louisa asked.

Frinton had one of the biggest estates in the south of England.

'Just a patch of land and a house. A few tenant cottages, you know the sort of thing,' Frinton said modestly.

'I do love the country.'

'Perhaps you could come and visit me some time.'

Robert nearly jumped out of his chair. Frinton had either just indecently propositioned Louisa or was halfway to a marriage proposal.

'That sounds lovely.'

'No,' Robert said.

Louisa and Frinton turned to Robert in surprise, as if they'd both forgotten his presence.

Louisa raised her eyebrows, then turned back to Frinton with a sunny smile.

'Please excuse Lord Fleetwood, I think he's probably tired from the ball last night.'

Now she was making him sound like a dod-
dery old guardian. He was only a couple of years
older than Frinton.

'Maybe we could go for a stroll, leave Lord
Fleetwood in peace?' Frinton suggested.

'That would be most agreeable,' Louisa said.

Robert felt his heart plummet into his boots.
She actually liked this twit. Not that Frinton was
the worst of the gentlemen of the *ton*, but he certainly wasn't right for Louisa.

Frinton stood and offered Louisa his arm.

'I'll come, too,' Robert said quickly, all too
aware Mrs Crawshaw wouldn't stop any untow-
ard advances from Frinton. He cursed himself
for dismissing the severe, prim Mrs Hempshaw
as a companion. At least he would have been
able to rest easy with her accompanying Louisa
for a stroll.

'That's really not necessary,' Louisa said.
'Mrs Crawshaw will come with us.'

'It is necessary,' Robert said in a voice that
brooked no argument.

As he walked a few paces behind Louisa and
Frinton, Robert felt his mood darken. This was
the worst day imaginable, having to watch Louisa smile at another man, laugh at his jokes, hold
his arm. Robert wanted to be the one she was
walking with, not consigned to trudge behind

her and her admirer, the ever-vigilant guardian only there to guard her honour.

He watched as Louisa lifted her head to hear something Frinton was saying. Robert remembered exactly how she'd looked when they'd been on Mrs Knapwell's balcony. She'd tilted her chin up then, too, and looked at him with desire in her eyes. It physically hurt to think of her looking at another man like that. He felt sick of the thought of Frinton's lips on hers, his hands over his body.

Robert knew he had to do something, but Dunton's words echoed around his head again. Louisa would want a family, a home. If he couldn't give that to her, then she deserved someone who could.

Just not Frinton.

'Miss Turnhill,' Robert called out, 'we need to return home.'

Louisa and Frinton stopped walking and turned to look at him.

'We forgot your engagement with Mrs Knapwell,' Robert improvised. 'You promised to meet her this afternoon. It would be rude to let her down.'

Louisa frowned for an instant, then smiled sunnily. 'Don't worry yourself, Lord Fleetwood. When I spoke to Mrs Knapwell this morning we rearranged for another day. I've got the entire afternoon free.'

Robert contemplated marching over to Louisa, picking her up and throwing her over his shoulder. At this point he'd do almost anything to get her away from Frinton and back home.

'But if you are otherwise engaged please feel free to return home,' Louisa said. 'I'm sure Lord Frinton is perfectly capable of looking after me.'

Robert very much doubted it. He would be willing to bet his entire estate the cad would try to seduce Louisa the first chance he had.

'I'd be very happy to take responsibility for Miss Turnhill,' Frinton said.

'I'm not going anywhere,' Robert replied bluntly. 'I'm free all afternoon.'

Louisa smiled again. 'Wonderful.' Then she turned her back on Robert, slipped her hand into the crook of Frinton's arm and continued her conversation.

After a few more minutes of walking they entered Hyde Park. Robert was immediately taken back to his first day with Louisa. He could picture the scene with such precision it was as though it had happened only minutes ago, not weeks. He hoped they would not walk down the Serpentine to where he and Louisa had paused. He didn't think he could bear watching her look out at the view on the arm of another man.

'Miss Turnhill.'

They all turned at the same moment. Dunton was striding towards them, a broad smile on his face.

'Fleetwood, Lord Frinton.' He nodded in greeting.

'What are you doing here?' Robert asked suspiciously. Between Dunton and Mrs Knapwell they had him squarely under surveillance. Perhaps they were worried for Louisa, thought him an unfit guardian to be left alone with such a sweet young girl.

'Nice to see you again, too, Fleetwood,' Dunton said. 'I thought a stroll around the park would clear my head after last night.'

Robert scowled at him. He was sure Dunton's presence here wasn't a coincidence.

'Once again you look ravishing Miss Turnhill,' Dunton said, turning back to Louisa. 'I know it's awfully rude of me to interrupt, but when I saw you over here I had a fantastic idea.'

Louisa looked at him eagerly. Robert watched her as she smiled at his old friend and felt a coil of dread in the pit of his stomach. Louisa was hopefully too smart to fall for some cad like Frinton, but Dunton was a good man. A man someone like Louisa could perhaps see herself spending the rest of her life with.

'Mrs Knapwell mentioned the other day you were hoping to have a riding lesson, Miss Turnhill, but that she interrupted that plan.'

Louisa nodded.

'I've got my horse here with me today.' Dunton motioned over to where a young boy stood holding a magnificent-looking beast. 'I was wondering if you would like to go on a short ride, just to see if you enjoy the experience.'

Three sets of eyes looked back at Dunton as if he were mad.

'Miss Turnhill is hardly dressed for riding,' Frinton said, obviously annoyed at having his courting interrupted.

Robert could see Louisa stiffen as Frinton answered for her. He knew for sure she would take Dunton up on his offer now.

'What a splendid idea,' Robert said, clapping his old friend on the back.

Louisa's eyes narrowed as she turned her attention to Robert, clearly wondering what he was playing at.

'I'd love to,' Louisa said eventually. 'That's if you don't mind too much, Lord Frinton.'

Frinton could hardly say no when asked so nicely. He motioned for her to go ahead.

Louisa reached out to take Dunton's arm, but before her hand could connect with his jacket, Robert slipped himself in between the pair.

Without looking at her, he offered her his arm and felt a thrill of pleasure as she took it.

'You asked that I be the one to teach you to

ride,' Robert said softly as he led her towards Dunton's horse.

'I don't mind Major Dunton—'

Robert cut her off with a steely look.

'When was the last time you were on a horse?' he asked.

Louisa thought for a moment. 'The week before my parents died. I was ten.'

'That's nine years ago,' Robert said softly. 'It's a long time. You won't have forgotten the basics, but you need to remember horses are dangerous beasts. They can be headstrong and they can get scared. I will be the one to teach you.'

She didn't object any further.

They reached the spot where Dunton's horse was grazing, a small boy holding on to the reins.

'This is Galahad,' Dunton said as he caught up. 'Galahad, this is Miss Turnhill. Be nice.'

The horse gave no indication he was listening.

'He's rather big,' Louisa said. Robert could detect a hint of nervousness in her voice.

'I'll be right there with you,' Robert said quietly. He saw her relax a little and loved that he was the one that was able to give her confidence, to make her believe in herself.

Without another word Robert swung himself up onto the horse. Dunton looked at him with raised eyebrows, but didn't say a word. The men had known each other long enough for Dunton to realise when there was no point arguing with Robert.

'Trust me?' Robert asked Louisa.

The few seconds before she replied were agonising. Robert had visions of her shaking her head, telling him she didn't trust him. He wouldn't blame her, he hadn't given her any reason to trust him these last few weeks.

Then Louisa gave an almost imperceptible nod of her head. Robert reached down and grasped her fingers in his own. As their skin met, Robert felt the tiny frisson of desire he always did when he touched Louisa.

He grasped her by the wrist and swung her up in front of him. Within a second she was seated in between his thighs, both her legs hanging down over the left side of the horse.

'Not quite how I remember side-saddle,' Louisa murmured.

It wasn't the first time Robert had ridden with another person on his horse. A few times in the war he'd had to gallop to safety with one of his wounded comrades thrown across the front of the horse, but it was the first time he'd had someone as lovely as Louisa up there with him.

Robert suddenly realised this was a very bad idea. He'd condemned himself to agonising minutes of having Louisa close to him, nestled in between his thighs. He would have to grip her by the waist, press his body up against hers, all the while putting on a stony exterior so the world wouldn't know the terribly erotic thoughts he was having.

'Comfortable?' he asked quietly.

Louisa nodded but didn't say a word.

'Do you really think this is the best time?' Lord Frinton asked from down below.

'Please don't feel as though you have to wait, Lord Frinton, there's no telling how long Miss Turnhill's lesson will be,' Robert said.

Before Frinton or Dunton could protest further, Robert urged the horse into a gentle trot.

'Lord Frinton is probably right,' Louisa said after a few seconds. 'This isn't the right time for a riding lesson.'

Robert could think of so many reasons to turn back, but he didn't want to. If he were truthful to himself, he wanted to ride off into the countryside with Louisa between his thighs and keep going until no one came looking for them.

'Would you like me to turn back?' Robert asked.

He found he was holding his breath whilst he waited for her answer.

Louisa shook her head. 'Everyone will be gossiping about us, though,' she said.

'Let them gossip.' At this moment in time Robert was content to just enjoy Louisa's company. They could deal with the consequences of his rash actions later on. 'We'll go to one of the quieter areas of the park so not too many people see us.'

Slowly Louisa began to relax into his arms. Robert was acutely aware of every part of her body that touched his: her leg pushed up against his thigh, her waist underneath his arm, and now as she sank into him, her body against his chest. It felt wonderful, exquisite, right.

'I've missed you,' Louisa said so quietly Robert barely heard her.

'I've always been here.'

Louisa shook her head. 'Not like this. I've missed being like this with you.'

It was said with such sadness Robert just wanted to pull her close to him and tell her he'd never let her go again.

'You understand why it has to be this way, don't you, Louisa?' Robert asked.

'No.'

He didn't know where to begin. 'You're the best person I know,' he said slowly. 'And you've had such a bad life, people have been cruel to you.'

Louisa nodded. 'Until you came along.'

Robert ploughed on, wanting to make her understand. 'You deserve happiness, a future.

You deserve to be showered with love every day, from a man who can give you every part of him.'

Louisa sat quietly, waiting for him to go on.

'I can't give you that, Louisa.'

'Why not?'

Robert could barely explain it to himself, let alone find the words to make Louisa understand.

'The war, what happened in St Mamede, it changed me. For two years I've barely lived. I've stumbled through life, avoiding everything but the most necessary of human contact.'

'You've lived these last two weeks,' Louisa said quietly.

He couldn't deny it. Ever since Louisa had walked back into his life, Robert had felt the spark ignite inside him. It was as though he were coming out of a long hibernation, slowly reawakening and starting to appreciate the world again.

'I wouldn't make you happy, Louisa,' Robert said.

'And you think being married to a man I don't love would?'

Robert felt himself stiffen as her words sank in. Did she mean she loved him? He stared at her face. She was looking resolutely off into the distance, refusing to meet his eye.

'I wouldn't make you happy,' he repeated more to himself than her.

'I think we should go back.'

'Louisa…'

She turned towards him suddenly and fixed him with a hard stare.

'You are good enough, Robert. You deserve happiness and love in your life. Yes, you had a tough time in the war, but now it's time to move on, to forgive yourself.'

'Louisa, I can't…' Robert felt his voice catch in his throat.

'I'm not saying you should forget what happened. You should never forget what happened, that forms part of who you are. But there's no point in living if all you do is punish yourself and those who care for you.'

Louisa reached up and stroked his cheek lightly with her fingers. 'If you don't love me, Robert, then that's fine. But if the only reason you keep pushing me away is because of some misplaced sense of guilt, then that's not good enough.'

Louisa slipped from his arms and off the horse. 'Don't follow me,' she said without looking up. 'I can walk back from here. I'm going to stay with Mrs Knapwell for a few days, give you time to think.'

Robert watched her as she stalked over the grass. He had a lot of thinking to do.

Chapter Twenty-Four

Five days. Five whole days and not a single word.

Five days ago Louisa hadn't planned on giving Robert an ultimatum. When he'd swept her up on to the horse and into his arms she'd felt a momentary sense of everything being right with the world. She knew she was meant to be in Robert's arms. She hadn't been able to stop herself from telling him that she missed him.

Louisa had known what he was thinking: that he wasn't good enough, that he still had to atone, to punish himself for what happened in St Mamede. She felt that was a stupid reason to deny them both the happiness they deserved.

So it had all slipped out. She'd told him she cared for him, hinted she wouldn't be happy with any man but him. And then he'd let her walk away.

Louisa wondered what he was doing now. An image of Robert sitting with another woman flashed into her mind, but she knew she was just being silly. She didn't have to worry about unfaithfulness with Robert, more the fact that he didn't think he deserved to be with anyone.

When she'd returned to the main part of Hyde Park, she'd requested that Major Dunton accompany her back to Mrs Knapwell's house. He'd done so willingly, without asking any further questions, allowing her precious time in which to mull over her conversation.

The past few days had dragged. Mrs Knapwell had done her best to keep Louisa distracted and entertained, but Louisa knew she'd been poor company for the older woman.

'He'll be there tonight,' Mrs Knapwell said as she entered Louisa's room.

Louisa shook her head.

'He will.'

She wasn't sure what she wanted any more. The first couple of days after their conversation in the park Louisa had hoped Robert would arrive at Mrs Knapwell's house and sweep her into his arms, begging her to forgive him, telling her what a fool he'd been.

When that hadn't happened Louisa had grown angry. She'd opened herself up to him again and he'd just allowed her to walk off without even checking if she was safe.

Now she didn't know what to think. Part of

her wanted him to be at the ball tonight, at least she would get to see him. The other part of her knew it might break her heart, seeing him and knowing that he had finally rejected her once and for all, whatever the reason.

Louisa tried to smile bravely. 'If Lord Fleetwood is there, then at least we will be able to sort out housing arrangements,' she said, trying to be practical.

'You know you can stay with me for as long as you want, Louisa, I enjoy your company.'

'You've been so kind.'

'Nonsense,' Mrs Knapwell said. 'I think of Lord Fleetwood as a son and now I've come to think of you as a daughter. I just want the pair of you to be happy.'

As the days went by Louisa thought that was more and more unlikely.

'Now let's have a look at you.'

Louisa obediently stood and did a slow twirl.

'Perfect, no man will be able to ignore you tonight.'

Louisa didn't care about the hundreds of nameless gentlemen who would be attending Lady Gillingham's ball tonight. All she cared about was Robert.

Mrs Knapwell reached out and adjusted the lace trim around the neckline of the dress. This was Louisa's favourite evening dress. It was maroon silk, with a white-lace trim. The neck-line scooped low over her bust, and the skirt was full but not overwhelming.

There was a quiet knock on the door and one of the maids popped her head into the room.

'There's a gentleman downstairs waiting,' she said quickly, before hurrying off.

Louisa felt her heart pounding in her chest. Robert had come for her. He'd come to accompany her to the ball.

She bit her lower lip in anticipation; she'd both dreaded and wished for this moment all week. Now it was here, she didn't know what to do with herself.

Mrs Knapwell motioned for Louisa to go down, hanging back to give the couple some privacy.

Louisa descended the stairs slowly. When she was halfway down she could see someone standing at the far end of the entrance hall. Immediately she knew something was wrong. This wasn't Robert. This man was slightly shorter than Robert and his hair wasn't as dark. Louisa felt all the anticipation draining from her body.

'Miss Turnhill,' Major Dunton said with a bow, 'I can see you were expecting someone else. I'm sorry to disappoint you.'

Louisa shook her head, not trusting herself to speak for a second.

'I thought I would escort you and Mrs Knapwell to the ball.'

'That's very kind of you,' Louisa said automatically.

Dunton looked at Louisa hard for a few seconds. 'He's a damn fool,' he exclaimed quietly, taking Louisa by surprise.

Louisa didn't say anything. Major Dunton ran his hand through his hair and shook his head.

'A damn fool,' he repeated. 'You haven't heard from him in the last few days?'

Louisa shook her head.

'Fleetwood always was obstinate, but I've never known him to be downright stupid before.'

'Maybe it's just not meant to be,' Louisa said, trying desperately to stop the tears springing to her eyes.'

Dunton eyed her with a mixture of disbelief and pity.

'It's meant to be,' he said sternly. 'For two years Fleetwood has hardly conversed with anyone, has barely gone out in public if he could help it. You come along and he's transformed back into his old self. It's meant to be.'

'I don't know how to make *him* see that.'

They stood in silence for a couple of minutes, both contemplating what seemed like an impossible task.

'I've already beseeched him to stop living in the past, asked him to forgive himself.'

Dunton nodded. 'And to a point he has. He's allowed himself to laugh and smile these last few weeks. He just needs that final push.'

'Mrs Knapwell suggested I try to make him jealous by encouraging other men.'

'Fleetwood is too honourable for that to work,' Dunton said. 'If he thought someone would make you happy, then he'd step aside.'

'But he knows no one would make me happy except him.'

'You've told him that?'

Louisa nodded morosely.

'Then we have to make him see it.'

'How?'

'Marry me. Or at least let us become engaged.'

Louisa stood with her mouth hanging open.

'I'm sure this isn't how you expected your first marriage proposal to go...'

'Major Dunton...' Louisa trailed off.

'I'm perfectly serious. Let us become engaged.'

'You don't have to do this.'

Dunton shrugged. 'What's the worst that could happen?'

'Robert might not protest and you'll be stuck with me.'

'So I get a beautiful fiancée out of the bargain. Doesn't sound too bad to me.'

Louisa looked at him long and hard.

'Look, if it doesn't work we can stay engaged for a few months, then you can quietly break things off. What have we got to lose?'

'I'm not sure about it.'

'I just think if Fleetwood thinks he's about to lose you for good, then it might spur him into action at last.'

Louisa considered Dunton's offer. She could see why he was suggesting it. If losing her permanently was actually played out in front of Robert's eyes, then he might realise exactly what kind of life he was condemning himself to.

Part of her protested. It screamed that if she was having to work this hard for Robert's affection, then maybe it wasn't meant to be. Then she pictured his face just before his mouth lowered on to hers and she knew he wanted her, he simply wasn't allowing himself the happiness he deserved quite yet.

'If you're sure,' Louisa said.

'Positive.'

Dunton raised her hand to her lips and kissed her on the knuckles.

'We'll announce our engagement at Lady Gillingham's ball tonight.'

An hour later Louisa's heart was in her chest. Their carriage had just pulled up outside Lady

Gillingham's massive town house and they were awaiting their turn to descend. Major Dunton hopped from the carriage, then offered both Louisa and Mrs Knapwell his arm. As Louisa placed her hand at his elbow, she wished not for the first time that it was Robert standing next to her.

She missed him. She'd been angry he hadn't followed her and upset he hadn't declared his love for her, but most of all she'd missed him. She missed seeing his face at breakfast every morning, she missed teasing that first smile of the day from him, she missed listening as he explained something to her. She missed all of him.

As they entered the grand entrance hall, Lady Gillingham stepped forward to greet them.

'Delightful to see you again,' she said, grasping Louisa's hand as if they were old friends. 'It was such a pleasure to meet you at Mrs Knapwell's dinner party.'

Louisa smiled politely, remembering she had not taken a shine to Lady Gillingham then.

'Is Lord Fleetwood not with you?'

Louisa saw the predatory look in the older woman's eyes and immediately felt her body tense.

'Lord Fleetwood was not sure whether he would be attending this evening,' Louisa said nonchalantly, 'so he asked Major Dunton to accompany me and Mrs Knapwell.'

'How very thoughtful,' Lady Gillingham said, visibly disappointed. 'I suppose Lord Fleetwood may come on his own later this evening.'

'Perhaps.'

They moved on into the crowded ballroom. Louisa felt deflated. Lady Gillingham's response meant Robert wasn't here yet. He might not even show up at all and then all this would be for nothing.

'Stay strong,' Dunton whispered in her ear as he led her into the ballroom. 'Fleetwood will be here.'

'How do you know?'

'He loves you,' Dunton said simply.

Louisa shook her head in disbelief. If he loved her, surely he wouldn't put her through all of this?

'He loves you. And it's been almost a week since he last saw you. He won't be able to stop himself from coming.'

Louisa wasn't quite so sure. He could have visited her anytime at Mrs Knapwell's house. He'd known exactly where she was for the last few days and hadn't once tried to contact her.

'Dance with me,' Dunton said, 'whilst we're waiting.'

Louisa nodded and let herself be led over to the dance floor. She wasn't concentrating, but

Major Dunton made up for her lapses and expertly twirled her round and round.

Louisa's eyes were fixed on the door. Every time a new guest appeared in the doorway, her heart leapt into her throat, only to sink when she realised it wasn't Robert.

The music was just finishing and Major Dunton was bowing in front of her when Louisa froze. Robert had arrived. She almost knew it before she'd even seen him. Her body was aware of the exact second he entered the room. Louisa forced herself not to stare, instead smiling prettily at Major Dunton and taking his arm as he led her from the dance floor.

She wondered how their meeting would go. He was her guardian. It would be the most natural thing in the world if he came straight to her side and enquired after her health. Suddenly Louisa felt overwhelmed, as if she needed a few more minutes to compose herself. Dunton must have felt her stiffen on his arm. He leant in towards her and squeezed her hand.

'Be strong,' he whispered.

Louisa watched as Robert spotted them. His frown deepened and he started to push his way through the crowds of people.

'I need to speak to you,' he said without any preamble.

'Good to see you, too, Fleetwood,' Dunton said amicably.

Robert ignored him. 'Louisa, I need to speak to you.'

She knew the kind thing to do, the right thing to do, would be to end this torment and go somewhere a little more private to speak, but for an instant Louisa wasn't feeling charitable or particularly good. He'd made her wait for so long that she felt as though he deserved some of the same treatment.

Dunton looked down at her, as if asking whether she wanted him to leave.

'Whatever you need to say you can say in front of Major Dunton,' Louisa said firmly.

'I most certainly cannot.'

They stood staring at each other for a long few seconds.

'Come with me, Louisa.'

'No. I'm staying here with Major Dunton.'

'Dunton,' Robert said, his voice low and slightly menacing.

'Sorry, old man, you heard the lady. After all, I have to do what the fiancée asks.'

Louisa watched Robert's face carefully as Dunton's words sunk in. His first expression was one of disbelief, his second barely concealed anger.

'You two are engaged?' Robert asked eventually.

His gaze locked on to her and Louisa had to fight the urge to squirm uncomfortably.

'We're engaged.' Louisa confirmed.

'You're not,' Robert said.

'We are.'

They spoke in low voices so no one else could hear, but both were intense with emotion.

'You are not engaged, Louisa.'

Louisa sighed. 'I'm not having this conversation with you all night.'

'You forget, I'm your guardian. I have to agree to any engagement before it can go ahead.'

Louisa smiled at him. 'What happened to giving me my freedom, letting me do whatever I choose?'

Robert ran a hand through his hair. 'Freedom is all very well and good if you make the right choices.'

'And it would be wrong to marry Major Dunton?' Louisa asked quietly.

'Yes.'

'He's a good man.'

'The best,' Robert agreed.

'Then you should be happy for me.'

'I'm not.'

They stood looking at each other for another few seconds.

'Dance with me,' Robert said, more as a command than a request.

Slowly Louisa reached out and took his arm, aware of the thrill that passed through her body as her hand grasped his arm.

'One dance, Lord Fleetwood, then I must return to my fiancé.'

Chapter Twenty-Five

One dance would have to be enough.

'I've missed you,' Robert said softly into Louisa's ear as he pulled her closer. 'The house has been quiet without you.'

'You've had Mrs Crawshaw for company.'

'A poor substitute.'

'You knew where I was,' Louisa said accusingly. 'You could have come at any time.'

Robert pulled her even closer, not caring any more what other people might say.

'I've been awful to you, Louisa,' Robert admitted, 'but I think eventually you'll forgive me.'

It felt so right holding her in his arms. He wished the music would go on for ever so they would never have to step apart.

He ran his hand down her back, stopping just above the curve of her buttocks, loving the way she physically shuddered with anticipation.

'You knew where I was,' Louisa repeated. 'You didn't come.'

'And interrupt your little engagement with Major Dunton?'

Louisa reddened and Robert knew he'd hit a nerve.

'You're not going to marry him, Louisa,' he said in a tone that brooked no argument.

She didn't want to marry Dunton. Robert knew that as well as he knew his own name. She loved him, she'd told him so when they'd been alone in the park. She loved him and once again he'd rejected her. Now this was her way of striking back at him. He didn't blame her for it. He'd been an absolute brute towards her.

He wasn't sure if the engagement was her way of making him hurt or a misguided attempt to make him jealous. He rather thought the latter. Despite what he'd done to her Louisa didn't have a cruel bone in her body. Dunton had probably suggested the scheme himself as a way to make Robert realise what he was missing. His old friend was generous and selfless and would step up if he thought he could help in any way.

Robert didn't need to succumb to their plot to feel jealous. The last few days without Louisa had been agony.

He twirled her round, catching her expertly and pulling her closer so their bodies were almost touching. Louisa's breathing was laboured and her cheeks flushed. Her eyes were wide and her mouth slightly open, just inviting him to kiss her.

Despite an overwhelming desire to claim her as his, Robert knew he couldn't do so in the middle of the dance floor. It would be scandalous and Louisa would never forgive him for making her the talking point of the *ton*.

'You're looking very beautiful tonight,' Robert said quietly as they glided past another couple.

Louisa didn't reply. Robert knew he was going to have to work harder.

'The most stunning woman in the room.'

She snorted.

'To me you are.'

His heart almost stopped as she looked up at him, her eyes full of questions. He was going to make her his. First she would break off this sham of an engagement with Dunton, then she would agree to be his for ever.

Robert wasn't even too concerned that she was hardly speaking to him now. He had time. He had all the time in the world to convince her they belonged together.

'You were right,' he whispered in her ear.

She looked up at him, waiting for him to continue.

'I'm a fool.'

'I've never said that.'

'I'm sure you've thought it plenty of times over the last few days.'

He saw her grimace and surmised she'd called him far worse names in her head.

'I am a fool. A blind, wooden-headed, foolish man.'

Louisa said nothing.

'I'm more foolish than King Midas when he asked for the golden touch, more idiotic than the Trojans when they accepted the wooden horse into Troy, more half-witted than Jason when he spurned the unhinged Medea.'

He could see Louisa was trying to hide a smile.

'In short, I've been a fool, Louisa, and I wouldn't blame you for never wanting to see me again.'

She still didn't say anything. Robert ran his thumb across the palm of her hand, revelling in the softness of her skin. It felt like heaven just to touch her again. All he wanted to do was sweep her up into his arms and whisk her away to some private sanctuary, never to let her leave his sight again.

'But sometimes we fools get lucky, we get a second chance.'

He looked at her hopefully. She gave an almost imperceptible nod. Robert's heart soared. She was going to forgive him.

'When this dance is over I'm going to take you by the arm and escort you somewhere private,' Robert said, bending his head so his words were only audible to her. 'Then we will talk. But for the next few minutes I'm just going to enjoy having you in my arms.'

He saw all sorts of emotions flit over Louisa's face: confusion, hope, disbelief. She was beautiful. She'd changed so much since he'd found her those few short weeks ago in the Lewisham Asylum. Louisa was now a strong, confident woman. There was no trace of the self-doubting girl he'd found chained to the wall. And she had started to trust, as well. Despite everything he'd put her through she was still willing to give him a chance. He knew he was lucky to have found her.

Slowly Robert began tracing small circles on Louisa's back with his fingers. He knew she could feel his touch through the thin layers of fabric. She bit her bottom lip, as if finding it hard to concentrate, and her eyes glazed over a little.

He loved that he could have this effect on her. He felt strangely possessive; he wanted to be the only one who ever touched her like this, the only one who ever made her breathing become shallow and desire flood into her eyes.

The music reached a crescendo and they stepped the last few steps of the dance.

Robert bowed and Louisa automatically curtsied.

'Will you give me a chance?' Robert asked.

It felt like hours before Louisa gave a sharp nod of her head.

Robert felt his heart soar as he tucked Louisa's hand into the crook of his elbow and led her from the dance floor. They walked quickly, skirting round groups of people, trying not to make eye contact so they wouldn't get pulled into conversation.

Robert went out into the hallway and led Louisa down into the private part of the house. He tried a door handle, found the room to be unlocked, then pulled Louisa inside. Finally he turned, felt for the key and locked the door behind them.

Chapter Twenty-Six

Louisa waited until her eyes had adjusted to the darkness before turning to face Robert. He was standing with his back to the door, looking like a lion ready to pounce.

Louisa felt her mouth go dry and tried to swallow, knowing she should say something, confront him, but unable to find the words.

'I behaved awfully,' Robert said as he took a step towards her.

She nodded and took a step backwards, knowing that if he got to close she would lose all sense, all reason, and right now she needed to talk to Robert, not fling herself wantonly into his arms.

'By rights you should be refusing to speak to me,' Robert continued, 'but I'm a lucky man, you're too kind to let me suffer, to shut me out.'

Louisa took another step back and still didn't know what to say.

'When you confronted me in Hyde Park you said a lot of things I didn't want to believe.'

She'd only spoken the truth.

'And I've spent these last few days thinking long and hard about my future. And about the past.'

'You need to stop thinking about the past all the time, Robert,' Louisa said softly.

'I know. You're right. You've been right all along. I've just been too stupid to realise it.'

'You know what happened in St Mamede wasn't your fault,' Louisa pressed him.

Robert grimaced. 'If I'm honest I think there will always be a small part of me that blames myself for what happened. They were my men, after all. I was ultimately responsible for them.' He paused and took another step towards her. Louisa sensed that what he was about to say next would be very important. 'But I also realised that I can't keep living in the past. What happened happened and no amount of self-loathing or deprivation is going to change that.'

Louisa wanted to reach out and comfort him, encourage him to go on, but she sensed this was hard enough for him to say as it was and didn't want to interrupt his flow.

'These past couple of years I've shut myself away and I realise now that was the wrong thing to do. I should have been living my life to the full. I should have been thankful I survived.'

Louisa found herself nodding and no longer backing away.

'The day I met you I felt as though I'd come alive again. It was as though I'd been frozen for two years, just going through the motions. You breathed the life back into me.'

Louisa thought of how much they'd been through together and knew what he was saying was true. Robert had changed since they had first met, and she supposed some of that could have been because of her influence.

'I fell in love with you, Louisa. I fell in love with you almost immediately.'

Louisa felt as though her heart was about to explode with happiness. He loved her.

'But I denied it to myself, thinking I didn't deserve you. Thinking I didn't deserve the happiness I knew you would bring me.'

He stopped a couple of paces in front of her. Louisa wanted him to reach out and pull her into his arms, but she knew he needed to get everything off his chest first.

'I made up all kinds of excuses, reasons why we couldn't be together, but in reality it was because I thought I didn't deserve to be happy.'

'You do deserve to be happy,' Louisa said quietly. 'You're a good man, Robert, and after everything you've been through, the one thing you do deserve is happiness.'

'When you confronted me in the park, I was a mess,' Robert admitted. 'I wanted you so badly, I couldn't stand the thought of you being with someone else, marrying someone else, but I still couldn't forgive myself for what had happened in Portugal.'

'What changed?' Louisa asked.

'I forced myself to try to live without you,' Robert said. 'It was impossible. I would crave your company at the breakfast table, your presence in my study as I worked, your smiles and your laughter. I missed you so much it hurt.'

Louisa felt the love for this man swell and grow inside her. He'd missed her just as she'd missed him. He'd craved her company as she'd craved his.

'So I forced myself to sit down and examine the reasons we couldn't be together. The reasons I was using to condemn myself to a lifetime of unhappiness.'

Louisa held her breath.

'And I realised you were right. Regrets are not enough of a reason to cause two people this much unhappiness. I needed to start living in the here and now, to stop revisiting St Mamede in my thoughts and put the past behind me.'

Louisa stepped forwards and took his hand in hers.

'I can't promise I will ever be able to forget what happened in St Mamede, but I will do my very best to stop it from ruling my life.'

'I wouldn't want you to forget,' Louisa said softly. 'What happened to your friends and men was awful, they deserve to be remembered. But they deserve to be remembered by a man who is getting on with his life, living it to the full in honour of the lives they gave.'

Robert nodded and for the first time in the weeks she had known him she could see he actually agreed with her.

'I need you, Louisa,' Robert said, his voice hoarse with emotion, 'I need you so badly.'

Louisa felt as though she were about to burst with happiness.

'I know what I've done to you is unforgivable, but I'm willing to spend the rest of my life proving that I'm the man for you, proving you can trust me.'

He reached out and grasped her by the hand. Their bodies were still a couple of feet apart and Louisa realised he was giving her the chance to reject him, to push him away. He wanted this to be her decision.

'When you found me in the asylum, I was a mess,' Louisa said slowly, needing Robert to hear what she had to say. 'Half the time I wondered if I was actually mad and the other half I spent wondering how long until I did go mad.'

'You were never mad, Louisa, I knew that from the first.'

She smiled at him and gripped his hand even tighter. 'You believed in me, and that made me believe in myself.' She paused, wondering how best to put what she had to say.

'That first night at your house I was so scared of being hurt I didn't even stop to consider the safest place might be with you. I just didn't want to have to rely on anybody else. I'd been hurt and betrayed so badly I thought the best thing I could do would be to strike out on my own.' She smiled softly up at Robert, trying not to think about where she would be now if he hadn't followed her. 'You saved me, from that horrible man and from my own foolishness.'

She could see the anguish in Robert's eyes as he thought about the attack he'd only just been in time to fend off.

'And then you showed me what it was like to be cared for, what I had been missing all those years.'

Robert took a step forwards and stroked her cheek with the tips of his fingers.

'You deserve to be loved and cherished and worshipped,' he said quietly.

Suddenly his lips were on hers, kissing her passionately and possessively. Louisa allowed herself to melt into his embrace, savouring the warmth of his lips on her skin, the taste of his mouth and the pleasure of having him so close.

After thirty seconds Louisa broke away. She needed to finish telling Robert how she felt. She needed to make him understand.

'I've loved you almost from the very first,' Louisa said, 'but I was so afraid of getting hurt I tried to deny it.'

'Then I pushed you away,' Robert said, his voice full of regret. 'Can you forgive me for being such a fool, Louisa?'

'When we were on the rooftop of the orphanage, I thought my heart would never mend,' Louisa said. 'I gave myself to you and you rejected me—it was like my worst nightmare. I told myself I'd been right all along, that trusting someone else would only end in tears.'

Robert looked as though he'd been shot. Louisa could see he hated the idea of causing her so much pain.

'And then I began to realise why you pushed me away. And I knew my fears or your regrets were not a good enough reason for us to be apart.'

'So wise,' Robert said, reaching up to curl a

stray strand of hair around his fingers. 'So beautiful and kind and wise.'

'I think we should make a pact,' Louisa said. 'I should promise to trust you and you should promise to start living in the here and now.'

'Can't I promise to love you?' Robert asked.

'You can promise that, too.'

'And will you love me?' he asked, his smile seductive. Louisa knew she would never be able to deny this man anything.

'I've tried not to love you,' Louisa said, 'and it was impossible. I think I will love you until I die.'

Robert stepped forwards again and took her in his arms. This time the kiss was leisurely and contented. Louisa felt his body press against hers and she knew with certainty that this was right. She was meant to be with Robert. They were completely right for each other.

Chapter Twenty-Seven

She was pretty amazing, this woman of his, Robert thought. She loved him, she'd loved him for weeks. He'd been such a fool, wasting precious days, hours, seconds that could have been spent revelling in her company. He heard a soft moan escape her lips and knew in that second he had to have her.

He pulled his lips away from her sweet mouth and started to trail kisses down her neck. He loved it when she shivered beneath his touch. He wanted to see her undressed, naked to his eyes, to see the little goosebumps rise on her skin as he trailed his tongue over her most sensitive places.

Her skin was so soft, so smooth. He started to picture her laid out beneath him, with every inch of her body accessible to him. Robert felt himself let out a groan; just the idea of Louisa naked underneath him was almost unbearable, the reality would be exquisite.

He grabbed Louisa's hand and pulled her to the sofa. There were only two lamps flickering in the room, illuminating it with a faint glow, but it was enough. Robert wanted to see Louisa undressed, bathed in brilliant sunlight, but there would be time enough for that. They had all the time in the world to enjoy each other.

Robert trailed a finger down Louisa's neck, feeling her writhe underneath his touch, urging him to go lower. His finger caressed the skin over her collarbone, then trailed lower, teasing her by running around the neckline of her dress. Robert could feel Louisa straining upwards, trying to encourage his fingers to explore further, to dip into her dress and caress the contours of her breasts.

'Oh, Robert,' Louisa murmured, just the sound of her voice firing an even deeper passion within him.

He kissed her again, savouring the sweet taste of her lips beneath his, then pulled away.

'Stand up,' he said, unable to be more eloquent.

Louisa stood, facing him. Slowly Robert reached out and spun her round so her back was towards him. He ran his hands down the length of her spine, feeling the curve of her bottom beneath the layers of her dress. He knew he couldn't wait much longer. He needed to have

Louisa soon, but the small voice of reason reminded him where they were. He wasn't going to be able to stop himself from making Louisa his in the most primitive of ways, but he would restrain himself so she could walk out of here afterwards and not have the entire *ton* know what they had been doing.

Carefully he started to unlace her dress. He cursed the intricacy of the design. Although it looked stunning on, Robert just wanted the damn dress off her; he wanted to see Louisa in all her natural glory.

As the dress loosened Robert paused, taking a second to run his hand from the nape of her neck down her back. Although she still had her undergarments on he could feel the heat radiating from her skin and he knew he was getting ever closer.

'Robert,' Louisa said, her voice strained.

He didn't know what he would do if she asked him to stop now. He wanted her so badly, desired her more than anything else in the world. If she asked him to stop, it would be agonising.

'I need you,' she said.

A fire of desire roared inside Robert and his resolve to undress her gently slipped away. He tugged at the laces and fastenings that secured her undergarments, pulling her dress off over her head at the same time. He heard ripping but was too caught up in the moment to care.

Robert spun Louisa back round to face him. Layers of her clothing were piled on the floor and now she was just clad in a simple chemise of cotton. It was thin, so thin he could see the outline of her nipples through the material.

'Are you sure you want this?' he asked, knowing he had to be chivalrous, but equally aware it might break him if she said no.

'I want this,' Louisa whispered. 'I want you.'

Robert didn't need any more encouragement. He stood in front of her and ran his hands down her body, taking in the swell of her breasts, her taut abdomen and the crease where her body met her thighs. Louisa shuddered with anticipation and within seconds Robert had whipped the rest of her clothes off.

He looked at her for a long few seconds, his beautiful siren standing in front of him, enticing him in.

'Robert,' Louisa said, her voice barely more than a whisper, 'this hardly seems fair.'

She motioned to his fully clothed body and took a step towards him. Robert groaned as her fingers started tugging at his shirt, pulling off his jacket. He resisted the urge to help her, instead enjoying Louisa's touch all over his body as she struggled to undress him.

'You're beautiful,' he said as she brushed up against him in the process of pulling his shirt over his head.

Then she was in his arms, her bare chest pressed up against his, both their hearts pounding in unison. Robert kissed her everywhere he could lay his lips: on her mouth, her jaw, her neck, her chest. He heard her gasp as he lavished attention on her breasts.

Breaking away for just a second, Robert scooped Louisa up into his arms and carried her over to the sofa.

'I want to enjoy this,' he murmured.

He heard her gasp as he straddled her, still clad in his breeches, but his manhood very obviously straining to get out.

He lowered himself down so his body was covering hers, then began to tease her.

'Robert,' Louisa urged. 'Please.'

'Please what?' he asked.

'Please.'

'What would my lady like?' He paused, pulling away slightly. 'To be kissed here?' He peppered kisses across the base of her throat. Louisa groaned. 'Or here?' He moved lower and ran his tongue down in between or breasts. 'Or here?'

Louisa let out a low moan of pleasure as he caught a nipple between his teeth.

'Does my lady like that?' he asked.

Frantically Louisa nodded her head, pushing his head back into position.

Robert let out a low chuckle, pleased Louisa was finding so much pleasure so soon. He grazed her nipple with his teeth, then drew back, switching his attention to her other breast.

'Oh, Robert,' Louisa said, 'that feels so good.'

'This is only the start,' he promised her.

Robert could feel his own desire mounting to almost unbearable levels, but he knew Louisa was the important one this evening. He had to show her pleasure such as she'd never known before. There would be plenty of time for him later. And over the rest of their lives.

He pushed himself up slightly and slowly started to run his hand over her abdomen towards her most private place. Louisa's breathing was coming in short, sharp gasps and Robert smiled as she inadvertently thrust her hips towards him to try and meet his hand.

She looked so beautiful, lying so wantonly beneath him. He couldn't believe he was so lucky. This stunning, lovely woman wanted him. And for the rest of their lives she would be giving herself to only him.

Robert began to tease her again, running his fingers across the top of her thighs and across her lower abdomen. Her skin was silky smooth and her muscles jumped beneath his touch.

'Touch me, Robert,' she begged him.

He was too much of a gentleman to refuse.

Grinning wolfishly, Robert ran his fingers over her most private place, trailing the tips of his fingers in a feather-light touch.

'More,' Louisa begged.

Her face was flushed and more lovely than he'd ever seen her.

Robert couldn't restrain himself any longer. He dipped his head and tasted her. He felt Louisa shudder beneath his kiss and writhe against his mouth. Slowly he caressed her, building in speed as she pressed herself against him. Every moan and mewl of pleasure just stoked the fire within Robert until he was certain he could take no more. But first he was determined to satisfy Louisa. She was the priority, she was the focus.

Her breathing was coming in short sharp gasps now and Robert could tell she was close to climaxing. He ran his tongue backwards and forwards, making her writhe with each contact, circling and dipping in.

Louisa suddenly gripped his head and Robert felt her body tense beneath him. She shuddered and arched her back, bucking up towards him.

After a few seconds Louisa's muscles relaxed and she crumpled back on to the sofa.

'I need you, Louisa,' Robert said, finally giving in to his desire.

Her fingers fumbled with his waistband, trying desperately to pull down his breeches. Robert helped, pushing the material from his waist, until his manhood sprung free.

'I need you,' he repeated.

Instinctively Louisa shifted slightly and opened her legs. Robert pressed himself on top of her, their bodies fitting together as if they had been made for each other.

Robert knew he had to go slowly, this would hurt Louisa whatever he did, but he wanted to make it as good as possible for her.

He pressed up against her and felt himself slide inside. Already it felt as though he were in heaven. Deep down he knew he'd been waiting weeks for this very moment and finally it was here.

Robert paused, ready to warn Louisa of the pain she would feel, hoping he could make it all worthwhile for her.

Before he could say a word, Louisa reached up and pulled his mouth on to hers, kissing him so deeply and passionately Robert forgot everything else. He pressed deeper into her, feeling her stiffen as he passed her maidenhood.

'It will get better, my love,' he whispered into her ear. 'I promise it will get better.'

It took all of Robert's resolve to stay still for as long as he did, he was almost mad with desire, but he looked into Louisa's beautiful face and told himself this time was for her.

After a few seconds he felt Louisa relax beneath him and he slowly started to thrust forward. He couldn't tear his eyes from Louisa's as he moved backwards and forwards inside her, loving how she bit her lip with pleasure when he was buried deep.

Robert knew he couldn't last much longer. She'd worked him up into such a frenzy that he'd been mad with desire for so long now. Just as he knew his climax was inevitable, he felt Louisa stiffen beneath him, her eyes squeeze shut and her muscles spasm inside.

Her climax sent him over the edge and Robert felt pure ecstasy as he released inside her.

Robert collapsed on top of her, taking in deep breaths and allowing a calm feeling that everything was right with the world to flow over him.

After a minute or two he opened his eyes and found Louisa smiling up at him.

'That was wonderful,' Louisa said.

'You're wonderful.'

She grinned at him and Robert felt himself grinning back. He didn't think he'd ever been so happy in his entire life.

'I'm sorry your first time was on Lady Gillingham's sofa,' he said apologetically. 'I just couldn't resist you.'

Louisa lifted her head from the arm of the sofa and kissed him long and hard on the mouth.

'I don't want you to ever apologise for not being able to resist me. It makes a girl feel quite desirable.'

'You're more than quite desirable.'

Robert shifted, aware Louisa was probably feeling a little uncomfortable underneath him.

'We're not going to be able to go back to the ball looking like this,' Louisa said as Robert stood up.

He looked down at both of their naked forms.

'You think people would notice if we step out without our clothes on?'

Louisa rolled her eyes at him. 'Even when we're dressed, it'll be obvious what we've just been doing.'

For a second Robert nearly told Louisa he didn't care, let them gossip. He was going to marry her, spend his life with her—what did it matter if people knew what they'd been doing? Then he looked at her worried face and saw how concerned she really was. Louisa didn't want to be thrust into the spotlight as the young ward who had been compromised by her guardian at Lady Gillingham's ball. She just wanted to quietly slip away and confirm her love for Robert in private.

'Let me help you get dressed,' Robert said, trying to think of a solution.

With more care than when he'd been taking Louisa's clothes off Robert helped her to dress. After a few minutes she was clothed, but looked in no way presentable.

Robert hurriedly threw on his own clothes, knowing he wouldn't be able to get his cravat looking anything like when his valet tied it.

'We might be able to slip out the back way,' Robert said.

Louisa looked dubious.

'I want you to wait here for me. Lock the door after I've gone and don't open it for anyone. I'm going to see if we can get my carriage brought round to the back entrance.'

He bent down and kissed her softly on the lips, pulling away reluctantly after a few seconds.

'Don't forget to lock the door,' he said as he slipped out into the darkened corridor.

He waited until he heard the turn of the key in the lock, then crept into the darkness. Lady Gillingham had one of the biggest town houses he'd ever been in. She'd assigned one section for the ball and kept the rest private so Robert was quite confident he wouldn't bump into anyone he shouldn't whilst he was creeping around in this part of the house.

Robert felt his way along the corridor in the darkness until he found a set of stairs right at the back of the house. He checked over his shoulder, then started to descend, hoping he would run into a friendly footman.

'Can I help you, sir?' a young man dressed in a smart uniform asked as he reached the bottom of the stairs.

Robert grinned. He had enough cash in his pocket to make sure this young man helped him and kept quiet about it.

'I've got myself into a bit of a predicament,' Robert said quietly, 'and I'm hoping you'll be able to help me.'

He got some of the notes from his pocket and held then out to the young man.

'What is the problem, sir?' the footman asked, pocketing the money immediately.

'I need to make a quick exit with a friend of mine. We can't go out the front door...' Robert trailed off as the footman glanced down at his rumpled appearance and a smile of understanding crossed his face.

'I could ask for your carriage to be brought round the back,' the footman offered helpfully.

'Perfect.' Robert held out a few more notes. 'For your trouble,' he said, 'and your discretion.'

'What's the name, sir?'

'Fleetwood.'

'I will go and arrange it immediately. If you would like to bring your friend down here in five minutes, I can show you where to go.'

Robert shook the young man's hand before turning and retracing his steps up the stairway.

'Lord Fleetwood, what on earth are you doing below stairs?' Lady Gillingham's voice made him jump as he reached the darkened hallway.

'Just got a little lost,' Robert said, flashing the widow one of his rare smiles.

'I have been looking for you for some time,' Lady Gillingham said. 'I thought we might take up where we left off a few weeks ago. I think you were going to make me a proposition.'

Robert really didn't have time for this right now, but he couldn't have Lady Gillingham getting too suspicious.

'You know I'm interested in you. As I said before, I do like a man with an air of mystery about him.'

'I'm not mysterious, Lady Gillingham.'

'Please call me Emilia, we are to be good friends, after all.'

'I wouldn't want to keep you from your guests,' Robert said, knowing Louisa would be wondering where he was.

'I can neglect them for a few minutes longer, especially if it were to forward our friendship.'

Robert didn't know why this woman was

being quite so persistent. It wasn't as if he had ever encouraged her, or at least not in the last few years. They had flirted somewhat before Robert had left for the war, before Emilia Ruddock had married Lord Gillingham, but that seemed like a lifetime ago.

'Maybe another time,' Robert said, trying to gently push his way past her.

'Lord Fleetwood, I warned you before, I always get what I want. Stop trying to fight me and I promise you'll enjoy it.'

The image of Louisa lying naked beneath him flooded back into Robert's mind. He knew he would never want anything to do with a woman like Lady Gillingham, not when he had his own perfect woman waiting for him.

'Lady Gillingham,' Robert said pointedly, 'I suggest you give up this ridiculous pursuit. I'm not now, nor ever will be, interested in you. I am in love with a wonderful, beautiful woman and I plan on spending the rest of my life making her happy.'

Lady Gillingham recoiled as if he'd slapped her. Her lips curled into an unattractive sneer.

'You'll regret treating me like this, Fleetwood,' Lady Gillingham said, then turned on her heel and stalked off.

Robert quickly made his way back to where

Louisa had locked herself and tapped quietly on the door.

'It's me, my love,' he whispered through the wood.

He waited for a few seconds, then heard Louisa unlock the door, grinning at her dishevelled form as she peeked out.

'A friendly footman is getting our carriage brought round the back,' Robert said, pulling her out into the dark corridor. He wanted to get to the safety of his carriage before Lady Gillingham came back for more.

As they strode through the darkness hand in hand, neither Louisa or Robert saw Lady Gillingham standing in the shadows, watching them with icy eyes and a frown of displeasure.

Chapter Twenty-Eight

Louisa wrapped her arms around her body and hugged herself. Robert was just giving an extra bribe to the footman who had fetched their carriage in return for him keeping quiet about the whole affair. After a few seconds Robert bounded up into the carriage and banged on the roof, signalling they were ready to depart.

He sat down beside her, then thought better of it. A second later Louisa felt herself being picked up and deposited on Robert's lap.

'Where were we?' he murmured into her ear.

She looked at him, puzzled.

'I think we'd just got started, don't you?'

Louisa's giggles turned to sighs as Robert lowered his mouth on to hers. She loved the feel of his taut body beneath her hands, the hard muscles that were only hers to touch.

She wriggled a little on his lap and felt the stirrings of his manhood beneath his trousers.

'See what you do to me, Louisa?' Robert asked.

She felt powerful and humble at the same time. She loved that she was the one to arouse him, that it was she he desired, but she also felt blessed that he had decided to shower her with his love and affection.

She wriggled a little more and Robert groaned.

'Sit still, you little minx, otherwise I'll have to do very wicked things to you in this carriage with the streets of London as a witness.'

Louisa liked the idea of wicked things.

She turned and ran her lips across his jawline, relishing the feel of the rough stubble that had already begun to grow. She caught his earlobe between her teeth and sucked, causing Robert's hands to tighten around her waist and pull her even closer. Then she ran the tip of her tongue down his neck, tasting him and feeling the beat of his pulse pounding beneath the skin.

'We'd better get home soon,' Robert whispered.

'I'm quite enjoying myself,' Louisa said mischievously.

She saw the glint in Robert's eye and immediately knew he was going to make her beg him for more before the journey was finished.

His hand slid over the material of her skirt and grasped her ankle gently.

'Madam isn't wearing any stockings,' he observed. 'How convenient.'

In her rush to get dressed Louisa hadn't bothered to replace her stockings, instead balling them up and stuffing them into her small bag.

'What lovely smooth skin you have,' Robert said, tracing a pattern with the very tips of his fingers around her ankle.

Slowly he worked his way up her calf, alternating between massaging the muscles and caressing her skin ever so softly.

Already Louisa could feel herself urging him to go higher. She wanted him to touch her where no other man had, to make her scream and writhe in ecstasy, then plunge inside her and join his body with hers.

'Do you like this?' Robert asked, as if he were behaving like the perfect gentleman.

'Mmm-hmm,' Louisa managed to mumble.

'Or would you prefer it if I stopped?'

She couldn't think of anything more cruel.

'I'll carry on, just for a little while,' Robert decided.

His fingers climbed a little higher, dancing over her knees and moving on to her thighs. Louisa felt herself open her legs ever so slightly, inviting him in.

'Not yet, my love,' Robert whispered into her ear. 'It's all about patience.'

His fingers moved backwards and forwards over her skin, causing Louisa to shiver. It was as though her skin had become unbearably sensitive; she was deriving such pleasure from his simple touch.

Suddenly his fingers grazed over her most private of places and Louisa felt her body shudder. But as soon as Robert had touched her his fingers had moved on, back to caressing the skin on her legs.

'Again,' she whispered, knowing she sounded wanton and unladylike, but not in a position to care.

'Again?' Robert asked. 'What would you like again?'

'Touch me again.'

'But I am touching you,' he teased.

'Touch me there.' Louisa felt herself blushing, but she needed his touch. She felt as though she would go mad without it.

Thankfully he complied, brushing his fingers against her ever so gently. Louisa felt her hips rise involuntarily to meet him, pressing him into her warm folds.

'Sit still, madam,' he chided. 'What did I tell you about patience?'

Louisa could only moan as he stroked her, brushing his fingers backwards and forwards and making her crave more and more.

'Oh, Robert,' Louisa whispered, arching her back and letting her head drop backwards.

'Oh, Robert, stop?' he teased her, momentarily stopping his caress.

'No,' Louisa whimpered, 'I want more.'

'My lady is greedy,' he said, covering her lips with his own in a possessive kiss.

Louisa felt as though her body was being assaulted from all sides. Robert's lips were gentle against hers, his mouth nipping and biting and working her up into a frenzy. And beneath her skirts his fingers were still moving slowly backwards and forwards, never speeding up, but still making the tension build steadily inside her.

Louisa opened her eyes and looked down at Robert. He was hers, all hers. He'd promised if he were her man he would be faithful to the last, and now he was touching her she knew it would be true. She couldn't believe how lucky she was, how happy she was. Only a few weeks ago she hadn't wished for anything more than her freedom. Now she had something so much more wonderful.

'Don't stop, Robert,' she murmured as he drew his lips across her jaw and down her neck.

'Never,' he promised her.

Louisa reached beneath her with her free hand and started to fumble with his breeches. Every time her hand brushed against the bulge beneath, Robert let out a ragged breath. Her inexperienced fingers took twice as long to undo the fastenings as his would, but before too long her hand was inside.

Robert let out a low, primal groan and Louisa felt the power she had over him. She grasped the silky smooth hardness of his manhood, revelling in how it pulsed and swelled beneath her hand. Slowly she ran her fingers up and down, watching Robert's face as she teased him just as he was teasing her.

'Oh, Louisa,' Robert murmured into her ear.

'Oh, Louisa, stop?' she teased him as he had her earlier.

'Never.'

She felt him shift beneath her before he lifted her by the hips and positioned her over him. Slowly Louisa sank down on to him, only stopping when he was completely inside her. She loved the feeling of being in control, of being in charge of giving Robert pleasure.

She gasped as he slipped his hand back under her skirt and started to stroke her again. Louisa started to writhe in ecstasy and felt herself instinctively moving up and down. She started slowly, revelling in each thrust, enjoying each and every sensation. Then the sensations became overwhelming and Louisa gave in to the wild passion that had built up inside her.

Their bodies moved in perfect unison, coming together over and over again. Louisa looked down at Robert and felt love and desire all melt into one. Suddenly Louisa felt a jolt of pure pleasure radiate through her and she threw her head back. At exactly the same moment Robert stiffened and she felt him pulse inside her.

Louisa's muscles all trembled and went weak and she found herself collapsing forwards onto Robert's chest. She lay panting for a few seconds, trying to catch her breath and ride the waves of pleasure that were still buzzing through her body.

'I hadn't meant for your second time to be in a carriage,' Robert said after a few minutes. 'Just as I hadn't meant for your first time to be on a sofa.'

Louisa raised her head and kissed him languidly on the lips.

'You just couldn't resist me?' she asked jokingly.

'Exactly.' Robert was completely serious. 'I fear I won't be able to touch you when we're out in public in case it precipitates a scandalous show.'

'Maybe we just shouldn't go out in public.'

'What a fantastic idea,' Robert said.

Louisa couldn't think of anything more perfect than spending her days closeted in bed with
Robert. Perhaps every so often they could emerge
from the bedroom to have something to eat, but
other than that they would be complete recluses.

They pulled up outside Robert's house and
Louisa tried in vain to make herself look vaguely
respectable. After a few seconds she gave up.

'I wouldn't worry,' Robert told her. 'The servants have probably been taking bets for weeks
on how long it would take us to get together.'

He hopped down from the carriage and
reached up. Instead of helping her down to the
ground he swept her into his arms and carried
her up the steps. Louisa was giggling so much
she didn't even see the footman's face as he
opened the door.

'Good evening, sir,' Smith, the footman, said
as they entered the hallway. 'And you've brought
Miss Turnhill home again. Wonderful to have
you back with us, Miss Turnhill.'

'Miss Turnhill is back for good,' Robert said
quietly, so only Louisa could hear.

'Can I get you anything, sir?'

'I've got all I need, thank you, Smith.'

And with that Robert whisked her up the

stairs and into his bedroom. He kicked the door shut behind him and lowered her on to the bed.

'I love you, Louisa,' he said as he began to undress her for the second time that evening.

'I love you, Robert.'

Chapter Twenty-Nine

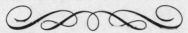

Louisa didn't think she'd ever been happier in her entire life. She opened her eyes to find sunlight streaming through the curtains and Robert gazing down at her.

'Good morning,' Robert said, leaning in for a leisurely kiss. 'Did I tell you that I loved you?'

Louisa pretended to consider the question for a minute or two.

'I'm not sure. Maybe last night someone might have declared their love for me…' She trailed off as he covered her mouth with his own.

'How did you sleep?' he asked.

'Perfectly.'

She'd lain awake in his arms for a few minutes before drifting off into the most contented sleep ever.

'I didn't have any nightmares,' he said quietly.

Louisa turned over so she was facing him

directly. 'I will do everything in my power to stop you from having another nightmare again.'

'Anything?' Robert asked.

'Anything.' She put a finger to his lips just before they could cover hers. 'But first I need some breakfast. I'm ravenous.'

Robert groaned, then conceded. 'Actually, I'm starving myself.'

They both got out of bed and reluctantly started to dress. Louisa was amazed she didn't feel self-conscious about being naked in front of Robert in the cold light of day, but every time she caught him staring she could see the love and desire in his eyes.

'Ready for breakfast?' Robert asked when he'd finished securing the fastenings on Louisa's dress.

'I hope there's poached eggs,' Louisa said dreamily, her stomach starting to gurgle in anticipation of the meal.

They descended the stairs arm in arm, walking past Smith the footman and trying to ignore his delighted grin.

'I'll tell cook you're ready for breakfast, sir,' Smith said once they were seated, 'and I'll ask her to make it a hearty one.'

Louisa could see Robert was too happy to even think about reprimanding the footman for his suggestive comment.

'I should send a note to Major Dunton,' Louisa said as she sat down.

'I think Dunton is clever enough to work out what happened,' Robert said with a grin. 'And that his ploy to make me see what I was missing wasn't really needed.'

'I suppose you did work it out on your own eventually,' Louisa murmured, closing her eyes as Robert took her hand and planted a kiss on her wrist.

While they waited for breakfast they sipped on rich coffee and held hands. Louisa felt herself shiver as Robert traced a pattern around her palm and wondered whether she had the strength to skip breakfast and pull Robert back upstairs.

As she was contemplating doing just that Smith reentered the room with the first of the dishes.

'A letter arrived for you earlier this morning, Miss Turnhill,' the footman said as he placed the white envelope before her.

'Who delivered it?' Robert asked.

'I'm not sure. It was just lying inside the door and when I looked out there wasn't anyone to be seen.'

Louisa eyed the fancy script on the front of the envelope with curiosity as she tucked into her poached egg. After a few bites she put down her fork and opened the envelope. Next to her Robert picked up the morning paper and began to read.

Inside was a letter, addressed to her. She flicked through to the last page and was surprised to find it signed not with a name, but just 'a friend'.

Intrigued, Louisa pushed her plate away and began to read.

20th May
Dear Miss Turnhill,

Although what I have to write may seem unpleasant, I am writing only as a friend. I want to assure you I have your best interests at heart. As a woman who has been hurt before I wish to save you the pain and heartache betrayal can bring.

I cannot reveal my identity to you, but suffice it to say I am a woman who knows Lord Fleetwood intimately.

Louisa felt the blood drain from her cheeks, but forced herself to read on.

We were acquainted before Lord Fleetwood went off to war and more recently we decided to renew our friendship. Lord Fleetwood often spoke of you and it was clear from the very start he cared deeply about you, as a guardian should for his ward. It was during one of our many discussions about how best to deal with the unfamiliar demands of having a ward that the subject of your past came up.

Louisa thought she might be sick. Surely this was some cruel joke.

I wish to assure you I would never reveal the details of your past to anyone, but as someone who cares deeply for Lord Fleetwood I urge you to consider what such a revelation would mean for him. Although he has kept on the edges of society for the past few years he will no doubt one day wish to return to his peers and embrace the privileges of his rank.

If you were to continue your relationship with him and it were to be revealed you were a resident in the Lewisham Asylum, the damage to you both would be irreparable.

Louisa took a sharp breath and out of the corner of her eye she could see Robert looking at her with concern. She forced her eyes to remain on the letter and continued to read.

*And the truth will come out. Lord Fleet-
wood let the details of your past slip to
me—before long he will reveal it to someone else. Please consider your next actions
carefully and remember it is not only you
who will be disgraced by the secrets you
keep.*
    Yours sincerely,
    A Friend

Louisa felt her hands start to shake and the
panic rise up inside her. Someone knew. Someone knew all the sordid details about her past.
And this mystery woman was saying Robert had
been the one to tell her.

Louisa tried to think rationally. She tried to
tell herself that Robert wouldn't do that, that he
wouldn't tell anyone about her past. She stole a
glance at him and saw the reassuring expression
on his handsome face.

'Louisa, what's wrong?' he asked, his words
heavy with concern.

She nearly handed the letter over to him, but
at the last moment changed her mind. If Robert
hadn't told this woman, then how had she found
out? Only a very few people knew about her in-
carceration in the Lewisham Asylum. Certainly
if someone was interested enough they might

have been able to find out where she had been all of last year, but why would they bother?

Smith reentered the room.

'This was left outside, sir, with a note asking for it to be delivered to Miss Turnhill.'

Smith handed over a folded newspaper. Louisa set the letter down on the table and took the newspaper with shaking hands. The morning was getting stranger and stranger.

She opened out the paper and scanned the black ink, realising after a few seconds it was one of the weekly gossip pages published anonymously and devoured by the *ton*. These gossip pages contained no real news, just scandals of who was having affairs with whom and who had committed a society *faux pas*.

'What is it, Louisa?' Robert asked.

Louisa's eyes rested on the headline of by far the largest article in the paper.

Lord Fleetwood's Ward a Lunatic

She felt the bottom fall out of her world. She didn't even need to read the rest of the article, the headline was enough.

Louisa's chest felt unbearably tight, as though some large animal were sitting on her, crushing her. She could feel the blood pounding in her head. Her vision was going blurry and her fingertips were starting to tingle.

'Louisa, you're worrying me,' Robert said, reaching out to take her hand.

Louisa shied away from him, pushed her chair back from the table and stumbled to her feet.

She needed air. She felt as though she couldn't breathe. Unsteadily she made her way out into the hall and towards the front door.

Robert followed her, reaching out to try to take her by the arm.

'Don't touch me,' Louisa said quietly.

The look of hurt on his face was nearly enough to bring Louisa to her senses. Nearly, but not quite.

'Leave me alone, Robert,' Louisa said, hearing the mounting hysteria in her voice.

'Never.'

'Please, if you care for me at all, leave me alone.'

'What's wrong?'

She shook her head, unable to put into words all the awful thoughts that were spiralling through her mind.

'Read the paper,' she said instead, then turned and fled out of the door.

Louisa ran. She picked up all the layers that made up her skirt and ran. She knew she had to get out of sight as soon as possible, otherwise Robert would follow her, convince her to go back with him. That was the last thing she needed right now.

She let her instincts take over and threaded her way through the streets. She splashed through puddles and dodged between groups of strolling people. She didn't care if they recognised her and wondered what she was doing. The whole world knew her dirty little secret now, nothing she could do would make it any worse.

Louisa must have run flat out for at least fifteen minutes before the hammering of her heart made her slow to catch her breath. She glanced over her shoulder to check if anyone was following her. She half expected to see Robert striding down the street, ready to whisk her into his arms.

Panting, Louisa made her way to an empty doorway and lowered herself onto the step. She sat with her head in her hands and tried to figure out exactly what had happened.

The whole world would now think she was mad. It wouldn't matter to them that she had been wrongly imprisoned, that her guardian had sent her away to get his hands on her money. Everyone would just see the fact that she'd spent over a year in a madhouse and assume she was insane.

'I don't care,' she said quietly and immediately knew she was lying to herself. She did care.

She cared more than she would ever admit. The last few weeks had been like a fairy tale. She'd been Louisa the debutante, not Louisa the inmate. For the first time in her adult life she'd felt normal. It had been amazing. She should have known it wouldn't last.

Louisa glanced down the street again just to check Robert wasn't striding towards her. It was empty. She didn't know whether to be relieved or upset.

It was the letter that was really bothering her. Of course the announcement in the gossip pages was awful. She hated the idea of people talking about her over their breakfast tables, but she'd be able to cope with that if it hadn't have been for the letter.

She wondered who had sent it. And why. What possible reason could they have for telling her that her past would catch up with her and hurt Robert in the process?

Louisa tried to figure out who this woman could be. She had said she was intimate with Robert, hinted that they had discussed Louisa and her past as one would only with a lover. Maybe they'd discussed her past and how to deal with her across a pillow after they'd made love.

Louisa felt the tears start to fall down her cheeks. That was what hurt the most; she'd been convinced Robert loved her. He'd told her he did.

He'd looked into her eyes when they'd made love and made her feel special. But how special was she to him? Had he looked at this other woman the same way before revealing the details of Louisa's past to her? Perhaps they'd cooked up the idea of Robert seducing Louisa, marrying her, together, as a way to keep a lid on the scandal.

Louisa stood suddenly, unable to take any more. Her imagination was whirring and each different scenario was worse than the last.

Slowly she started to walk down the street, her chin almost resting on her chest and her eyes fixed on the ground. She didn't know where she was going just as she didn't know the truth of how the details of her past had come to grace the pages of the society newspaper, but she did know she was once again truly alone.

Chapter Thirty

Robert stared after Louisa's fleeing form for thirty seconds before realising the implications of the situation. Louisa was running alone through the streets of London. In a few seconds she would disappear around a corner and he might not be able to find her.

Letting out a string of expletives, he dashed out the front door, down the steps and sprinted along the street, following Louisa. She'd rounded a corner and was out of his line of sight for ten seconds. Robert crashed around the same corner and saw a flash of colour as her skirt swished around the next street. Robert picked up his pace, knowing he couldn't afford to lose sight of her. The last time she'd run off into the streets of London, she'd been attacked, and if he hadn't come upon her, who knew what awful things would have happened.

Robert dashed around the next corner and felt

his heart pound in his chest. He couldn't see her. He scanned left and right, desperately trying to catch sight of her retreating form, the swish of her skirt or any clue as to where she had gone.

With panic rising inside him, Robert jogged to the end of the street, checking each side road for any sign of Louisa. He felt cold dread at the thought of Louisa on her own in London.

'Have you seen a young woman, dressed in blue?' He grabbed hold of an elderly gentleman. 'She was running?'

The old man gave him a disgusted look and shook Robert's hand from his arm. Robert moved on to the next couple.

'Have you seen a young woman, dressed in blue?' he asked, praying one of them would nod and point him in the right direction.

No one had seen her, or at least no one was admitting to having seen her. He supposed they probably thought him a violent husband, searching for the wife who finally had plucked up the courage to run from him.

Robert was desperate now. He jogged from street to street, his head turning from side to side. Deep down he knew he had lost her, but he couldn't quite admit it to himself.

After nearly an hour of frantic searching Robert had to accept he didn't have a clue where

Louisa was. He felt helpless; he was meant to protect her and he didn't even know where she had gone.

He started to retrace his steps back home, harbouring the faint hope Louisa might have changed her mind about whatever had spooked her and returned before him. Maybe she would be sitting at the breakfast table, sipping coffee, waiting for him to join her. Robert allowed himself that glimmer of hope, but he knew it wasn't going to happen.

As he was climbing the steps the front door opened and Robert saw the concerned faces of all his servants.

'Did you find her, sir?' Smith asked.

Wordlessly Robert shook his head.

'I think you need to see this.'

The footman handed Robert the paper Louisa had been reading just before she had fled. He glanced at it and saw the headline, in bold letters, and immediately understood. Someone had found out about Louisa's past and had spilled everything to the *ton* in the worst way possible— through the scandalous gossip pages.

'There's more, sir,' Smith said gently.

Robert felt the realisation that Louisa really had gone hit him and reached out a hand to steady himself. Immediately the footman was by his side, guiding him into his study. Robert brushed him away, but gratefully took the glass of whisky Smith poured for him.

'I'll give you a few minutes, sir.'

Robert was left alone with the newspaper and the letter Smith had thrust into his hand before he had left the room. Taking a deep breath, he read the gossip article carefully, looking for clues as to who could have found out the details of where Louisa had spent her last few years.

Lord Fleetwood's Ward a Lunatic!

This author was thrilled to meet Lord Fleetwood's young ward at Lady Gillingham's ball last night. Miss Louisa Turnhill is a delightful young lady with impeccable manners. So imagine this author's surprise when Miss Turnhill's background was revealed by a trusted source.

Miss Turnhill caused quite a stir when she arrived late to the Season. The official reason for her tardiness was given to be that she was in mourning for her late guardian. In fact, although it is true her guardian was recently taken from this world, this author has been able to confirm that until very recently Miss Turnhill was a resident of the Lewisham Asylum for the mentally insane. She spent just over a year as a patient at the institute.

An inside source revealed Miss Turnhill was not just incarcerated for the de rigueur complaint of melancholia either. She is reported to have suffered from mania and psychosis and was kept under physical restraint!

No wonder Lord Fleetwood seemed so keen to keep his new ward quite so close— we're just surprised that the brooding bachelor decided to let her loose on society at all.

Robert let out a primal growl and threw the paper across the room. It was drivel. Ridiculous drivel. He couldn't believe someone would write such hurtful things about his sweet Louisa.

He was going to find whoever had written it, and whoever the 'trusted source' was, and he was going to strangle them. It would be a better death than they deserved.

Robert turned his attention to the letter Louisa had received that morning. The handwriting was distinctly feminine, but Robert didn't recognise it as any close acquaintance.

As he read through the letter his frown deepened. No wonder Louisa had run off like that.

Her past had been revealed to everyone in London and twisted to make her look as though she was mad. But worse than that, and the reason Robert had suspected she had run away, was that whoever had written the letter had made it sound as though it was *he* who had betrayed her confidence.

Robert thought of Louisa alone and heartbroken, wandering the streets of London. Surely she would realise he would never do anything to hurt her. Surely she would realise the author of the letter was lying.

He hoped so, but Robert knew that at the moment Louisa was hurting. She had allowed herself to trust and now it was as though that trust had been torn to pieces before her eyes. Maybe when she had the chance to accept what had happened, to think about it rationally, maybe then she would realise Robert would never do anything to hurt her, but right now she was upset and betrayed.

Robert knew if he could just find her, talk to her, he would be able to make her understand that he would never do anything to hurt her. She would see how much he loved her and realise the letter contained nothing but lies.

But to do that, he first had to find her. And in a city of over a million people he had no idea where to start.

* * *

Robert knocked firmly on the imposing front door. After a couple of seconds it swung open and a footman ushered him inside.

'Lord Fleetwood to see Lady Gillingham,' Robert said curtly.

The footman led him through the grand hallway to a drawing room, right next door to the room where he had made love to Louisa for the first time. Robert wished they could be back there, when Louisa was safe in his arms and she believed he loved her.

'I will inform Lady Gillingham of your presence,' the footman said, leaving the room.

Robert paced backwards and forwards, all of his pent-up rage preventing him from sitting down. He kept glancing at the clock on the mantelpiece, watching as the seconds ticked by, ever conscious that every minute that elapsed was another minute Louisa was on her own on the streets of London.

'Lord Fleetwood, what an unexpected surprise,' Lady Gillingham said as she swept into the room.

'You're poisonous,' Robert said without any preamble.

Lady Gillingham pretended to look shocked at his words. 'Now, Lord Fleetwood, that's not a very nice thing for one friend to say to another.'

'We're not friends,' Robert said, 'and we never will be. You're an evil human being.'

'Is this about that Turnhill girl?'

Robert felt the rage boil inside him. He couldn't believe Lady Gillingham was standing so calmly in front of him, discussing her hateful actions as if she'd just let it slip that Louisa took sugar in her tea.

'So you admit what you've done?' Robert asked.

Lady Gillingham sighed. 'Do we have to be so dramatic about this? It's not as though I've hurt the girl.'

'Not physically.'

'People deserve to know who they are socialising with. We've invited her into our homes, put our loved ones at risk.'

'You know she'd never harm anyone. Don't pretend you did this for the greater good.'

Lady Gillingham smiled and stepped towards him. 'No, I suppose you're right. I wrote to the gossip pages for entirely selfish reasons.'

She reached up and placed a hand on Robert's cheek. He had to stop himself from punching her. He didn't hit women, but Lady Gillingham was testing his self-restraint today.

Instead Robert encircled her wrist with his hand, locking her in his steely grasp.

'It's worked, hasn't it? I've got you right where

I want you, here with me.' She pressed her body close to his and Robert had to stop himself from physically shuddering at the repulsiveness of the contact.

'Lady Gillingham, I wouldn't be intimate with you if you were the only woman in London. You disgust me. You're cruel and unkind and that permeates through. It makes you ugly.'

Robert pushed her wrist away from him and watched as Lady Gillingham staggered backwards as if he'd physically struck her.

'You can't stand the thought that someone else would be more attractive than you so you try to sabotage them. It's petty and frankly ridiculous of a woman of your status.' Robert wondered whether any of his words were getting through. 'How did you find out?'

Lady Gillingham smiled and spread her arms wide. 'Your visit to the asylum didn't go unnoticed. A fancy carriage in that part of town is almost unheard of. After that it was child's play getting the odious proprietor to talk.'

Of course Symes would have been eager to spread malicious gossip about his former charge.

'Why did you do it?'

Lady Gillingham recovered some of her composure and gave him a slow, self-satisfied smile. 'She was in my way,' she said simply.

'When did you become so cruel?' Robert asked.

'Oh, it happens to us all, Lord Fleetwood. Even your precious little Miss Turnhill will do something you disapprove of one day. When she's been sold into a loveless marriage with a man forty years older than her, she'll be made to realise her only worth is her body, just like a common street whore. Then even when her husband dies, the only men interested in her will be the ones who think because she's been married she's fair game.'

Robert shook his head and refused to feel sorry for her. 'It's no excuse,' he said. 'You've ruined another person's life.'

Lady Gillingham stared at him defiantly, but Robert could see her steely exterior was about to crack.

'And people would treat you with more respect if you didn't constantly live up to their expectations.'

She glanced down for a few seconds and Robert could see she was trying to get herself under control.

'This is what's going to happen,' he said, feeling much more in control of the situation. 'You're going to write to whomever your contact is at the gossip pages and insist they set the *ton* straight.'

Lady Gillingham shook her head slowly, but Robert carried on regardless.

'You will tell them the truth.'

'I did tell them the truth,' Lady Gillingham said petulantly.

'You told them half the truth. I want it published that Louisa was wrongly imprisoned by her guardian who wanted her inheritance. She is not in the least bit mentally unwell or unstable.'

'The damage is done now, there's no point.'

'There is a point. And I don't care for your opinions, you'll just do as I say.'

'Why should I?' Lady Gillingham asked, a small note of defiance left in her voice.

'Because if you don't I will make sure every newspaper publishes a long list of your lovers. It might be acceptable for a widow to have affairs if she is very discreet, but you'll be hounded from society if the details are made public.'

Lady Gillingham turned white and reached out a hand to steady herself.

'You will make sure the correction is published tomorrow, on the front page, along with an announcement that Miss Turnhill and I are engaged to be married. You will be named as the source and you will admit to having got your facts wrong.'

Robert fixed her with a steely stare before striding from the room. He knew however much she didn't want to, Lady Gillingham would get the correction printed. Most of the damage to Louisa's reputation would be irreparable, but it was worth trying to salvage what he could. And, Robert was hoping Louisa might see the announcement herself and realise it had all been an awful mistake and that he loved her with all he had.

Chapter Thirty-One

Louisa had passed the last few hours in a daze, wandering without any set direction or destination in mind. She knew her clothes set her apart from many of the Londoners going about their daily lives. She stood out and as the day wore on Louisa realised that wasn't necessarily a good thing.

She glanced around her, aware for the first time in hours of her surroundings. She wasn't in the reputable part of London anymore. At some point she had crossed the river and with it the invisible divide between the rich and poor.

This is where I belong, Louisa thought, looking at the grimy buildings and depressing facades. The people were dirtier, too, the dirt ingrained in their faces and the strains of living in poverty evident in the premature wrinkles on their skin.

'Spare some change for a poor old woman.'

A wrinkled crone grabbed hold of Louisa's arm and pulled her closer.

Louisa shrugged the woman off. 'I'm sorry,' she said, desperate to get away. 'I don't have any money.'

It was true, she realised. In her haste to get out of Robert's house, she had left without taking anything of use with her. She didn't have any money. She didn't even have a shawl or wrap, nothing to keep her warm as the evening drew in.

Go back, the small voice in her head told her.

Louisa stumbled onwards, wondering if she was being stupid. She knew how dangerous it was for a young woman to be on her own in London, but she also knew she couldn't go back, not yet. She had to get some things straight in her head before she could even consider going back to Robert.

'What's a pretty lady like you doing in a place like this?' a soft voice said into her ear.

Louisa jumped and pulled away, but a restraining hand was placed on her arm.

'Let go of me,' she said, her voice coming out in a strangled whisper.

'He asked you a question. Would be rude not to answer, little miss.'

Another man appeared on her right side and gripped hold of her sleeve.

'Just keep your mouth shut and don't make any noise. You're coming with us.'

Louisa glanced frantically around, trying to catch someone's eye. The street was crowded, but everyone was taking pains to avoid eye contact.

'Let's go,' her first assailant growled.

Louisa felt something sharp pressing against her ribcage and nearly let out a scream when she realised it must be a knife.

'Remember, don't you go making any fuss and it'll all turn out better for you.'

Louisa doubted it. She wasn't so naive she didn't realise as soon as she allowed herself to be led away from the relative safety of the crowded main street she was as good as dead.

'What do you want?' she asked, trying to keep the tremor from her voice.

'Just a little of what you've got.'

Louisa took a deep breath. She knew she had to do something, but her heart was already pounding with fear. She made to step forwards, as if she were complying with their request. Trying to forget about the knife that was pressed up against her flank, she told herself to be brave.

'That's it, nice and slow.'

Not allowing herself to hesitate Louisa spun suddenly, throwing her body away from the first of her assailants and his knife. She barrelled into a middle-aged woman and bounced off her again. At the same time she let out an ear-piercing scream, knowing that the more attention she could attract the better.

Her two assailants froze. Louisa took advantage of their hesitation and shouted at the top of her voice, 'Stay away from me.'

The second of her attackers stepped towards her menacingly and for a second Louisa wondered whether her actions had just made things worse. He was nearly upon her when the first man reached out and grabbed him by the sleeve. He shook his head, slipped the knife up his sleeve and melted into the crowd. The second man hesitated, torn between following his comrade and finishing the job they'd set out to do.

After an agonising few seconds he turned and ran off down the street, darting round a corner and disappearing from view.

Louisa felt her heart pound in her chest and her breathing became shallow. Her hands started to tremble as she realised what a close call it had been.

Hurriedly she started to walk down the street, wanting to put as much distance between her and her assailants as possible.

The light was starting to fade and Louisa knew it would be dangerous to stay out in the open all night on her own. She wanted to go back

to Robert, to safety, but she knew she had to figure out what she was going to say to him first.

She glanced around at her surroundings as
she walked and her gaze fell on a grimy building with a short, stubby steeple. She almost cried
with relief. A church could offer her a few hours'
sanctuary from the dangers of the streets.

Louisa tried the door and was relieved when it
swung open, letting her inside. She entered cau-
tiously, allowing her eyes to adjust to the darkness before closing the door behind her. The
building was empty, but a few candles flickered
near the altar and Louisa quietly crept through
the church and took a seat on a pew. She bent
her head forward and rested it against the wood
of the pew in front.

'Do you seek sanctuary?' a soft voice asked
when she had been sitting there for a few minutes.

Louisa jumped and sat up straight. 'I'm sorry,'
she said, starting to stand.

'No, please, sit, I didn't mean to startle you.'

Louisa looked up into the friendly face of the
priest.

'This church is a place for quiet contempla-
tion. You take all the time you need.'

Louisa smiled her thanks and watched as the
priest walked away from her. She had a lot of

thinking to do and at least she now felt safe to do it.

'What should I do, Mama?' Louisa whispered into the silent church.

She knew she wouldn't get a reply, but she hoped her parents were somewhere out there, looking out for her.

She shouldn't have run away, she knew that much. It was a cowardly reaction and hadn't solved anything. She just hadn't been able to bear the thought of Robert betraying her, of his telling a lover about her past. She hadn't trusted anyone for such a long time and she had trusted Robert, let him in through her protective barriers. The idea of him betraying that trust had been heartbreaking.

But now she thought about it, would Robert really betray her? He was a good man, she knew that. And since rescuing her from the asylum he had always tried to protect her. He might have been a little slow off the mark admitting he loved her, but he'd never done anything to make her mistrust him.

She thought about the letter. At the time when she'd read it, she'd been so upset by the content, by the fact her secret was out, she hadn't stopped to analyse what other possible motive the writer could have. It had been wrong of her to believe this anonymous letter writer over Robert.

Louisa thought back to something her mother had told her a few months before she'd died. 'Trust your heart and your instincts,' she'd told Louisa. 'They're rarely wrong.'

Louisa closed her eyes and emptied her head and tried to follow her mother's advice.

Robert loved her. He loved her and wouldn't do anything to hurt her. She knew that from the bottom of her heart.

She remembered everything he'd done for her over the last few weeks, every stolen kiss and longing gaze. She remembered their lovemaking and she knew it was not just carnal desire that had lit his eyes as he looked at her. He loved her.

The letter must have been written by someone who wanted to hurt her, or to hurt Robert. The only problem was there was some truth in it; the revelation of her background would damage Robert much more than it would damage her.

She wondered for a second whether it would be better to leave, to set Robert free, but she knew she wouldn't be able to do it. And besides, it wasn't her decision to make. Robert would have to decide for himself whether he wanted to tie himself to someone who had been publicly denounced as a lunatic.

Chapter Thirty-Two

Robert checked his pocket watch and glanced up and down the street. He was early and he wondered how long he was going to have to wait. Not that he cared if he had to wait for hours if Louisa showed up at the end of it.

He was back where it had all started, at the Lewisham Asylum. He glanced up at the barred windows and imagined the poor inmates locked inside. Many would never see the outside world again. They were locked up and forgotten by those who professed to love them. It still made him angry every time he thought of Louisa spending all those long months in the asylum, treated barely better than an animal.

'Robert.' Louisa's voice made him jump. He'd been staring intently up at the asylum, remembering the first time he'd met Louisa and hadn't noticed her approaching from behind. 'I'm sorry to bring you back here. It just felt right to meet you where we first met.'

Robert turned and swept her into his arms, so relieved to see her. When he'd received the note asking him to meet her here, he'd thought it too good to be true. He wondered if it were a cruel trick, or worse, if someone had forced her to write the note so they could demand a ransom for her.

'I thought I'd lost you,' Robert said, breathing in the scent of her hair, his hands running over her back, pressing her much closer than he strictly should.

Louisa gently pushed him away.

'I'm sorry for running away,' she said. 'I saw that awful announcement and I just couldn't think straight.'

'Louisa, I would never...'

She reached up and pressed a finger against his lips. 'I know,' she said.

Robert felt the relief flood through his body. He hadn't realised quite how tense he had been. For hours he had been wondering exactly what she would say to him when they met. Every possible scenario had run through his mind. He hadn't dared to hope Louisa would believe he had nothing to do with the announcement in gossip pages.

'I love you.' Robert didn't know what else to say.

'I know.'

Robert felt his heart start to pound as the seconds ticked by without Louisa telling him she loved him back.

'Robert, I need to say something and I need to say it without you interrupting me. Please.'

He felt the panic rise inside him. She was going to tell him she was leaving. Or that she didn't love him. Or that she believed everything that was written in that horrible letter.

'I have a problem trusting people,' she said.

Robert waited, knowing there must be more to come. He'd known she had a problem trusting people from the very first time he'd set eyes on her.

'I thought I would never trust another human being again in my life. And then I met you.' She smiled at him softly and for a moment hope flared in his heart. 'I tried not to trust you. I tried so hard not to fall in love with you, but somehow you broke through all my defences.'

Robert held his breath, wondering what she would say next.

'Then yesterday I saw that awful announcement in the paper and read the letter.'

'Louisa, I...' Robert started, but trailed off as he remembered he'd promised to let her say her piece without interruptions. The hand that held that morning's society pages dropped back to his side.

'Immediately I returned to my distrustful state and that wasn't fair.'

Robert frowned, not quite understanding.

'You haven't given me a single reason to distrust you in all the time I've known you. You've always been true and honest. My reaction was unfair to you and I wish to apologise.'

His frown deepened; he hadn't expected their conversation to go anything like this. He allowed the hope to flare again inside him.

'I know it will take a long time for me to let go of my issues with trust, but with your help I know I can succeed. That's if you'll still have me.'

So many questions raced through Robert's mind, but he knew now wasn't the time for them. He stepped forwards, slipped an arm round Louisa's waist and pulled her towards him.

'I promise I will spend my entire life helping you to trust me,' he said.

Louisa smiled tentatively as Robert lowered his head, brushing his lips against hers in a sensual and loving kiss.

'I haven't told anyone about your past, Louisa,' Robert said as he pulled away from her momentarily.

'I know. I know you wouldn't do anything like that.'

'And I don't have a mistress or a lover.'

Louisa smiled at him. 'You don't have a lover?' she asked, some of the humour back in her eyes.

Robert immediately thought of Louisa on top of him in the carriage and felt the first stirrings of arousal.

'I have a fiancée,' he said firmly.

She cocked an eyebrow. 'Is that a proposal?'

Robert looked around him. In a way it was poetic, proposing where he had first met her, even if the asylum was the least romantic place on earth.

'Louisa, will you make me the happiest man on earth and marry me?' he asked sincerely.

'You'll be hounded from society,' she replied.

'I don't care. As long as I've got you.'

'I love you,' she said.

'You still haven't given me your answer.'

'Yes.'

Epilogue

Three months later

Louisa had been told by everyone she'd met that a bride was meant to feel nervous on her wedding day. She smoothed down the silky fabric of her dress and smiled. She didn't feel in the least bit nervous, she just felt happy.

She'd got her happy ending. Robert was the kindest, most loving man she could wish for and she loved him with all her heart. Every time he looked at her, Louisa could see her love for him reflected in his eyes.

He stood next to her, showing her off to all the *ton*, making sure everyone knew he was proud to be married to her.

'What do you say we get out of here?' Robert whispered in her ear.

'We've only been here ten minutes,' Louisa whispered back.

Robert stifled a groan as the next well-wisher came to shake his hand and compliment Louisa on her dress.

The wedding had been a grand affair with what seemed like half of London in attendance. Louisa would have been just as happy with just a few treasured guests—Mrs Knapwell, Major Dunton, Gertie, the little orphan, who was proudly showing off her new dress to anyone who would look—but Robert had insisted on a large wedding. He'd told her he wanted the *ton* to know he was honoured to have her as his bride.

For their part everyone who had been invited had shown up, all craning to get a view of London's most talked-about couple. In the past Louisa might have hated this notoriety, but nothing could dampen her happy mood today. Today she had married the man she loved.

'I've got a surprise for you,' Robert whispered, dropping his hand from the small of her back to the curve of her buttocks and squeezing gently through the material of the dress.

'Robert,' she said scoldingly, 'you know I'm a stickler for propriety.'

He chuckled, paused to murmur a response to their next well-wisher, then leant in closer to Louisa, so she could smell his distinctive scent. His presence so close still made her feel giddy.

'Not that kind of surprise,' he reprimanded.

'Although, if you prefer, we can go straight to the bedroom...'

'Another sort of surprise?' she asked. 'Now you intrigue me.'

'A surprise?' Gertie asked as she came scampering back towards Robert and Louisa. 'I love surprises. What is it?'

Louisa grinned. Now Robert had both her and Gertie to contend with.

'It's a surprise for Louisa,' Robert said, winking at Gertie as if she were a coconspirator.

'For Mama?' Gertie asked.

Louisa felt her heart squeeze in her chest as Gertie said the words. They hadn't completed all the formalities yet, but one day soon Gertie would be their daughter. Every time Gertie addressed her as 'Mama', Louisa felt the tears spring to her eyes.

'So can we leave?' he asked.

Before Louisa could answer, Gertie nodded vigorously. 'I want to see the surprise.'

Louisa glanced at the room full of guests, most of whom they hadn't greeted yet, and felt a bubble of rebellion rise inside her.

'They have all come for the spectacle,' she said quietly. 'Why not give them something to talk about?'

'I love you,' Robert said, grinning at her.

Without any further warning Robert spun,

scooped Louisa up into his arms and turned to face their assembled guests.

'Ladies and gentlemen,' he said, his voice booming over the conversations of the guests, 'thank you all for coming. I think it is high time I took my beautiful wife somewhere a little more private. Please stay, enjoy the party. Eat, drink and be merry.'

Before the crowd could recover, Robert strode out the double doors with Louisa in his arms and Gertie beaming by his side.

Louisa giggled. 'They'll be thinking you're mad, too, now.'

'Must be my wife's influence rubbing off on me,' he said with a grin.

'So, what's my surprise?' Louisa asked.

'A wedding present of sorts, but not a conventional one.'

Louisa tried to guess what it could be with no success.

'I've got you intrigued now, haven't I?'

He led her outside to his waiting carriage and helped her up. Once she was seated he lifted Gertie by the waist and set her gently inside the carriage.

'Where are we going, Robert?'

'Wait and see.'

Louisa watched the familiar London streets pass by before her eyes.

'Can I not have a little clue?' she asked.

Gertie clapped her hands in glee. 'Two clues,' she said. 'One for Mama and one for me.'

'I'll give you a choice,' Robert said, a mischievous glint in his eye. 'You can either have a clue or I can spend the journey kissing your mama.'

'That's a clue in itself,' Louisa said before Gertie could answer. 'We can't be going all that far.'

Gertie pulled a face. 'I want the clues,' she said. 'Kissing is icky.'

Robert grinned. 'You won't be saying that when you're older.'

Gertie scrunched up her nose. Louisa felt as if her heart was about to burst. She loved her little family so much.

'Stop delaying and give us a clue,' Louisa said.

'So my wife doesn't want a kiss?'

'Kissing is icky,' Louisa said, her eyes meeting with Robert's.

'I'll make you withdraw that statement later,' Robert said quietly. Louisa felt the familiar heat rising up her body as she always did when Robert looked at her like that.

Gertie sighed dramatically and rolled her eyes.

'I think young Miss Gertie is indicating she

would like that clue now,' Louisa said, not able to tear her eyes from Robert's.

'Too late.'

For a second Louisa was too caught up in the moment to realise what he'd just said.

'We're here.'

Louisa peered out of the window, trying to figure out where he had taken them.

The carriage slowed to a stop and Louisa recognised the building they had pulled up outside.

'Robert, what are we doing here?' Louisa asked.

'Where are we?' Gertie asked.

'I know it's a strange wedding present,' Robert said, 'but I thought you might appreciate it.'

He opened the carriage door and helped her and then Gertie down.

'I don't understand.'

'I bought it for you.'

Louisa turned to him with a frown. 'You bought it for me?' she asked.

He nodded.

She looked up at the asylum and slowly understanding suffused through her body. 'So no one else would have to suffer the way I did,' she said.

He nodded. 'What you went through was inhumane.'

Louisa flung herself into Robert's arms and peppered kisses all over his face and neck.

'Thank you,' she said. 'It's the best present ever. We can make it so much better. We can ensure the patients get treated with respect and dignity.'

Gertie put her hand in Louisa's, sensing this was a big moment.

Louisa looked up at her husband and knew she couldn't have married a better man. Instead of buying her jewels or trinkets, he'd understood what really mattered to her. Thanks to him she would be able to turn the place where she had suffered the most into a calming and peaceful sanctuary for those who were afflicted with illnesses of the mind.

'I've got a present for you, too,' Louisa said.

Robert looked at her with curiosity as she placed his hands on her abdomen. For half a minute he just stood there, looking puzzled, before realisation dawned in his eyes.

'You're…we're…' He couldn't get the words out.

'I'm pregnant,' Louisa said, loving the happiness spreading across Robert's face. 'About three months.'

'Pregnant?' Gertie asked.

Louisa nodded, hopeful the young girl would be happy.

'I'm going to have a sister?'

Louisa nodded again, waiting for Gertie to react.

'Or a brother,' Robert said.

'I'd like a sister, please,' Gertie said, 'then we can play together and she can share my doll and we can be best friends.'

Louisa felt the relief seep through her body. Gertie was already looking forward to being a big sister. And she could tell Robert was more than happy with her news; he had biggest grin she'd ever seen on his face.

'You're perfect,' Robert said, stooping down to kiss her, 'You've made me the happiest man alive twice over today alone.'

Louisa looked up at her husband and smiled at him serenely. No matter what he said, she knew she was the lucky one. She was loved by the one man she adored and already she had a perfect little family.

* * * * *

MILLS & BOON®

Two superb collections!

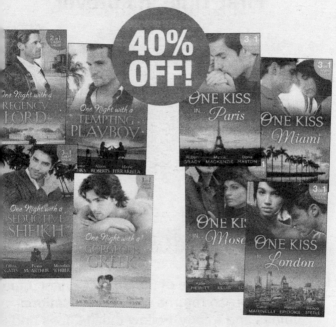

MILLS & BOON®

HISTORICAL

AWAKEN THE ROMANCE OF THE PAST